WESTERN A
BKM Bro

NEWARK PUBLIC LIBRARY - NEWARK, OHIO 43055

W9-BVO-365

WITHDRAWN

Large Print Par

Parker, F. M.

The assassins

DATE DUE
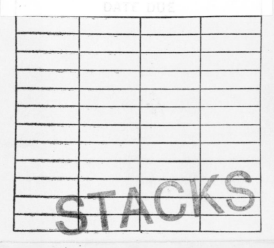

STACKS

DUE IN 28 DAYS

Newark Public Library
BOOKMOBILE
900 W. MAIN ST.
NEWARK, OHIO 43055

THE
ASSASSINS

THE ASSASSINS

F. M. Parker

G.K.HALL & CO.
Boston, Massachusetts
1990

Copyright © 1989 by F. M. Parker.

All rights reserved.

Published in Large Print by arrangement with
New American Library, a division of Penguin Books USA,
Inc.

G.K. Hall Large Print Book Series.

Set in 16 pt. Plantin.

Library of Congress Cataloging in Publication Data

Parker, F. M.
    The assassins / F. M. Parker.
      p.   cm.—(G.K. Hall large print book series)
    ISBN 0-8161-4999-2 (lg. print)
    1. New Orleans (La.)—History—Fiction. 2. Large type books. I. Title.
[PS3566.A678A97 1990]
813'.54—dc20
                                              90-32777

Prologue
The Making of the River

THE drifting snow of the white ice desert of the great glacier was less hospitable than the drifting sands of the hottest desert.

For tens of thousands of years the water of the oceans had been sucked up by the winds of the world and flung as snow onto the breast of the continent. The snow turned to ice, more than two million cubic miles of it smothering the land. The level of the oceans dropped two hundred feet.

Piled nearly two miles thick in its central dome, the ice became plastic under its own crushing weight. Mobile now, the ice flowed outward to cover two-thirds of the land surface, and extended far out into the Arctic and Atlantic oceans. The glacier drowned mountains six thousand feet tall and obliterated two mighty rivers, one flowing east and another north, and beheaded a third river that went off to the south. Even the strong rock crust of the planet was depressed two thousand feet.

Millennium after millennium passed as the glacier held the continent captive. Powerful winds blew constantly off the huge ice field, stirring raging blizzards in summer as well as winter. The beheaded south-flowing river was often frozen solid to its rocky bottom.

The shifting balance of heat and cold on the earth tilted to the warm side. The quantity of ice flowing to the periphery of the glacier became equal to that which was melting. The glacier halted its advance and stood and did battle with the sun for thousands of years.

The glacier lost the battle and surrendered to the sun. In six thousand years the front of the ice retreated five hundred miles.

A multitude of streams of water rushed away from the seventeen hundred miles of melting glacier terminus, spreading like a tangled skein of blue-green silk through rock and sand moraines. The giant rivers that had been overrun by the ice flowed strongly again. They fought one another for mastery of the broad continental watershed.

Once an arm of thick ice blocked the east river for eight thousand years and created a gigantic lake. To the west large depressions were uncovered by the retreating glacier. Ice melt poured into the deep cavities to form a series of mighty lakes.

The land surface began to rebound from the depressed level to which the glacier had crushed it. The bottoms of the lakes rose. At times the high walls of the lakes would be breached and a flood of unimaginable quantity spilled out. Most of the water poured into the river flowing south, and it became the greatest river on the earth.

The braided network of the upper reaches of the south river finally coalesced downstream into one tremendous channel several miles wide and hundreds of feet deep. The channel ran brim full of swift water straining to return to the sea.

For long distances behind the retreating glacier the land lay barren and abandoned by all plants and animals. Choking dust storms raged, swirling away carrying the fine loess two miles into the air and many hundreds of miles beyond its source. The sun was obscured for months. In the darkness, massive sand dunes fifty feet tall and miles long were birthed.

The south river cared nothing about the darkness, but hurried onward, pulled relentlessly by the implacable gravity of the planet. It dumped its titanic load of sand and silt into the Gulf of Mexico. A delta of massive proportions grew swiftly, now below sea level, now above.

The lusty river full of tumbling, churning water refused to be held to one channel and frequently shifted its huge meandering body into new courses. It flung its mouth from side to side, sometimes tens of miles apart in a day, and spewed out its load of continental debris first here and then there. Often the delta expanded thousands of feet in a year, until it was scores of miles wide and extending ten times that far into the gulf. The river changed the very size and shape of the continent.

The glacier died. The river shrank. Yet it was still a great stream, and near its mouth was a half-mile wide and two hundred and fifty feet deep. For ten thousand years the river flowed thus.

Natural levees formed on the banks of the river. Each time the stream poured over its banks, the current slowed at the margin of the channel and dropped its load of fine silt. An embankment, a levee, was built. The river in normal flow was confined within these impervious banks of clay. Outside the levees and lying below the level of the river was a region of extensive swamps and lakes, a labyrinth of water and land.

At times deep crevasses broke the levees, and the river plunged through, flooding the land for miles and holding it in a watery prison for weeks. The land animals drowned.

Then one year white man found the river. He traveled its length and named it Mississippi from the name the Indians gave it, misi-great and sipi-water. In his foolhardy, reckless way, the white man began to build a town in the mud flats that lay twice the height of a tall man below the level of the river. Only a fragile levee protected the town, called New Orleans, from the gargantuan destructive powers of the river.

Often the river rampaged through the town, for the presence of the white man did not prevent the levees from failing.

Have you ever been in New Orleans? If not,
  you'd better go.
It's a nation of a queer place; day and night a
  show!
Frenchmen, Spaniards, West Indians, Creoles,
  Mustees,
Yankees, Kentuckians, Tennesseans, lawyers
  and trustees,

Negroes in purple and fine linen, and slaves in
  rags and chains,
Ships, arks, steamboats, robbers, pirates,
  alligators,
Assassins, gamblers, drunkards, and cotton
  speculators;
Sailors, soldiers, pretty girls and ugly
  fortune-tellers;
Pimps, imps, shrimps, and all sorts of dirty
  fellow;

A progeny of all colors—an infernal motley
  crew;
Yellow fever in February—muddy streets all
  year;
Many things to hope for, and a devilish sight to
  fear!
Gold and silver bullion—United States bank
  notes,
Horse-racers, cock-fighters, and beggars without
  coats,
Snapping-turtles, sugar, sugar-houses, water
  snakes,

Molasses, flour, whiskey, tobacco, corn and
    johnny-cakes,
Beef, cattle, hogs, pork, turkeys, Kentucky
    rifles,
Lumber, boards, apples, cottons, and many
    other trifles.
Butter, cheese, onions, wild beasts in wooden
    cages,
Barbers, waiters, draymen, with the highest sort
    of wages.

Colonel James R. Creecy

1

Vieux Carré, Old Square, New Orleans,
June 3, 1847

THE door of the Gator's Den, a free blacks' gaming parlor, opened, and the yellow rays of gaslight spilled out into the dark night. The mutter of men at craps and cards drifted out the opening and reached Lezin Morissot, who was in the deep shadows of the carriageway of the deserted house a block away.

A large black man stepped from the Gator's Den and stood on the brick sidewalk. Someone shoved the door closed behind him and night fell again upon Dauphine Street.

Morissot watched the man take a deep breath of the slow, damp wind coming off the Mississippi River, and glance both ways along the street. Even in the frail light, the hulking form of Verret was recognizable. He turned to the right and leisurely strode off.

Morissot moved back a step into the deeper darkness of the carriageway and leaned against the brick wall. He calmly planned his strategy for killing. Now and then he peered out at Verret, faintly silhouetted in the night. The man came steadily on.

Morissot had stealthily followed Verret from

early evening and into the night, until the man had finally ceased rambling about the Vieux Carré and settled down to play cards in the Gator's Den. Morissot had entered the gambling place himself and played cards for an hour at a table near Verret. Over his cards, he had studied the man. It was nearly morning now, and the man would be heading but one place, home and bed.

Reaching into the pocket of his jacket, Morissot removed a garrote. He uncoiled the steel wire and took the wooden handles, one attached to each end, into his hands. When Verret felt the wire around his neck, there would be no escape. Morissot the assassin liked the silent, deadly weapon.

He glanced up at the dark sky. A thick overcast, hanging close to the earth, crept off to the south. It was a good night for Verret to disappear.

For a moment, Morissot wondered about Verret. He knew him only as one of the many black crew bosses on the docks. Why did someone want him dead? But then Morissot let the question slide away. He was being paid a handsome sum to see that the man vanished. That was the simple beginning and end of it. Still, at some primal level he felt that the man's death would in some unknown manner mean danger to him.

Morissot's senses began to sharpen, to expand, as they always did when he took a killing weapon into his hands and prepared to strike his victim. His keen eyes checked the fronts and the wrought-iron balconies of the two-story houses lining the street and set flush against the sidewalk. He smelled the house slop, garbage, and human excrement in the drainage ditch in the center of the dirt street. A bat dived out of the blackness and darted in close to inspect him. He heard the whisper of its leathery wings stroking the air as it veered upward and away. Verret's footfalls sounded on the sidewalk.

Two Spanish sailors with three sheets in the wind came staggering out of a cross street that led from the nearby red-light district with its brothels and saloons. They began to sing in loud, off-key obscenities, their voices echoing along the canyon of Dauphine Street. They lurched together and, supporting each other, crossed Dauphine and disappeared down a side street in the direction of the docks. The drunken voices faded away.

Verret had halted and turned to stare at the sailors. Now he faced about and continued on toward Morissot. He seemed more alert.

Morissot cast one last look both directions. The street lay abandoned in the late hour of the night. But the day was only minutes below the horizon, and soon a throng of people would pour out of the houses. The killing must be accomplished quickly.

The assassin spread the handles of the garrote to widen the wire loop. He stepped to the edge of the carriageway darkness near the street and pressed tightly against the brick wall.

The burly form of Verret passed in the night. He was humming a low tune to himself.

Morissot sprang from his hiding place and in

behind the man. He raised the garrote and brought it down swiftly over the man's head. Jerked it savagely tight. With a mighty heave, Morissot yanked Verret into the carriageway.

Verret's hands flew up to tear away the choking band around his neck. His fingers dug at the wire embedded in his flesh. Abruptly he stopped the futile effort. He whirled to catch his attacker.

Morissot, his muscles bulging as he tightened the garrote ever tighter, spun with Verret, staying clear of the larger man's hands.

Verret tried again and again to break free, lunging left, right, plunging ahead to suddenly pivot, desperately grabbing for the man at his back. Morissot moved with him, always just out of reach. The two men spun in a silent macabre dance of death in the murk-filled carriageway.

Few men were Verret's equal in strength. But the garrote had cut deeply into the tendons and veins of his neck. Stars began to explode in his brain. He had but one last chance to live. He hurled himself toward the ground. There he could roll and catch his assailant.

Morissot, with the knowledge gained from many killings, did not try to stop the fall of the big man. He stepped away from Verret and pulled to the side, changing the man's downward momentum into a swing to the side. Verret's head crashed into the brick wall of the carriageway with a thud.

Morissot rode the man down to the ground. His knees landed with crushing force in the center of the strangling man's back. In the darkness,

Morissot held the garrote tightly, and he sawed it hard from side to side to cut off the last bit of air to the lungs and stop the final drop of blood flowing through the large jugular vein.

For a full three minutes, Morissot held the choking garrote. Then he released the handles and unwound the wire from Verret's neck. He stowed the weapon away in a pocket and rolled the man to his back. Stooping, he caught an arm and with ease hoisted the big body to his shoulder.

Silently Morissot passed along the short carriageway to the enclosed courtyard at the rear of the vacant house. He called softly out ahead through the darkness to his horse. The beast must not become alarmed at the smell of death and the corpse across his shoulder and make a racket.

The overcast of the sky parted and bright moonlight speared down, bathing the courtyard in bright light. Morissot froze and stood motionless, the corpse of Verret dangling. If someone should step out onto the balcony of the house across the street, Morissot would be completely visible.

The speeding clouds healed the momentary tear in the overcast. The sky and moon vanished and night poured black and dense into the courtyard.

Morissot went on. Verret's limp body was placed in the rear of the light wagon that was hitched to the horse. Morissot spread a blanket over the still form and then laid his fisherman's poles, lines, and net on top of everything.

He stepped up into the wagon and spoke to the horse. The animal tossed its head once with a jangle of bridle metal and went out the carriageway, pulling the vehicle into the street.

Morissot began to whistle in a soft tone, the tune Verret had been humming just before he died.

The wagon with its grisly load reached the border of the Vieux Carré. As Morissot guided the horse across the broad thoroughfare of Canal Street, three black stevedores heading for the wharves on the Mississippi River came into sight. Morissot recognized them in the rising dawn.

" 'Mornin', Lezin. Going fishing mighty early, ain't you?" called one of the men.

"Can't even see to bait a hook yet," added a second man.

"I've found the fish favor a man who's there just at daybreak," Lezin said. He did not slow. The three were a nosy, talkative lot.

"How about givin' us a ride to the river?" asked the first man.

"Walkin's good for you," Lezin replied shortly. He lifted the reins and slapped them down on the horse's back.

"Lezin Morissot, you're a nigger with a mean streak in you," the first man called.

Lezin ignored the fellow. The men knew him as a river fisherman. They must never learn more than that.

He entered Baronne Street of the Garden District. The homes of the rich white Americans lay on his left. In ten minutes he had skirted around

6

those big fine houses and come to an area of cultivated fields separated by bayous full of stale black water. Another ten minutes and he halted the wagon in a grove of giant cypress and sycamore trees on the bank of the Mississippi.

Morissot jumped down from the wagon and uncovered Verret's corpse. Unceremoniously he caught the man's jacket at the collar and dragged him out of the vehicle and to the edge of the water.

Tim Wollfolk awakened to the rumble of the deep Mississippi River flowing past close beside him. He tossed aside his blanket and climbed erect.

He was three days riding south of Baton Rouge, Louisiana. The evening before, he had made camp on the top of the river levee. The embankment, some fifty feet wide, fell away steeply to the river. While on the opposite side, it sloped down at a gentle angle to the old floodplain and the main road. A dense woods, still dark with lingering night shadows, lay beyond the road.

Thick gray clouds hung close overhead. To the north rain hung like curtains along the full length of the horizon, and was moving directly down the broad river valley. Tim smelled the threatening rain. The storm would be upon him in an hour.

He glanced down river. There, somewhere within four or five miles lay the one-hundred-and-thirty-year-old city of New Orleans with its one hundred thousand inhabitants. Tim's pulse increased. Soon he would enter that great port city.

7

He would locate the lawyer, Gilbert Rosiere, and claim his inheritance.

Two weeks earlier, Tim had received a letter from the New Orleans lawyer informing him that his uncle, Albert Wollfolk, had died and that Tim was the main beneficiary of his will. Rosiere indicated that properties of value were involved.

Tim's mother had died when he was but a boy. His father had died in an explosion of the boilers of a steamboat five years past. That had left his Uncle Albert as Tim's last living relative. He felt a bitter sorrow for not having known his uncle before his death. Now Tim stood alone as the last of the lineage of Wollfolks.

Tim had quit his job as accountant in the Lynch and Lynch Steamboat Company at Cincinnati, Ohio, and purchased a ticket on the steamboat *Rainbow*. In five days the boat had reached Baton Rouge. Wanting to see the land and plantations at a close range, Tim had left the riverboat. He bought a saddle horse and rode south, marveling at the huge cotton and cane plantations with the elegant mansions. As he drew nearer New Orleans, the land had become swampy and the broad cultivated fields fell away behind. The road often wound through dark bayou country and long stretches of forest.

The horse snorted a sharp blast of air and stomped the ground. It stood tense, ears thrust forward and staring across the road at the woods. Tim looked in the same direction to see what bothered the animal. He saw nothing threatening in the woods, only the indistinct boles of the trees and the leaf-filled branches swaying to the wind.

Probably the horse had caught the scent of a prowling panther or maybe an alligator. Tim had heard the animals were present and sometimes took livestock. An alligator rarely killed a human.

He turned and walked down the slope of the levee to the river's edge. For the past few days the Mississippi had been rising slowly from springtime storms. The water had continued to climb during the darkness of the night and now hurried past in a tide of brown, muddy water nearly three-quarters of a mile wide. Patches of floating foam and brush rushed by. A large tree torn loose from its hold on some distant upstream piece of land wallowed and rolled as it was shoved along by the current. A flock of ducks glided in to inspect the river, then climbed up and away from the rolling waves kicked up by the jostling, swirling currents. They flew off searching for quiet water. A rattlesnake driven from its den and caught by the river swam by in a sensuous, undulating twist of its long body.

Tim was used to the flooding Ohio; still he was amazed at the titanic flow of the Mississippi pouring past.

He knelt to wash his hands in the cold water. After a quick bite to eat, he would ride into New Orleans.

"Hey, fellow, turn around," a loud voice shouted from the top of the levee.

Tim twisted to look behind in the direction of the call. He jerked, startled, for three men with pistols in their hands stood staring down at him. The pistols pointed straight at him.

"Stand up," shouted the same voice, coming from a tall skinny man, "and get your hands above your head where I can see them."

"What do you want?" questioned Tim, rising slowly to his feet.

"Now, how about that?" the first man said. "He wants to know what we want." He grinned without mirth.

"We want your money, fool," said a second man.

"Then maybe we'll have you take a long swim in the river," the third man said.

The three men laughed as if the threatened robbery was some huge joke.

Tim's heart thudded within his ribs. "I only have fifty dollars," he said. "It's there in my belongings near the blanket."

"Clovis, see if he tells the truth," directed the skinny man.

Clovis quickly stooped and rummaged through Tim's possessions. "His pocketbook is here," he said. He counted the coins and paper money. "Fifty-two dollars and some change."

The skinny leader of the robbers jabbed his pistol in Tim's direction. "Damn little money. Turn your pockets wrong side out. Hurry it up."

Tim dug into his pocket and turned them outward. "I only have this knife and some lucifers." He held them up for the men to see.

10

"He might have his loot in a money belt, or he may be carryin' it in his boot," Clovis said.

"Go down there and check," ordered the leader.

Clovis scrambled down the steep face of the levee. He warily approached the well-muscled young man. "Now, don't try anything," he warned. "Throw that knife away."

Tim dropped the knife and matches to the ground. His fear grew. These men would not simply walk off and leave him alive. It was obvious they were practiced robbers. They would know dead victims would tell no tales to the law.

Clovis, holding his pistol cocked and pointed at Tim's head, reached out to feel for hidden money.

It's now or never, thought Tim. His hand flashed down and caught Clovis' outstretched arm in a viselike grip. He spun the robber around and at the same time dodged to the side to get from in front of the man's pistol.

The gun fired with a brain-jarring explosion. Tim rocked to the mighty concussion. The burning gunpowder scorched the side of his face. The acid smoke stung his eyes.

But he was not hit by the bullet. He jerked the man again to keep him off balance and caught him by the gun hand. Bodily he lifted Clovis and swung him to a position so that his body, though smaller than Tim's, would be a partial shield between him and the two remaining robbers on top of the levee.

A horrible blow struck Tim in the left shoulder. He staggered back under the punch of the bullet. He caught himself in knee-deep water. His feet slipped on the steeply down-shelving bottom of the river, and he almost fell. The swift current pulled at his legs.

"I thought you'd try something," yelled the bandit leader. "But you made a mistake. I can shoot your eyes out at this range."

The angry voice added strength to Tim's arms. Trapped as he was against the river, he knew there was little chance to survive. But damn them all to hell, he wasn't dead yet. He wrenched the pistol from Clovis' hand and swung it to point up the slope at his enemies.

The bandit leader fired again as Tim's side showed for an instant from behind Clovis. The bullet went true to his point of aim.

Tim felt the bullet skittering across his ribs, ripping muscle loose from bone, and tearing free from his back. His breath left him with a swish.

Clovis felt Tim's grip loosen. He broke away.

Tim was hurled backward by the slam of the hurtling chunk of lead. His feet found no bottom in the deep water.

Tim sank at once, the cold water of the river enclosing him like ice. Down, down he went, the swift current catching him, tumbling and rolling him, adding confusion to his pain-filled brain.

At some great depth, Tim's shoulder bumped the bottom of the river. Knowing for an instant which direction was up, he tried to stroke to the surface. But his left arm refused to respond to the frantic commands of his mind, and his clothing and boots were like lead holding him down. He tumbled helplessly along the gravelly bottom of the river.

<hr>

2

TIM let the powerful current of the river take him where it willed. Using his one good hand, he struggled at a boot until it came free. Laboriously he tugged at the second. It too finally came loose. Fighting his pain, he jerked his belt buckle open and kicked out of his trousers.

With his lungs ready to burst, he shoved off from the river bottom and fought upward, clawing at the slippery water with his right hand.

He broke free of the suffocating water. He sucked a mighty draft of the life-giving air. God, how delicious!

He paddled and kicked weakly, barely holding himself afloat. He looked around. The river torrent had swept him away from the shore and was racing downstream with him. He had been carried around a bend of the river and out of sight of the outlaws.

Above Tim a giant sycamore, a century old and weighing ten water-soaked tons, ponderously swapped ends in the muddy current. The tree had been undercut from its high bank above the river and carried off by the flooding water. Hammered by thousands of blows during its two hundred miles of travel in the turbulent river channel, the tree had all its bark stripped away, limbs beaten short, and the tough knotty roots worn to less than a yard in length.

The tree rolled, drowning one-half of its roots and surfacing the other portion. It stabilized with the massive bulk aligned with the flood, an enormous battering ram charging downstream.

Tim did not see the behemoth sycamore bearing down upon him. It struck him a bone-cracking blow on the injured ribs, driving him under the water. A sharp root caught in his shirt and held him down.

The delicate balance of the tree was destroyed by the weight of the man. The tons of wood began to rotate. The momentum built, then rolled toward a new balance point.

Tim ripped free as the tree turned. He battled to the surface, spitting out the foul-tasting water that had slopped into his mouth.

He grabbed a short length of wood floating nearby and clutched its meager buoyancy to him. He began to kick across the current for the shore. For each hard-earned foot gained toward the bank, the river swept him a hundred downstream.

Tim felt the cold and his wounds turning his muscles to wet strings. How much blood was he losing? Surely a large amount. He started to doubt that he could reach the bank which sped so swiftly past. The fear built renewed strength. He kicked onward.

Tim's legs gradually ceased to move. Only his hold on the piece of wood endured. He floated onward.

Bit by bit his mind became numb and nearly useless. His grip on the world and the chunk of wood slipped away from him. He sank below the surface of the water. Down he went through the cold, twisting current.

His feet touched the deep bottom of the river. Weakly he kicked upward, his one good hand reaching for the surface that he knew he would never see again.

His lungs were exploding. He had to breathe. His mouth opened and water flooded into his lungs. He was drowning.

Lew Fannin dreamed. A scowl formed about his closed eyes. Suddenly he became taut, every muscle hardening, and the trigger finger of his gun hand closed once, twice, three, four times.

Abruptly Lew sat bolt-upright. His eyes flashing around, he stared hard in every direction out through the cold gristle of the dawn and into the brush and trees surrounding his camp. He glanced down at the five-shot Paterson Colt revolver in its leather holster beside his bedroll. He grinned sourly at himself. This was the third time he had refought his last battle with outlaws.

The night was spent. He rose and packed his few belongings. He saddled his big gray horse and swung astride. Without a signal from the man, the horse moved off in a swift walk along the road at the base of the levee.

Man and beast had been together all the days of the animal's life. It had grown to sense the state of

15

the man. Now the tumult within the man's mind communicated itself to the horse and it tossed its head and chomped on the metal bit in its mouth.

Lew spoke quietly to the faithful horse and slapped it playfully on the neck. "All right, old fellow, we're almost there."

The horse nickered, swished its tail, and broke into a gallop on the road winding through the deep woods.

Lew relaxed, the riding of the gray soothing him as it always did. He would take the horse with him to Mexico.

Louisiana was the most aggressive of all the states in forming regiments of fighting men to send to the war in Mexico. The state paid a twenty-five-dollar bounty to each enlistee for joining. Lew had heard that a company of mounted riflemen was being recruited in New Orleans. He planned to join and sail south to help General Winfield Scott whip the Mexicans.

A month earlier such an action would not have interested him much. He had been in the Texas Rangers for four years. He had always wanted to be a lawman, one of the small elite band of Rangers enforcing the law over the vast state of Texas. A nation until it had recently become one of the states of the Union.

He had taken naturally to the hard life and gun fights with outlaws and sometimes with the tough Comanche braves. His most recent assignment had been at Adamsville on the Lampasas River in the center of bandit country. His last arrest had taken

him on a long journey after four rapists and murderers across Comanche territory to the Red River.

Lew had pushed the gray horse relentlessly along
the tracks of his quarry. He came upon them as
they crossed to the north side of the Red River
and out of his jurisdiction. He pulled back into
the trees and hurried upriver. There he crossed on
a rock-bottom ford and swung back east and caught
the four outlaws.

The men had fought him fiercely and he killed
two of them. By then the blood of battle was in
Fannin's eyes and he remembered the dead victims of the criminals. He refused to allow the
remaining two murderers to surrender, but forced
them to fight him. He killed everyone.

As Fannin traveled the long weary days back to
Adamsville with the corpses swollen and bloated
in death, he reflected upon his merciless killing of
the outlaws. That violence was a worrisome trait
in him. He began to think of a change of jobs.
However, he knew he would always be a warrior
and not a farmer or office lackey.

The Ranger captain read Fannin's report and
roughly reprimanded him for crossing the Red
River into Oklahoma and for not taking the last
two rapists prisoner. Fannin knew without doubt
that the captain was correct. But he was not certain he could ever allow justice be denied to a
victim by a criminal merely crossing a river. He
thought the savage deaths he had brought to the
outlaws were justified. Fannin immediately re-

signed and began the long journey east to New Orleans.

The concept of justice was important to Lew. He remembered his first lesson in justice and honesty. As a seven-year-old youth, he had tried to pick the pocket of an old man on the streets of Chicago. But the man felt the fingers digging for his wallet and, swifter than Lew had thought possible, whirled and caught him by the hand.

The old man lifted Lew off his feet and held him dangling from his arm. "Lad, stealin's a bad thing, and you're a poor thief. Where are your folks? I'm going to take you home and tell them what you tried to do."

"I don't have family. But I stay with a man. He's a damn fine thief. Here he comes now. You'd better let me go, for he's going to beat the hell out of you, old man."

Lew smiled inside his head at the remembrance. That gray-haired, sixty-year-old man beat the younger man to the pavement in less than a minute. Then, catching Lew by the hand, he had dragged him along with him.

The man's wife had stood in the center of the room staring at Lew. "What in God's name are you going to do with that dirty ragamuffin?"

"He's got no family and we got no kids. I thought we'd take him back to Texas with us. He's had some bad friends. I think it's our Christian duty to use our last years raising and teaching him to be fair and just to all men."

And so Lew traveled to Houston with the old

18

couple. For nine years he lived with them, until their deaths, the woman following swiftly after the man.

They were the only two people Lew had ever loved. He took their name, Fannin, and considered it a very great honor.

Lew crossed the broad Mississippi River on a ferry boat at Baton Rogue and headed south toward New Orleans. Once it had rained all day without letup and he had taken a night's shelter in a roadside tavern and lodging place.

The road entered a swampy zone and became deep with mud. Lew pulled the horse down to a walk and guided it out of the mud and up to the top of the levee flanking the river. He went on through gradually thinning woods.

A quarter-mile ahead, or a little less, a man climbed out of his bedroll on the levee and looked about. Then he walked down the bank to the river's edge. Fannin thought the clothes of the man resembled those of a horseman he had seen at a distance traveling ahead of him the day before. The fellow moved like a young man.

Three men broke from the woods on the inland side of the levee and ran up to the top of the embankment. Fannin thought he could make out pistols in their hands. They talked with the first man. After a minute or two, one of the men went down the face of the levee. The first man began to struggle with the armed arrival.

The first man was being attacked, or was it an arrest? Fannin had heard that travelers on this stretch of forested road were sometimes robbed, even murdered. The instincts of the lawman to investigate rose in Fannin. He spurred the gray to a run through the trees. He pulled his Paterson revolver and held it ready across the saddle in front of him.

The crash of a heavily charged pistol shattered the stillness of the morning. The two struggling men stumbled out into the edge of the water. A second shot erupted and the first man was flung into deep water. He vanished below the surface.

Fannin raced out of the trees and dragged his horse to a sliding stop near the men on the levee. He reined the mount to the side so that the barrel of the Paterson lying on his lap pointed straight at the three.

"What's happening here?" Fannin questioned. "Why did you shoot that man?"

The men had heard the pounding iron-shod hooves of the running horse and had spun to face the rider. The third man scrambled up the slope to stand with his cohorts.

The leader suppressed his surprise at the sudden appearance of the stranger. His face hardened and he shifted his cocked pistol for a quick shot.

Fannin saw no badges on the chests of the dirty, scruffy trio. Their expression was not that of lawmen, but rather of men caught doing murder. Fannin felt the wolf rising in his chest at the ruthless killing of the traveler.

"What man did we shoot?" asked the leader. "I see no body. All that's here is an empty camp."

He spread his thick lips and a mouthful of broken teeth showed in a wicked, jeering smile.

With panther-cold eyes, Fannin watched the men. A prickle ran over his body as his anger built. Without a corpse, murder could not be proved. And there were three of them to swear no man had been in the camp. He glanced along the bank of the river to see if by some slim chance the man who had been shot had lived and swum back to the shore. There was only weeds and the lapping muddy water.

The leader of the outlaws measured the young man in the broad-brimmed Texas hat and wearing the big silver spurs. He appeared confident, uncaring that there were three of them against him. Overconfident, for he should be easy to kill. The leader saw the Texan turn his view to look along the bank.

"Kill him," shouted the leader. He jerked up his pistol.

Fannin had expected the assault. He raised his Colt and burst the leader's heart. He rotated the barrel of the weapon to point at the next man, who was swiftly raising his gun. Fannin fired, the lead projectile shattering the thick sternum bone of the man and plowing onward through the soft lung tissue and out the back.

The third man halted the movement of his pistol, holding it only partway lifted. He stood looking directly down the black open bore of Fannin's gun.

The outlaw slowly shifted his stare from the gun

to Fannin's face. He shuddered as he saw the chilling enigmatic gray of the Texan's eyes. The danger in the man was absolute.

The man is a murderer, thought Fannin. He will rob and kill again. There is no justice for the dead traveler. He held his anger at bay as he pondered the situation. What could be accomplished if he took the man into New Orleans? Nothing, except a long inquest, and Fannin might himself be in trouble for killing two men.

Fannin's lips drew back and his teeth showed cruelly white. The man was guilty without a doubt, for Fannin had seen the murder committed with his own eyes. The outlaw should die for his crime. Who should be the executioner?

Fannin shot the man through the forehead. He fell backward, to sprawl on the steep bank of the levee.

Fannin dragged the three dead men down to the edge of the Mississippi. He searched them, taking a pocketbook with fifty-two dollars from one of them. The others had only a few coins. He found no identification. That was all right, for Lew did not want to know their names.

Fannin flung the corpses one after the other into the river. The leader went in last. As the man sank, a chuckling sound came from the water.

"I think killing them was a good idea too," Fannin told the river.

He washed his hands in the water, using the sandy silt of the bank to scour them clean.

3

LEZIN MORISSOT knelt in the brush on the brink of the Mississippi River. He was on the outside curve of a giant looping meander of the river, and the mighty current struck there full-force and deep. He felt the ground tremble to the pounding of the floodwater that lapped at his knees. Anything caught by the swift water would be carried to the Gulf of Mexico within hours.

He searched the clothing of Verret's corpse. He found a purse containing several gold coins and a roll of paper money. The man had won in his last night at cards.

Morissot shoved the money into his pocket. Nothing else possessed by the dockworker had value, and they were thrown far out into the river. Not one item that could identify the dead man should stay with him.

Morissot lifted the body by the belt and shoved it headfirst into the river. The water swirled over the black curly head and broad back of the man. The feet disappeared last, the river engulfing the entire corpse, adding it to the jetsam and flotsam and other debris carried in its liquid brown bosom.

For a moment Morissot remained kneeling,

swinging his view downstream as he watched the spot in the fast current where Verret had sunk. The body did not resurface. Lezin began to rise.

Directly in front of Lezin, a white hand stabbed up from the water. It rose until it extended half a forearm high. The fingers were rigid and stiff. Lezin dodged back from the object.

The fingers slowly closed and opened, as if trying to clutch something. Almost immediately the hand began to sink. The water rose to the wrist.

Morissot's long arm snaked out. Even as he did so, he felt his fear. But Verret's corpse could not have turned white and made its way upstream. It could not now be passing by to entice and trick Morissot into catching its hand so that it could pull him in and drown him.

Morissot's strong grip snagged the white hand. Instantly he was yanked toward the swirling water by the pull of the body deeply immersed in the river current. Morissot flung out his left hand and grabbed the stem of a bush near him.

Stretched out over the water, Lezin clung to the cold hand. If the hand had closed on his, he knew he would have let go of his own hold and tore free. But the hand seemed lifeless.

The body surfaced, thrust up by the water. It hung in Morissot's clutch, half-naked and startlingly white. Facedown, it plowed the water. Lezin heaved the white man onto the shore.

The body lay motionless. Lezin wondered if he had pulled in a dead man. For how could a man live beneath the water? Perhaps he had imagined the hand closing and opening. The river current must have in some manner caused that movement.

The white body quivered. The man was real and yet alive.

Morissot stepped astride the man, encircled his waist with his arms, and hoisted him nearly a yard off the ground. Muddy river water gushed from the man's lungs and mouth. Morissot dropped the body, only to jerk it up forcefully and hold it there while the brown liquid drained out the open mouth. He repeated the action again.

The body lay flat, face turned out of the dirt, and Morissot vigorously and rhythmically pumped the lungs by pressing and then releasing the wide back. One minute dragged into two as he worked to bring life back into the body. Blood started to flow more swiftly from the wounds on the shoulder and back. That was a good omen.

A mighty spasm convulsed the body, immediately followed by a giant belch of water. The lungs began to expand and contract on their own, sucking starvingly at the air.

Morissot moved away from the white man and squatted, considering what he should do next. Had the man been shot and thrown in the river as he had dumped Verret there? Or maybe he had been shot while trying to escape the law. There was no ready answer to the puzzle. But whether the man was victim or criminal was not important to Lezin now. He would wait until the man regained consciousness and then question him.

He lifted the man and placed him where the corpse of Verret had lain a moment before. He covered the cold, still body with the blanket. Following the roads twisting around the bayous, he drove northeast toward Lake Pontchartrain.

Lew Fannin sorted through the scant possessions of the man slain by the robbers. Besides the camp gear, he found a fresh change of dress clothing, including coat and tie. Wrapped in a waterproof oilskin covering was an old tintype photo of a man, woman, and a boy of six or so. On the back the date 1830 had been scratched. A more recent tintype showed the same man, but obviously older. There was a bill of sale for a horse dated three days before, a single-page letter to a man named Timothy Wollfolk, with many smudge marks, as if it had been read many times, and lastly three letters of identification. Lew settled down to read the personal letter.

May 6, 1847
Mr. Timothy Wollfolk
802 Front Street
Cincinnati, Ohio
Dear Sir:
   I take this sad moment to inform you of the death of your uncle, Albert Wollfolk. He was buried yesterday in the Saint Louis Cemetery No. 3 on Esplanade Avenue. I hired a contractor to build a fitting tomb. Your uncle's eulogy and interment was most properly conducted.

*As Albert Wollfolk's attorney, I have informa-
tion to impart to you. Your uncle left a will and in
it you are mentioned. I might say, you being his
only living relative, are the main beneficiary.
There are some special bequests, but nothing that
can't be reasonably accomplished.*

*Several pieces of valuable property were owned
by your uncle. Should you not want to travel to
New Orleans, I would be pleased to sell these
holdings for you and forward the proceeds to you.
A power of attorney from you to me would be
required. However, I suggest you come to New
Orleans so that we may resolve this matter in
person.*

Please inform me of your wishes.

*Your Most Obedient Servant,
Gilbert Rosiere, Esq.
468 Ursuline Street
New Orleans, Louisiana*

Lew read the letter a second time. Silently he
sat and stared out over the wide river. He felt the
tragedy of the man's death doubly strong, for he
too was the last of a family line. A most strange
coincidence. It is too bad that you died, fellow, for
it appears you might have become wealthy.

Finally, Lew took a deep breath, his chest arching, then let it out slowly. The muscles along his
jaw ridged and hardened. He had been selected by
the lottery of cold black chance to avenge Wollfolk's murder. Now he had an opportunity to seize

wealth, perhaps a fortune. There were no relatives of Albert Wollfolk, and thus no rightful heirs who would be cheated. Lew would become Timothy Wollfolk.

He began to read the letters of identification, one from the minister of a Baptist church, a second from a banker, and the third from an officer of a steamboat company. Each described various characteristics of Wollfolk or his life. Fannin studied them thoroughly. Every bit of information would be required if he was to succeed in impersonating the young Wollfolk.

As Lew finished the letters and returned all to their waterproof covering, rain began to fall, fine misty droplets settling out of the dark clouds. He sprang up and began to gather the possessions of Timothy Wollfolk. No. Now they were Lew's possessions.

The rain increased, big drops plummeting down. Lew slid into his slicker. He examined Wollfolk's horse for a brand or other identifying marks. There were none. He released the animal and slapped it away into the nearby woods. The dead man's saddle and bedroll went into the river. Everything else was packed with Lew's belongings on the gray horse. He left at once for New Orleans.

The black clouds hung close to the earth and dumped a drenching downpour upon Morissot. He ignored the storm, only now and then calling out to the horse to hurry it along. The animal tried to obey, slipping and sliding on the greasy mud as it pulled on the wagon which cut deeply into the dirt road.

Morissot turned off the main traveled way and up a narrow lane through large dripping trees. Shortly his home, a two-story house, came into view in a small meadow. A tall brick wall completely enclosed the house and an ample yard.

The horse halted and Lezin jumped down to open the heavy double iron gates to the carriageway. He clucked to the animal and it followed him to the courtyard and the rear of the house.

Morissot hoisted Tim to his shoulder and carried him up the outside staircase to the iron railed balcony that completely encircled the house. He entered a large room.

"Marie, come help me," he called.

With a patter of quick steps, a young woman hurried into the room. "Father, what has happened? Who is that?"

"No questions now. Run and fetch Jonathan. Tell him to bring his needles and thread, and his healing herbs. Tell him nothing else. Hurry, daughter. The man is badly hurt."

Marie grabbed a shawl from a hook on the back of the door and hastened out into the rain.

Lezin moved across the room with his burden and into a bedroom. He gently laid the man down on the bed.

The old black man, Jonathan, pressed the wounds to encourage them to bleed. He had discovered that the blood itself sometimes tended to cleanse wounds and lessen the chance for infection. Then, with skilled precise stitches he sewed the raw red lips of the wounds together.

He arose and went to the kitchen, where he pounded pieces of three species of herbs into a powder. This mixture he moistened with water and carried back to the injured man. After liberally applying poultices over the wounds, he fastened them in place with clean cloth bandages.

Jonathan faced Lezin and Marie. "He is young and strong. Unless he becomes badly infected, he should heal and live. He will carry bad scars to the end of his days. Cover him with blankets, for he is chilled."

Jonathan's brow furrowed. "Should I know anything about this white man?"

"You have observed nothing strange here today, old friend," Lezin said. "If someone has seen you come here and asks you questions, merely tell them that Morissot the fisherman was clumsy and cut himself on his fishing knife."

"It is the same knife that you fell on and stabbed yourself in the back last winter?" asked Jonathan with a wry smile.

"The very same," answered Lezin. "That's a very unlucky knife." The man he had killed that time had been a very strong fighter, and also very lucky. Lezin had slipped in the struggle and his guard had dropped for a moment.

"So be it," replied Jonathan. He gathered his bags of herbs and needle and thread and walked to the door. Without looking back, he donned his tattered old rain slicker and went out the door.

Marie spread a blanket over Tim. She marveled at the whiteness of the man's skin that had been protected by his clothing. He was as fair as any woman she had ever seen. His hair was very light brown, almost blond.

Marie glanced at her father. "Why don't you want anyone to know that we are helping this man?"

"I pulled him wounded and naked from the river. That is very strange. Perhaps he has enemies who would come to kill him should they learn he is still alive. It is best that we wait until he can speak and tells us what he wants us to do."

"Very well, Father," Marie said. "I'll watch him first. You have been up all night and must be tired. Please go to bed." She looked down at the man on the bed, then back up at Lezin. "Oh, by the way, did you win at cards?"

"Yes, it was a very profitable night." He did not like to lie to her. But he must.

For a few seconds he studied her face, finely chiseled, delicate. Her skin was like ivory. The eyes were large and a dark shade of green. Long black hair was pulled back in a bun to the nape of her neck. A most beautiful daughter. Lezin tenderly ran the tips of his fingers along the smooth curve of her cheek. His hand was several shades darker than her face.

His heart cramped. Soon he would have to send her away from him. The remainder of his life

31

would be a terrible loneliness, an emptiness that no one could fill.

Lew entered New Orleans in the second hour of daylight. For half a mile he traveled through an area of large new houses with spacious grounds. Then he crossed a wide avenue with horse-drawn cars moving along it. A battered wooden sign labeled it CANAL STREET. He was immediately surrounded by the old houses of the Vieux Carré. Most were two or three stories with iron-railed balconies jutting out over the sidewalks. With the rain so recently ended and the water sluggishly draining away, the buildings seemed to stand on flooded lots.

Block after block Lew wandered the dirt streets lined with brightly colored stucco houses. Often the lower floors were used for businesses, offices, coffeehouses and cafés, grocery stores, and haberdasheries, and for half a hundred other purposes.

At the corner of Conti Street and Exchange Alley he heard the ring of fine steel striking fine steel. He dismounted and stood in the doorway of a fencing school and watched a thin, quick mulatto teaching a group of attentive young men the use of the rapier. Promising himself he would return and see more of these deadly lessons, he remounted the gray and rode on through the narrow streets.

Once he pulled to the edge of the street and waited while a chain gang of black men, guarded by two white men with pistols and long whips, worked their way along. With pitchforks and shovels the black men scooped up the dead animals and other waste and trash from the gutters and the drainage ditch and tossed them into the huge wagons that accompanied them.

Lew halted his gray horse and sat watching a company of soldiers pass in front of him along Barracks Street. The soldiers marched in a column of ten abreast, their arms swinging, mud-splattered boots lifting and falling in unison. They ignored the damp mist remaining after the rain, as did everybody else.

Traffic blocked by the parading soldiers piled up around Lew. There were scores of people on foot, several buggies, a few men on horseback, and an omnibus with every seat full. Lew glanced around at the Frenchmen, Spaniards, Anglo-Saxons, Kaintucks, Irish, Germans, and Italians. Not one person complained about the delay, but rather a sense of excitement seemed to hold everyone.

"Another company of riflemen for Scott's army," a man said to a companion.

"I hear as many as three thousand soldiers will leave today."

"Yes. Four transport ships, the *Telegraph, Galveston, James L. Day,* and the *New York* are scheduled to sail before noon," said the first man.

"The army barracks will be full again with recruits before nightfall," the second man said.

"Louisiana is more than doing its fair share. And Fort Jesup is overflowing with soldiers who have come downriver from other states. Scott will give the Mexicans such a whipping that they won't ever think again of trying to take back Texas."

"Texas doesn't need any help to beat the Mexicans if they come looking for trouble," Lew said to the men. "The country's filling up with Americans and there are plenty of fighting men."

"Maybe so. Maybe so," said the first man, turning. He examined the young man on the tall horse. His eyes dropped to the revolver on his side. "You planning to join up with the army?"

"I've given it some thought."

"Well, good luck to you."

Lew nodded, but did not continue the conversation. The column of soldiers ended. Lew let the marching men draw ahead before he fell in behind. They should lead him to the river and the fabulous waterfront he had heard so much about.

The street filled again with the townsfolk continuing on with their private errands. Black street vendors began to hawk their wares.

An old black woman with a large basket balanced on her head beckoned to Lew. She shouted out in a high thin voice. "I have sweet rice cakes, Texas man. Are you hungry?"

At the call, Lew felt the surge of his hunger. He had had a very small supper the past evening and no breakfast today. He reined his horse near the woman.

The black woman lifted the basket down from her head and removed the lid. She stepped forward and held the open basket up to Lew. "Take which one you want, or as many as you want," she said.

Lew selected one cake and bit into it. The taste was delightful. He took a second one. "That should do me for now," he said. "How much do I owe you?"

"That'd be four pennies," said the woman.

Lew gave her a dime and rode on, chewing the sweet cake. He felt good. He halted and dropped another dime into the tin cup of a blind white man playing a fiddle on the sidewalk.

As Lew drew closer to the waterfront, the crowds thickened, soldiers and sailors were everywhere. The streets were jammed with hundreds of drays, heavy clattering vehicles drawn by sweating mules, the axles groaning under tremendous loads. He halted for a few minutes at Jackson Square and watched a clown performing juggling tricks as part of a small circus.

Fannin came onto the waterfront and stopped in amazement. The liars in Texas had not lied large enough when they had described the docks of New Orleans. For a distance greater than Lew could see, for at least a mile and a quarter, and fading away in the mist, oceangoing ships and river steamboats were tied up to wharves. Beyond the stretch of wharves, the shallow draft riverboats had taken advantage of the slowly rising river and had simply pulled in and secured themselves against the dirt levee. With the river rising instead of falling, the boats would not become beached.

Every berth at the docks held either a river

steamboat or an ocean ship. At several docks, a second vessel was fastened to the first. Thus sailors and stevedores had to cross the decks of the first vessel to reach the shore. The multitude of the smokestacks of the steam-driven vessels and the tall graceful masts of the clipper ships was a forest hiding the Mississippi River.

Fannin swung down from the gray and tied it to a pile of cargo. He walked along the wharf among large mounds of crates, barrels, boxes, and bales of goods. He lifted his nose to the heavy mixed fragrance of river's edge, sharp smell of fermenting molasses, the scent of rich spices from the Orient, the odor of West Indian rum. He saw hemp, skins, salted meats, kegs of pork, barrels of pickled foods, tar, coffee, and other items too many to count.

As he walked, he noted the warehouses had been built back from the docks and above the river on top of the levee—hopefully out of reach of the unpredictable river. The giant mounds of cargo stored in the open were protected by large tarpaulins.

Stevedores toiled in long lines across the wide quay, coming and going up the slanting gangways loading and unloading the crowded vessels. Most of them were muscular half-naked black men carrying giant loads. Often they were chanting some kind of rhythmic words Lew could not decipher. Other dockworkers were Irish or German. Now and then they called out to their own kind in their strange foreign tongues. Mostly they labored silently.

Five hundred military wagons with wheels removed to conserve space were lined up in neat rows on the shore near a large cargo ship. One by one the wagons were being hoisted aboard by a clanking windlass driven by a chugging steam engine on the ship's deck. The wheels were being carried aboard by stevedores.

An adjacent vessel, a tall clipper ship named *Massachusetts,* was slinging bronze-barreled mountain howitzers into her hold. Another ship was loading kicking, squealing horses and mules, the drovers fighting them every step of the way up the gangway.

Fannin turned away from the docks. The sun had burned away part of the mist and now hung as a hazy red disk in the high heavens. It was time for Lew to claim Timothy Wollfolk's inheritance. His heart began to beat a tattoo against his ribs.

He remembered the black woman calling him a Texas man. With his big spurs and wide-brimmed hat and the Paterson Colt on his hip, he could never pass as a Cincinnati man.

On Saint Philip Street, Lew obtained a haircut and shave. Next door he bought a pair of shoes with low heels and a flat-crowned hat, with a brim more narrow than his Texas hat. He thought the clothing might be close to what a man from Ohio would wear. Finishing those chores, he rode along the street carrying his purchases and looking for a hotel.

A sign of room for let caught his attention at a house on the corner of Burgundy and Saint Philip. He paid for a day's rent of a room on the ground floor and stabled his horse in one of the small stalls behind the house.

Fannin examined himself in the mirror above the washbasin in his room. Wollfolk's clothing fit fairly well, only a little snug across the chest. The tightness of the tie about his neck felt strange. He inserted a finger and pulled it partially loose. He wondered how long he could pass as Timothy Wollfolk, a man he knew nothing about.

From now on, Lew Fannin would only respond to the name Timothy Wollfolk. Not a bad name, but not as good as the familiar Fannin.

He shoved the Colt inside the band of his trousers under his coat. The packet containing the pictures and letter went in the pocket of the coat. That was all the identification he had. He hoped no one looked closely at the picture of the boy and tried to see his characteristics in Lew. He closed the door and went along the street.

The game was beginning. If he was found out to be false, the law would think he had killed Wollfolk. He would be hung.

--------------------------------4--------------------------------

THE stuccoed, three-story building on Ursuline Street was a dark blue. A strange color, thought Lew, but not out of place in the Vieux Carré. An engraved wooden sign fastened to the wall near the door read, GILBERT A. ROSIERE, ATTORNEY AT LAW. The law office occupied the whole width of the ground floor.

Fannin entered and stood on the thick wool carpet and glanced around the spacious room. Two young men, bent over files of papers, sat at a desk. One man was white-skinned, the other quite swarthy. Behind them a door opened to a hallway, apparently to inner, private offices.

Both men looked up at Fannin.

"How may I help you?" asked the nearest man, a dark-skinned Creole.

"My name is Timothy Wollfolk. I have a letter from Gilbert Rosiere."

"Ah, yes, Mr. Wollfolk. Mr. Rosiere has been expecting some communication from you. He was not certain that you would come to New Orleans in person."

"I'm here," Fannin said shortly.

"I can see that," replied the man. "But unfortunately Mr. Rosiere is across the river in Algiers on a business matter and will not return until late today. I do know he would want to handle your case personally. Shall I make an appointment for you tomorrow early in the day? Would nine o'clock be satisfactory?"

"Nine it is." From the man's attitude, Fannin judged the inheritance must be large. He left the law office.

He stopped on the sidewalk. A large part of the

day lay free ahead of him. First a good meal and then he would widen his exploration of the city.

Lew ate fresh ocean shrimp, hot spicy vegetables, and crisp French bread. He finished the meal with two cups of strong coffee and a sweet French pastry.

He stopped at a tobacconist shop and breathed the pungent aroma as he waited for the proprietor to roll him half a dozen cigars. Timothy Wollfolk could afford the finest tobacco.

For hours Lew sauntered through the throng of people and vehicles on the avenues. The women were beautiful in silk and satin and also simple ginghams, but all with bows and ribbons; many smiled at him. He smiled back, but went on. Women would come later.

When Lew came to a way that led into a residential section of the city, he turned back into the business district. He passed the New Orleans Sugar Exchange, relatively quiet now in the off season of the year. The U.S. Mint on Gallatin Street held his interest. The fact the Mint was in New Orleans indicated the city was a powerful financial center. Farther along an iron foundry filled the air with smoke from its furnace, and from a sawmill came the shrill whine of the steam-driven saw blade ripping a log into lumber.

As the day grew old, Lew found himself approaching the dock area. He passed the ancient Cabildo, with its massive two bottom floors with their Spanish arches, and above, the delicate French garret floor and cupola. The building housed the seat of the city government. Nearby was Saint Charles Cathedral, its towering spires soaring into the sky. He crossed the crowded Jackson Square, where the night women were coming out in the dusk of the evening and strolling about and pairing up with the soldiers and sailors. Several of the women tried to catch Lew's eye, but his attention was not on them and they went on their way.

He looked downriver three or four blocks to the tall structures of Steinberg and Company, a dealer in hides and furs, and Jackson Brewery on Decatur and Front streets. Then his view moved over the long line of warehouses on top of the levee. New Orleans was a rich and thriving city. A man with money to invest, as he might soon have, could become very rich here.

Fannin had now made the circuit of the business district of the city and judged it two miles in a straight line along the river, and half a mile deep. The jostling people and hurrying vehicles, the narrow streets, and the half-mad activity at the docks were alien to his Texas life. Yet Lew was intrigued and attracted to the frenzy of the city.

The three young Creoles came out of the grog shop ahead of Lew. They were dressed in black trousers and white shirts closely tailored to fit their young, slender bodies. Thin two-edged swords hung in scabbards at the waist of each man. Laughing and talking, they moved off down the street.

One of the Creoles began to sing in a pleasant tenor voice as they walked along. The others laughed at his bravado of singing on a public street. But when he did not stop, his two friends took up the song, melding in a good, clear harmony.

Lew had no particular course, so he followed behind the Creoles through the gathering dusk. He enjoyed listening to the friendly camaraderie of the men. He felt his loneliness. He was a man with no friends.

The song ended and the men began to speak in French. Often they broke into ribald laughter at some joke.

The three men came to a city park and left the street to angle across the grass-covered space. The Creole who had begun the singing stopped on a low knoll. He ran his booted foot over the smooth grassy surface.

"This place would be an excellent spot for a duel," he said.

"I agree," a second man said. He pulled his rapier with an exaggerated sweep of his hand. The steel of the blade hissed as it slid from the leather scabbard. "On guard, you rascal," he said with false fierceness.

The first Creole laughed good-naturedly. He too pulled his sword, made a bow to the first man, and took a fighting stance.

He looked at the third man. "Gustave, you shall be the judge. Call out the rules and then watch me trounce this blackguard."

Gustave smiled broadly and asked in a loud voice, "Leandre, Maurice, is this duel to the death?"

"Yes," Leandre said in mock seriousness.

"Yes," Maurice said in equally severe mien.

"Then let the duel begin," Gustave said. He clapped his hands with a sharp sound.

The two Creoles came slowly toward each other. Playfully they struck, and parried, and counterattacked. The rapiers rang lightly metal on metal.

In feigned insult the younger duelist, Maurice, spoke to his comrade, Leandre. "Your sister is a whore."

"But I don't have a sister," Leandre said.

"Then for not having a sister, take this." Maurice reached out swiftly with his thin blade.

Leandre had not expected the abrupt change in the tempo of the game. The slender sword slipped through his guard, its finely honed point reaching in to nick his shoulder.

Leandre looked down at the seep of blood showing on his white shirt. "You play dangerously, Maurice."

Leandre stepped swiftly forward. His arm shot out, thrusting his sword at Maurice.

The younger man blocked the strike. But instantly, almost too fast to see, Leandre struck a second time. The keen tip of the sword drew blood on Maurice's chest.

"And there, my friend," Leandre said.

Maurice glanced at the slight wound and then

up at Leandre. "We shall see who loses the next drop of blood." He advanced upon Leandre.

Lew entered the park and walked toward the men. He noted the growing seriousness of the game.

The sword action continued. The blades moved with amazing swiftness, seeming to vanish as the men struck and parried. The sound of the metal hitting metal was harsh and cruel. In less than a minute, both men were bleeding from half a dozen shallow wounds. Still Lew could tell the two contestants were holding back from an all-out battle. Suddenly a rapid exchange of rapier strikes occurred. Maurice took a bad cut on the arm.

Lew had drawn close. Now he spoke to the young Creole named Gustave. "As the judge, are you going to allow your two friends to kill each other?"

The young man, unaware of Lew's presence, jerked, startled at the voice so near to him. He looked Lew over quickly. "Yes, you are right. It is up to me to stop it." He wheeled about and shouted out in a loud, worried voice. "Leandre, Maurice, stop! The duel is over. You both have won."

The swords of the contestants halted. The men looked at each other. A sheepish expression came to Leandre's face. Then he began to smile. The smile broadened and he laughed. A second later, Maurice joined him and they laughed together.

Leandre slid his sword into its scabbard. He

came forward and hugged Maurice. "Put your blade away," he said.

Maurice sheathed his rapier. He took a handkerchief from his pocket and bound it around his bleeding hand.

"Come with me," Leandre said. "And you too, Gustave. I know of another grog shop. I shall buy enough rum to get all of us drunk. Soon we will not feel these puny wounds."

The three young Creoles began to move across the park. Gustave cast a look back at Lew. He stopped, said something to his friends, and walked toward Lew.

"My name is Gustave Besançon. Thank you for what you did. The duel did need to be stopped. I am in your debt."

"I'm Timothy Wollfolk. You don't owe me anything."

"But I know that I do. Shall we fight to settle our disagreement?" He grinned widely at Lew.

"Some other time," Lew said with a laugh.

"Until then," said Gustave. He lifted his hand in salute and hurried to join his comrades.

Lew left the park, heading south toward the river. After four blocks, he encountered the natural rise of the levee. He walked up over the levee and down onto the quay.

In the late evening, the docks were mostly deserted, with the multitude of workers and drays drifting away from the river and melting into the city. Here and there lighted lanterns were being hung on ropes strung across the decks of ships,

45

down the gangways, and onward over the docks to some particular mound of cargo. On those lighted stretches, stevedores labored under heavy loads to and from the ships.

"It used to be that cargo was seldom loaded at night," said a man sitting on a pile of boxed cargo. "But now that New Orleans has been picked as the staging area and general jumping-off place for the invasion of Mexico, there are always gangs of men working on the docks."

Lew glanced at the man. He was old, with deep wrinkles in a tanned face. A pipe drooped in the corner of his mouth. A pistol in a holster hung on his side.

The old man noted Lew's view on his gun. "I'm a night watchman. There's valuable goods here. River pirates and thieves from the town would carry off half of it in a night if I wasn't here. You wouldn't be a thief, would you?" There was a twinkle in the man's eyes.

The question, even though it was made in jest, bothered Fannin. If he had to answer, there could be but one response: that he was planning to be a thief.

"How could one man guard all the docks? They must stretch along the river for better than a mile."

"I don't have to watch it all, only eight hundred feet of it. You see each dock-owner must hire his own guard."

Fannin seated himself beside the watchman. He seemed to want to talk. "Have you been in New Orleans long?"

"Since 1813, when I came down from the North with old Stonewall Jackson. I helped him to beat the hell out of the British soldiers. I was wounded and had to stay here a few weeks to heal. Got to likin' the city, so I just stayed on."

Lew gestured out over the wharves with their huge piles of cargo and beyond to the hundred or more ships. "I expect some businessmen are getting rich."

"Some are getting rich faster than they should."

"How's that?"

"There's only just so much dock space and even less warehouse room. The army and navy are paying two and three times the rate for tying up and using the docks and warehouses than was being charged just a few months ago."

"That will always happen when there's a shortage of something."

The old man puffed on his pipe. He looked squarely into Fannin's face. "You from around here?"

"No. Just got in today. From Cincinnati."

"I would expect the docks are busy there too."

Lew was caught off-guard by the query. And there would be more questions about Cincinnati, a city he had never seen.

"Yes. But not so busy as here."

Lew thought the man wanted to say something else. He waited. However, the watchman just looked both ways along the river and remained silent.

Lew let the time slide by without conversation.

A ship creaked as it wallowed to the current of the river and rubbed against the dock. A sailor came down a gangway from one of the ships and went out of sight over the levee. A guitar sounded from a ship down the river.

"Does Albert Wollfolk own any docks or warehouses?" Fannin asked.

The watchman turned to Fannin. "Why do you ask?"

"I'm Timothy Wollfolk. Albert Wollfolk was my uncle."

The man thrust out a hand. "Well, I'll be damned. I sure am glad to meet you, Tim. I'm Dave Cadwaller. I knew your uncle right well." He began to smile. "You're sitting on Wollfolk property at this very moment. Look up there." He pointed at the warehouse on the levee above them.

Through the growing dusk, Tim saw the sign on the building: A. WOLLFOLK, WAREHOUSE & DOCKAGE.

"Your uncle owns this eight hundred feet of river front that I told you I guarded. I work for your uncle. Or I should say, I did. The lawyer handling Mr. Wollfolk's legal business told me and everybody else to keep on working and the new owner would see that we got paid. Is that you?"

"It may be. I'm to see the lawyer tomorrow."

"Well, if you do end up owning this piece of old Mississippi River bank, you've got a good location." Cadwaller saw Lew's quizzical expres-

48

sion. "Albert Wollfolk was a smart man and knew the river better than most everyone else. He bought the best place for a dock. And that's right here. The river current comes in against the bank just strong enough to keep the sand and gravel swept away, but not so strong that the pilings of the docks get washed out. In other places along the shore the current is weak and the river bottom fills up and needs dredging. That costs money."

"So the profit is high," Lew said.

"Yes, and because of that, your uncle could underbid his competitors up and down the river. Of course, Mr. Wollfolk was sharp in other ways too, but not crooked."

"That's good to hear," said Fannin. "How did he die? The lawyer's letter didn't say."

"There are conflicting thoughts about that. The law says he died accidentally. There's a few others that ain't so sure."

"Why is there doubt?"

"Mr. Wollfolk was found early one morning in between the docks just down the river there. I heard the yelling when a sailor off one of the ships saw his body in the water. I hurried to see what was happening. The law comes and they pull Mr. Wollfolk out. I did see a big bruise on his forehead.

"Well, the law decides he walked off the end of the dock in the night and struck his head and simply drowned in the river. I don't believe that worth a damn. He knew every crack and knothole in his docks. He could walk every foot in the dark and never fall."

"Did you tell the law this?"

"You bet. They asked more questions around. Then that's the last I heard. But the ruling by the law stands as an accidental death."

"Were you on watch that night?"

"Yes, but there was some fellows fooling with cargo at the upper end and I was there talking to them for a spell. Whatever happened could have been then."

"Did you know my uncle was here on the docks?"

"Nope. And he almost always come by and said hello to me when he was here. I feel bad that this thing happened while I was on duty."

"Who were the men around the cargo that you were talking with?"

"Didn't know them and have never seen them since."

Lew waited for Cadwaller to continue speaking. But the man had withdrawn into himself and gave no indication of wanting further conversation. He pressed the lever down to raise the glass globe of his lantern and began to scrape the ash from the tip of the wick with his pocketknife.

Fannin climbed erect. "Be seeing you," he told the night watchman.

"Young fellow, I believe someone hated your uncle bad enough to kill him, or have him killed. Some of that hate may come your way. I'd keep an eye peeled."

Lew nodded. "I'll do that."

He walked off along the wharf in the deepening dusk. He glanced back once at Cadwaller. The man had lit his lantern. He was still working on the wick, the light flickering on his face as the flame was disturbed by the knife blade. The old watchman looked sad. Had he truly guessed the cause of Wollfolk's death? Or was his story a wild rambling?

Lew came to a place where the dock was blocked by a string of lanterns and a long line of stevedores. The laboring men carried kegs of gunpowder on their shoulders off the docks, up the swaying gangway, and down into the bowels of a steamship. Lew turned away from the lights and the men and angled across the dock in the direction of his lodging.

The gloom of the coming night gathered among the mountainous islands of canvas-covered cargo. On the eastern horizon a yellow moon showed the top curve of its round body. Lew increased his pace. Darkness would soon catch him in a strange city, and he had no light.

Lew heard booted feet on the wooden decking of the dock. He cast a look over his shoulder. Two men were swiftly overtaking him.

"Hey, fellow, wait up," one of the men called.

Fannin pivoted slowly to the left. As he did so, his right hand clasped his Colt, slid it out of his belt, and held it against the side of his leg. The old watchman's tale was making Lew cautious.

"What do you want?" Fannin asked, peering at the shadowy faces of the approaching men.

The two halted barely ten feet distant. Their eyes moved up and down Fannin, examining him very closely.

"Looks like he's the one," said the second man. He started to circle to the side.

Fannin's hand stabbed out at the man. "Stand where you are and tell me what you want." They must not be allowed to flank him.

"We just want to talk," said the man.

Fannin heard the lie in the voice. The men acted as if this was an old game they had played before. Fannin's muscles tensed for the fight.

Both men sprang forward, drawing short leather-covered clubs from rear pockets. They cocked their arms ready to strike Fannin with the lead-weighted blackjacks.

Lew brought up his pistol, thumbing back the hammer. He swung the gun to point at the nearer man. He was not going to let them break his head with the blackjacks. He could kill both of them before they could do that.

At the last fraction of a second, Lew moved the barrel of the revolver slightly to the side. He squeezed the trigger. A spear of red flame exploded from the muzzle of the gun, hitting the attacker in the arm. The man spun halfway around under the impact of the bullet.

Lew instantly faded to the side, to evade a possible blow from the second man, and rotated the Colt. The open bore swung like a snake's head searching for the next enemy to strike.

The sudden, unexpected crash of the pistol jolted the second assailant. He veered off from Fannin and kept right on running. Lew brought the pistol in alignment with the man and broke his shoulder with a bullet. The wounded man ran headfirst into a pile of cargo, bounced back, and fell.

The first assailant stood leaning to the side and watching Fannin with pain-glazed eyes. Suddenly his legs melted and he collapsed. His head hit the decking with a loud thump.

"You stupid bastards," Fannin said to the crumpled forms. "Two men with blackjacks can't beat a man with a pistol."

He heard running feet coming swiftly. He sprinted away up over the levee. He did not want the police to become interested in Timothy Wollfolk.

Lew slowed as he came down onto Front Street. He ambled past a group of men and women staring in the direction of the river.

"Mister, what was the shooting about?" asked a man.

"One of the night watchmen killed a big alligator," Fannin replied, continuing to move down the street. "It must have been at least twelve feet long."

"My goodness," exclaimed one of the women. "An alligator right in the middle of New Orleans."

"Now, Mary, it simply swam in on the rising water of the river," responded a man beside her.

"They've done that before. They never come over the levee and into town."

Lew found Saint Philip Street and turned up it toward Burgundy Street. Several blocks along, at a small cafe, he stopped and entered. He ate a bowl of thick soup containing large pieces of chicken, a dish of red beans, warm bread, and a tall glass of cold buttermilk.

The darkness lay dense on the street when Lew left the cafe. He struck off again on Saint Philip, walking cautiously for the frail moonshine only faintly illuminated the sidewalk. He overtook a lamplighter moving from one gas streetlight to the next, reaching up with his torch to touch them off. Lew walked off ahead of the lamplighter and into the darkness.

People passed, most of them carrying oil-burning lanterns to light the way. Other nightwalkers, like Lew himself without a light, went by, silhouettes without faces. No one paid him any attention.

He reached his lodging place and went into the carriageway. At the rear he entered his sleeping room just off the courtyard. He undressed in the dark and hung his clothing on hooks in a shallow closet.

For a time he lay on the bed and reviewed the violent events that had come his way in a few short hours. The words of the man on the docks kept coming back to him: "Looks like he's the one." What did that mean? Were they actually looking specifically for him? And the old night watchman saying Albert Wollfolk had been murdered. Who would want to kill him, and why?

Lew wondered what kind of a situation he was getting into. He might have to earn his inheritance. He smiled ruefully in the blind darkness at the thought. At least no one knew where he was staying, and he was safe for the night.

Somewhere inside the walls of the aged dwelling, there was a patter of small feet. Then a mouse began to gnaw, like a tiny saw cutting on a thin board.

Lew shoved the happenings of the day off to a far corner of his mind for later study. The sound of the mouse was somehow comforting. Bringing back memories of Texas. Sleep came at once to Lew.

5

THE second boxer climbed through the ropes and into the ring that was rigged up in the large loft of Jackson Brewery. The crowd whistled and stomped their feet on the wooden floor, eager for the bare-knuckle fight to begin.

"Five hundred dollars on Hadley," Stanton Shattuck told the bet-taker.

"Five hundred it is, Mr. Shattuck," said the man. He made a note on his pad of paper. "Don't you like the man from Philadelphia?"

"I don't know Kellum, so I'll go with the local fellow Hadley." Shattuck held out a sheaf of bills.

"I don't need to hold your money," said the bet-taker. "I know you're good for it if your man loses." He moved away taking other wagers and cramming the bills in a leather satchel hanging over his shoulder.

The referee shouted, calling the fighters together in the center of the ring. Both men bobbed their heads in acknowledgment of his instructions. They backed away to their corners.

The referee glanced at the fight promoter, who in turn looked at the two bet-takers. When he saw they had finished taking wagers, he nodded to the referee.

"Fight," said the referee, and backed hastily from between the boxers.

Kellum sprang across the ring. He pounced upon Hadley almost before the man could leave his corner.

Hadley jerked up his fists and dodged to the side. Kellum easily shifted directions, boring in. His fists lashed out, beating aside his opponent's defense. His fists moved like hammers. Two blows landed with solid thuds of knuckles.

Hadley stumbled, his eyes rolled up into his head. He fell to the floor.

For a moment the loft was caught in a hushed silence. Then a man shouted a curse: "Two god-damned licks and Hadley's out cold."

An angry roar burst from the spectators. The rafters of the brewery shook. The men began to push against the ropes of the ring. Some of them

56

caught hold of the bet-takers and the manager of the man from Philadelphia.

The manager wrenched free and jumped out into the ring. He yelled at his fighter. "I told you to carry this local son of a bitch for a few rounds."

"I didn't want to play around with him," Kellum said, glancing around at the shouting mob. "Besides they'll soon settle down."

Shattuck shoved away a man who was crowding him, and shouted out in a stentorian voice, "The fight was fair. Pay off the bets."

"Did you win, mister?" the man Shattuck had shoved called angrily.

"No. I lost five hundred dollars. But that doesn't make any difference. Kellum won."

"Mr. Shattuck is right," said the referee. "The fight was won fairly."

"Pay the bets," the fight promoter added his voice to Shattuck's.

The crowd grew quiet. Money began to change hands.

"Maybe the Philadelphia man would like to fight again, since Hadley didn't even make him sweat," Shattuck said.

Kellum laughed. He raised both hands above his head. "I'll fight any man in New Orleans," he called out in a loud voice.

Shattuck motioned to the man who had taken his wager before. "Am I good for another bet for a thousand dollars?"

"Sure. But on who?"

"On myself."

"But Kellum is a professional boxer," said the bet-taker in surprise.

Shattuck shrugged. "Mark my bet down." He began to remove his jacket.

"Shattuck's going to fight Kellum," the bet-taker called out.

"What's the odds?" a man questioned.

The bet-taker had heard rumors that Shattuck had once been a boxer. But that had to have been years ago. And Kellum had knocked Hadley out with ease.

"Three to one on Kellum," the bet-taker shouted so all the spectators could hear.

"Fight," said the referee.

Kellum came like a storm, hurtling across the ring, his fists poised to strike. Shattuck danced out of the way, blocking the blows Kellum threw as he came in pursuit. Then Shattuck halted. He would test Kellum, just a little bit.

Each man struck and blocked a series of blows. Only once did Kellum tag Shattuck, and that was with a spent blow that hurt almost not at all. Shattuck smacked Kellum twice in the face and glided smoothly off to the side.

Shattuck tasted the salt and copper of blood in his mouth. He smiled at the taste. It had been a long time since he had last fought. Now he had measured the man from Philadelphia. Shattuck knew he was the stronger. He could beat Kellum.

Shattuck drove in. Kellum blocked strongly, but somehow Shattuck's long-reaching fists were inside his guard and viciously smashing him. A savage wallop crashed into his face, slamming him to the floor.

Kellum leapt quickly up. Shattuck was there to meet him, swinging, nailing Kellum with a powerful right, hammering with his left. Kellum went down again.

Kellum climbed back to his feet. Stars were exploding in his head. He sucked in a tortured, scalding breath of air.

"You're no fighter," Shattuck said in a cold contemptuous voice. "I'm going to beat you to death."

Shattuck took deliberate aim and started to hit the bloody specter of Kellum's face. Oh, how he loved the game, the feel of his fists striking Kellum, the jar of the crashing impacts running so damn pleasantly up his arms.

Kellum tried to back out of reach of the pounding fists. A black curtain was falling, blinding him. He felt the ropes against his back. He hooked his arms over them. If he fell he lost.

His battered mind warned him that he should fall, or he would die. The warning came too late. Shattuck's right fist drove a sliver of Kellum's broken nose up into his brain.

"You're a goddamned fool, Lott," cursed Stanton Shattuck. His hands were balled into bony fists and he stood poised on the balls of his feet. "The two men you sent to cripple Wollfolk failed in the job and got crippled themselves. You should have gone yourself to see that the job was done right."

Beads of sweat hung on Lott's forehead. He knew Shattuck was ready to beat him, and there was absolutely nothing he could do to prevent the prizefighter from doing it. Fear came into the flat orbs of Lott's eyes, moving below the surface like slimy water creatures in the pale-blue pool.

The four men sitting at the nearby table in the room stirred uneasily. They knew Shattuck's violent nature.

Farr Rawlins was most distant from Shattuck. He was at the end of the table in the chair he always used for business meetings. He closely watched Shattuck standing with clenched fists, his yellow eyes glittering animal-like, muscles drawn to taut cords. The man would strike Lott a deadly blow.

Shattuck was a tall man in the prime of life. In his young days in New York, he had been a bare-knuckle boxer. After a series of wins, he had taken his money and gone into business on the docks of the Hudson River. He had brought his savagery from the prize ring to the waterfront. Even in that rough place, his brutality was unusual and became common talk among the dockowners and stevedores. In a few short years, he had amassed a fortune. Many competitors fell by the wayside. The bones of a number of them rested in the mud at the bottom of the Hudson River.

New Orleans, growing rapidly, had acquired the

name of Queen City. It was the unrivaled financial center and slave market of the South. The seaport city was second only to New York for the tonnage of cargo shipped from its waterfront. The vigorous growth of New Orleans and its unbridled violence had drawn Shattuck. Two years before he had sold his holdings in New York, traveled to New Orleans, and begun to purchase waterfront docks and warehouses.

Even Shattuck's fortune could buy but a minor portion of the waterfront. However, instead of the violent methods he used against his competitors in New York, he developed a new strategy. Over the months he had formed a cartel of the major waterfront owners. They called their organization the Ring. They agreed to work together to rig the bids for contracts for the use of dockage and warehouse space.

One major property owner, Albert Wollfolk, refused to discuss such an arrangement and continued to bid his eight hundred feet of docks and large warehouse independently of everyone else.

There were many contracts to bid for, and Wollfolk was no threat, until the army and navy arrived and began to seek huge amounts of space and cargo handling. The members of the Ring became fearful that Wollfolk's bids, being so much lower than theirs, would alert the military procurement officers to the collusion in bidding by the members of the Ring.

"It's over, Stanton," Rawlins said. "Nothing

can change the fact that Wollfolk escaped Lott's head-busters."

Shattuck, his anger white-hot, whirled toward the voice. He was ready to lash out at the person who had dared go against him.

Rawlins stared calmly back. There was an amused twist to his thin lips as he idly rubbed the thick curved handle of his cane.

Shattuck caught himself. These men were scoundrels. All had committed fraud and murder. All the killings had not been done by contract. The men had murdered with their own hands. He had some measure of control over them because the cartel he had organized was outrageously profitable, but much more important, they did not want to face him in a fight.

However, Shattuck did not control one man, Rawlins. The man was hard and tough, but crippled in one leg. A heavy cane held him upright when he walked. He was very rich, and the new money he made was but a marker, a method of scoring his success over his business foes and the military, which he deeply hated.

Shattuck had once tried to bully Rawlins. The crippled man had lifted his cane and pointed it at Shattuck. "My game leg prevents me from fighting you, so I'll just have to use my cane on you if you come near me."

Shattuck was confident he could take the cane away from Rawlins and beat him to death with it. Still, there had been some look in the man's eyes that had stopped Shattuck. He had never been able to sort out the basis for his decision not to spring upon Rawlins.

"Give Lott another chance," Rawlins said. "He has done many successful jobs for us."

Shattuck laughed, more a growl. He raked his view over the remaining two members of the Ring, trying to determine what they were thinking.

The Frenchman Russee Loussat looked worried. He had inherited his section of waterfront. The property had been in his family for several generations. Over the years the Loussats had done what was necessary to retain possession during the Spanish and American control of New Orleans.

Loussat enjoyed dueling, kept a quadroon mistress in the Ramparts, and raised a large white family in the east end of the Vieux Carré.

He came from an old and respected French family. Due to that, he represented several absentee French dock-owners. They gave him free rein to manage their properties, caring only that they remain very profitable.

The hatchet-thin face of the last man, Edward Tarboll, was unreadable, as usual. He had appeared in New Orleans several years back. He never talked about his past. But he had brought money, and that was sufficient in New Orleans. He too had recognized that the waterfront was the heart of the city, and that controlling a portion of it would bring him much wealth. He had quietly begun to purchase short segments that joined one another. By combining them he was the owner of a major stretch of docks.

Shattuck knew little of Tarboll's private life, only that he lived in a large mansion in the Garden District. It was staffed with a bevy of young black female slaves. Shattuck had heard tales from the Swamp that Tarboll had once been captain of a pirate ship. At times, when Shattuck was practicing with his pistol in one of the dueling gymnasiums, he would see Tarboll there. The man was an expert with both the sword and pistol.

"Lott, are you certain your two fellows attacked the right man?" Rawlins asked.

"Ask Loussat," Lott said.

Loussat spoke, "My nephew who works in Rosiere's office as a law clerk has been on the lookout for the young Wollfolk. He came to me and told me Wollfolk had arrived and what he looked like. I gave Lott this information."

Lott nodded. "That's right. Then I reason Wollfolk would go to the docks and check the property he owned. My men went there looking for him. They were to rough him up enough that he'd be in the hospital a few days."

"Then this Ohio lad puts your two toughs in the hospital," said Rawlins. "I'd like to have seen that."

"They weren't expecting him to pull a pistol. But he almost missed, just wounding them."

"Unless that was what he wanted to do," Rawlins said. "What does this Wollfolk look like?" questioned Shattuck.

"Young, mid-twenties," Lott said. "He's medium height, maybe a little taller, and thick through the chest. Gray-eyed and brown-haired."

"Very well, Lott," Rawlins said. "You can go. We'll call you when we need you again."

Lott gave Rawlins a grateful look and hurried from the room.

Shattuck was silent for a full minute, staring at the door through which Lott had disappeared. Then he turned a hard face to Rawlins. "We have just made a very dangerous mistake. The man should have been killed. We can't have failures."

"You are totally correct," Rawlins said. "Have Kelty kill Lott today. After your threats, he can no longer be trusted to remain silent about us."

Shattuck threw back his head and laughed. "You played a trick on Lott. He actually believed you were on his side."

"I didn't want you to kill him here. Kelty will do it someplace far away from us. Lott will just be another one of the twenty or so killed this week."

"We can have Kelty finish the job Lott failed at and disable Wollfolk," Tarboll said.

"Kelty would never take a job just to disable a man," Rawlins said. "He never leaves a victim alive."

"Albert Wollfolk was a problem and we eliminated him," said Shattuck. "Now we have this young Wollfolk to contend with. We must do something."

"He may not know the business and therefore will not be a competitor," Rawlins said. "It is very possible he will not bid against us for the rich military contracts. I think it best not to go after him again, but just watch him for a few days and see what kind of man he is. He may not be as troublesome as his uncle."

Shattuck looked first at one man and then the other. Loussat and Tarboll nodded in agreement. "All right," Shattuck said. He spoke to Rawlins. "I think Gunnard should slow down the work at Wollfolk's docks and warehouses even more than he has up to now. We can drive up Wollfolk's costs and make his contracts unprofitable. Gunnard can do that without Wollfolk ever realizing what's happening."

"Let's not underestimate Wollfolk again," said Rawlins. "How is Gunnard controlling the blacks?"

"They know he can kick them off the job any-time it pleases him. Also he has told them that the young Wollfolk hired someone to kill his uncle so that he could inherit the property."

"Are the blacks believing that?" Tarboll asked.

"The free blacks all liked Wollfolk, for he was a generous man to work for," Shattuck said. "He paid the best wages of any employer on the docks. He never whipped the slaves that he contracted from the plantation-owners in their slack season. All the blacks will dislike Wollfolk and will do what Gunnard tells them to."

"Then, for now we wait and watch," Rawlins said.

"And if he turns out to be trouble?" Shattuck asked.

Rawlins smiled his thin smile. "I think we all

know someone who can kill him in broad daylight, and it'll be completely legal."

"He will fall for the trap where his uncle was too wise," Loussat said.

"I'm certain he will," Rawlins said.

The tables, crowded with patrons, overflowed the Café Rubin and spilled out into the courtyard in the rear. Shattuck sat against the back wall beneath a large eucalyptus tree and listened to the noisy babble of the people. Now and then he sipped at his glass of wine. He was damned tired of waiting and would leave in one more minute.

A broad-bodied man with a full black beard came in by the small door in the wall of the courtyard. He threaded a path through the tables and immediately sat down, across from Shattuck. He said not a word, merely folding his big, calloused hands on the wooden top of the table.

"Hello, Kelty," Shattuck said. He was certain Kelty was not his true name. He was dressed in a gray broadcloth suit and white shirt. A hat was pulled down low on his forehead. Black eyes, glinting with an oily sheen, stared back from beneath the brim of his hat.

"You're an hour late," Shattuck said. He wondered if Kelty had spent the hour watching the men in the café and prowling the surrounding area searching for a trap that could be sprung on him.

"I'm here now," Kelty said, his voice a coarse rasping sound. "What do you want?"

"I want a man to take a very long trip. Would you help him to make the journey?"

"Yes."

One word, and a man's death was sealed. Kelty's terse method of conversing had not changed at all in the two years Shattuck had known him. He had first heard Kelty's name whispered by Russee Loussat as they had watched a boxing match. Loussat in a moment of excitement had referred to the killer instinct of the fighter that won the contest to the instinct of an assassin named Kelty.

Shattuck had questioned Loussat and learned the assassin could be contacted by leaving a name at a French bakery on Saint Peter Street. When Shattuck had tried that, the baker had refused to take the message. The man seemed much afraid. It had taken Shattuck two months to pull the elusive assassin into the open, and he had accomplished that by talking to people who told him to talk with other people. Finally he had left a message at the laundry on the Esplanade. Kelty had appeared one day, swinging into step beside him as he walked along the street to his office.

Shattuck made an agreement with Kelty to kill a man, not an important man. Shattuck wanted only to test Kelty. The targeted man vanished permanently.

"What is the man's name that should take a trip?" Kelty asked.

"Ed Lott," Shattuck replied.

"I know Lott. He's one of your men. A drunkard. You were a fool ever to have hired him."

Shattuck's temper rose. To be called a fool by Kelty was the worst of insults. He wondered if he could take Kelty in a no-holds-barred fight. He thought he could, but it would be a dangerous, and certainly a painful game to play.

"I want Lott to take his trip today."

"I'm busy for the next few days."

"It has to be today."

Kelty studied the well-dressed man. He sensed they were much alike. Shattuck had accumulated sufficient money to hire his killing done, that was the only difference. But if the need arose, Shattuck could easily revert to doing the deed himself.

Kelty spoke, "I always take time to plan my work. That's why I never fail."

"You can think of a way to do it safely, and do it sometime today. I'll pay a bonus of two hundred dollars."

"Do you know where Lott is?"

"An hour ago, or a little longer, I saw him going into the Pretty Lady. He's probably still there."

"Just in case he's not in the whorehouse, where does he live?"

"On Barracks Street." Shattuck gave Kelty the number.

"What about the body?"

"Leave it on the street, or in his room, or wherever. I don't care if it's found."

"All right. I'll do it. That'll be seven hundred dollars."

"Half now and half when it's done," Shattuck said, reaching for his wallet.

"No," said Kelty. "All of it now. You know I always keep my word."

Shattuck knew Lott was as good as dead. He took several bills from his wallet and slid them across the table.

Kelty palmed the money in his hand and left by the rear exit. Shattuck realized Kelty had been at the table less than two minutes. The assassin was a wary animal.

6

LOTT took his loving a dollar at a time with the redheaded whore in the Pretty Lady brothel. He left the room of the woman and walked along the hallway toward the front entrance. He staggered once and smiled to himself. He was a little drunk, and a dollar poorer, but he felt damn fine.

Instead of going back through the parlor, Lott unbolted the side door and stepped outside into the evening dusk. Mary Margret wouldn't like the door being left open, but who cared what the hell she liked. Lott moved off along the street.

"Hey, mate, you got two bits for a beached and broke sailor?" called a raspy voice.

Lott turned. A man in a U.S. sailor's uniform and carrying a ditty bag was walking toward him.

"I'm down on my luck temporarily like, but I got a billet on a ship starting tomorrow," said the sailor. "Then I'll have a place to hang my hammock."

The sailor slowed as two men passed on the sidewalk. Then he came on closer to Lott.

"Sure, I got a two-bit piece for a sailor. I was once a sea dog myself." Lott wobbled some as he dug into his pocket and began to finger through some coins.

The sailor swung the ditty bag to hold it under his left arm, the side toward the street. His right hand brought a knife from the mouth of the bag.

Lott looked up as the sailor bumped into him, crowding him into the wall of the whorehouse. A hot, searing pain ran through Lott's stomach, up high near his ribs. His lungs froze in midbreath.

Lott pushed at the sailor. Something awful was happening to him. He had to have room to breathe. But the sailor stood firm, holding him against the wall. Lott dropped the coins and struck at the man.

The sailor swiftly jerked his head aside and the blow missed. He withdrew the knife from Lott. Then very deliberately he plunged it up under Lott's ribs. The keen point of the weapon pierced the throbbing heart.

Lott moaned and his eyes went blank.

The sailor pulled his blade free and eased his pressure on Lott. The dead man slid down the wall, to lie on the sidewalk.

The sailor bent over Lott. "Sleep it off, mate," he said in a voice that could be heard in the street. He tucked the ditty bag more firmly under his arm. At the same time he shoved the knife into the open neck of the ditty bag. He went off nonchalantly along the street.

Half a block later, Kelty entered the open door of a rooming house. Once inside, he hastened his step down the center passageway and out the rear door. A passing hack halted at his signal, and Kelty climbed inside.

"To the waterfront and Saint Anne Street," he directed the driver. "I'll show you where to go from there."

Five minutes later, Kelty stood on a deserted section of the waterfront. He carried the ditty bag in between two mounds of cargo. Hastily he removed his suit from the bag and changed it for the sailor's uniform. The uniform and bag were crammed into a break in one of the crates.

Kelty strode across the quay, up over the levee, and down onto Front Street.

The onshore wind died before the merchantman *Boston Maiden,* chartered by the U.S. military, could reach the dock. Without headway and at the mercy of the strong current of the Mississippi, the ship veered away from its intended berth and started to drift backward. The captain of the merchantman began to shout through his megaphone at the harbor boats floating on the river and waiting for the call.

The four boats, manned by strong oarsmen, darted up to the ship. The boatmen captured the lines thrown down by the sailors on the deck and, pulling mightily on their oars, took up the slack. The downriver movement of the *Boston Maiden* was halted, reversed, and the ship began to inch back toward the dock.

Honoré Savigne, reporter for the *Louisiana Courier*, sat perched on the top of a tall mound of cargo near the water's edge. He held his pad of paper on his knee and was writing the introduction to his article on the arrival of the shipload of wounded and ill men from General Scott's invasion of Mexico. Now and then he would glance up at the huge sailing ship and the tiny ant men in the rowboats hauling it safely to shore.

Honoré slapped at the swarm of buzzing mosquitoes as he reviewed the course of the war. General Scott had captured the Mexican port city of Vera Cruz with negligible losses of men. Cerro Gordo, the next city sitting astride his invasion route, had been more costly, with nearly five hundred casualties. Now Scott was garrisoned in Puebla, seventy miles inland from the Gulf of Mexico, waiting for reinforcements and supplies from the States. Only minor skirmishes were being fought with the Mexican army. However, the return flow to the States of soldiers unfit for duty was swelling.

A fast mail packet had arrived in New Orleans from Vera Cruz two days earlier. The captain alerted the military and the hospital officials of the coming arrival of the *Boston Maiden* loaded with many sick and wounded soldiers.

A command was shouted on the ship. Thick

hawsers snaked down from the merchantman and dockworkers secured them to the stout cleats on the dock. Gangways were immediately swung out from the quarterdeck and fantail of the ship and lowered to rest on the dock.

Honoré jumped down from the pile of cargo and moved toward the *Boston Maiden*. Many walking patients had gathered on the ship's deck near the gangways as they were being lowered. Now the men came hurrying down to the dock. Medical corpsmen began to carry stretcher patients from belowdeck and down the slanting gangways. The ambulance wagons from the Marine Hospital and Charity Hospital came over the levee and rumbled out across the wooden dock.

Honoré bent over a soldier on one of the stretches and looked into the pain-filled eyes. "Welcome back to the States and to New Orleans, soldier," he said.

"What the hell can a one-legged man do in New Orleans?" asked the soldier in a bitter voice.

Honoré looked at the man's legs. One pant leg was empty and had been neatly folded four times and pinned to the cloth at the man's waist.

"That's up to the man," Honoré said. "What outfit were you with?"

"The Indiana 1st Volunteer Riflemen," the soldier replied. "Go away and talk with somebody else." The soldier turned his face from Honoré.

Savigne studied the one-legged soldier for a moment. The war was not grand and glorious for this man or for the several hundred other men limping

74

toward the ambulances, or lying on the stretchers too weak to stand.

He moved on. He stopped beside a man lying motionless on a stretcher. "How are you, soldier?" he asked.

The man did not speak, nor did he stir to slap at a large mosquito circling his exposed face. The mosquito landed, settled itself, and drove its probing snout into the man's skin. The mosquito began to drink hungrily.

Honoré stooped and brushed the mosquito away. He turned the tag pinned to the man's shirt so that it could be read. "Pvt. John Wilkinson" was written on the paper.

Honoré peered more closely at the soldier. His face was dark bronze in color. The lips were cracked as if from a long thirst, and blood oozed from them. Veins were distended in his forehead like thick, pulsing cords. He drooled a black liquid from the corner of his mouth.

Quickly Savigne stood erect and backed away. The man was infected with the deadly Bronze John, yellow fever. Honoré, in his thirty years of life in New Orleans, had seen too many instances of the black vomit to ever be mistaken what the symptom meant.

He walked along the row of stretchers, glancing into the faces of the soldiers. In the early stages of the disease, the symptoms could be confused with other ailments. However, in that single line of sick men, Honoré thought there were two other yellow-fever victims. He swept his view over the many returning soldiers he had not examined. There could be forty, maybe fifty cases of the disease among them.

More than half of these men would be dead in five days. In the crowded city, thousands more could die if they caught the fever. Fear came alive in Savigne, like some great snake uncoiling in his stomach.

The mosquito felt the jarring vibration as the merchantman bumped the dock. It stretched its wings once, then launched itself into the air, rising up from the wetness beneath the dock and through a crack between the planking into the daylight.

The scent of the creatures with the warm, moist bodies was everywhere. The mosquito was drawn inexorably toward the nearest human, one lying on a stretcher. He dived down, landing on the man's face. With an inborn knowledge, the mosquito sank its snout into the open pore of the man's skin. Inward he drove the sharp, searching point until it reached the flow of rich warm blood. The mosquito began to drink, swiftly sucking at the red liquid.

A hand swung at the mosquito. In a movement almost too fast to see, the insect jerked its snout free and darted away.

A moment later, the mosquito found the unprotected arm of a dockworker. It fed there greedily until its sting caused the man to strike at it. The mosquito dodged out of reach unhurt. Still hungry, it discovered yet a third man to feast upon.

Then, satiated, its stomach engorged with blood, it sank down once again through the crack in the dock planking to its resting place on the wet ground. It would soon feed again.

Honoré hastened across the dock to the physician directing the loading of the patients into the ambulance wagons. He knew the man from a previous meeting during the preparation of a story about the Marine Hospital.

"Doctor Carstensen, my name is Honoré Savigne. May I talk with you?"

"Yes, Mr. Savigne. I remember you. But I'm very busy and in a hurry. Some of these men need immediate attention after being cooped up in that ship for six days. Please speak quickly."

"Come with me, Doctor. I wish to show you something."

"Can't it wait?"

"No. This is very important, or I wouldn't waste your time."

"Very well. Lead the way." The doctor followed Savigne down the line of stretchers.

"Look, Doctor. The man has yellow fever. Shouldn't he be quarantined?"

Carstensen looked intently at the soldier. Then he raised his view to Honoré. A strange expression was on his face. "This man does not have yellow fever. He has been exposed too long to the devilish climate of Mexico."

"But he has all the symptoms," Honoré said. It was so obvious. Why couldn't the physician see it?

"He doesn't have the fever," Carstensen said in a stern voice. "And even if he does, why should we quarantine him? We do not know what causes the disease or how it is spread. Quarantine has never worked. Now I must get the soldiers to the hospital." He whirled and walked speedily away.

The last of the sick and injured soldiers were loaded. The scores of ambulance wagons rattled off the dock, divided at the top of the levee, one group heading in the direction of the Charity Hospital and the second toward the Marine Hospital.

Savigne watched the last vehicle vanish from sight. Carstensen was a respected and skilled physician. How could he possibly miss such an obvious diagnosis for yellow fever? Honoré shook his head in bewilderment. Was the answer simply that Carstensen did not want a panic in the city and was willing to gamble that only these few men would have the disease? Savigne would not print what he suspected: that deadly Bronze John had invaded New Orleans. But he would visit the hospitals in a few days. If the men died, then he would be certain, and he would tell the people of the city.

7

TIM rose up from the cold pit of liquid black of unconsciousness. His senses flickered on one by one. The pain came alive in his shoulder and side and throbbed with every heartbeat. His lungs felt raw and burned.

His memories rushed back, the man shooting him and the drowning in the river. But he must not be dead, for the pain was too real. He opened his eyes a crack and cautiously, without moving his head, looked around.

A mulatto man sat in a chair a few feet away. He was stropping the long blade of a knife on the leather top of his boot. His face was broad and bearded, and there was a scar over the left eye socket. Slightly lower and the blade making the injury would have blinded him in that eye. The man hesitated in the sharpening strokes of the knife, as if he were listening for something, then he began again.

The man looked fierce and immensely strong. With each swipe of the blade, the muscles of his powerful arms rippled beneath his brown skin. Was he enemy or friend? Tim would wait, feigning unconsciousness, until he had more time to evaluate the situation. He closed his eyes.

Morissot had sat for a long time listening to the white man's low, even breathing. Just now the rhythm had subtly changed, increasing slightly, and the breath deepening. Morissot knew with certainty that the man was awake. He was doing what Morissot would have done, say nothing upon coming back to consciousness in a strange place.

Morissot began to speak. "My name is Lezin Morissot. I'm a fisherman, and I found you nearly drowned in the river. What is your name?"

The white man made no sign he heard. The only movement about him was the rise and fall of his chest.

Marie heard her father talking, and she came from the next room to stand in the doorway. She glanced at her father, then at the still form of the wounded man. A questioning expression came to her face.

"This is my daughter, Marie," Morissot continued. "What is your name?" He was silent for a few seconds and then added, "Talk to me, for I know you are awake."

Tim opened his eyes and stared into the black orbs of the mulatto. The man nodded his head across the room.

Tim glanced in the same direction. A slender young woman with ivory skin stood watching him. In the slanting rays of the sun streaming in the window of the room, he saw her large round eyes were green. Her hair was a slice of midnight. Tim's breath caught at the beauty of the girl.

The girl smiled at Tim, and the smile increased her beauty to a dazzling thing. She came to stand beside her father.

"What is your name?" Marie repeated her father's question.

"Wollfolk, Timothy Wollfolk." How could this brown man have such a white daughter?

"We are pleased that you are better," Marie said.

"How long have I been here?" asked Tim.

"Since yesterday morning," Morissot answered.

"Are you hungry or thirsty?" Marie said.

"A little of both," Tim replied.

"I'll fix you something." She hurried from the room.

Tim's gaze followed Marie. The sight of her loveliness partially deadened the pain that cut at his body. He looked at Morissot.

The mulatto's face held an odd expression, one that Tim could not fathom. The man seemed to nod to himself, just the barest movement of his head, as if he had made some silent, inner decision.

"Marie is an excellent cook, even though she is young," Morissot said.

"I'm sure she is." Tim felt awkward because of the thoughts that had come into his mind about the girl.

"Why were you in the river?" questioned Morissot.

"Three men robbed me, and when I tried to fight them, one shot me. I fell into the water and was carried away. If it hadn't been for that, I would be dead. I'm sure they meant to kill me. How did you come to find me?"

"You came floating by while I was near the water. I pulled you out and pumped a gallon of water from your lungs. Then I brought you here."

"I must tell the law what happened," Tim said. "Maybe they can catch the men and get back my belongings."

"I doubt that. The law has not had much luck at catching robbers or murderers in New Orleans."

"Then what do I do?"

"Tell the law, if you want. But for now you must heal. You can stay here for a few days."

"I have no money." Tim knew he was naked beneath the blanket that covered him. "I don't even have any clothes." He tried to smile.

"You may wear some of mine. They will be a little large and loose, but should serve the purpose. Can you sit up?"

Tim struggled upward, favoring his left side. The pain rose to a crescendo that seared his brain. The room seemed to darken. Beads of sweat popped out on his face.

"Try harder," Morissot said. "Wounded men who move and walk heal most quickly. And Jonathan sews a tight stitch. You will only think you are ripping apart." He made no effort to help Tim, merely watching him.

At that moment through his pain, Tim hated the brown man. Damn you to hell, I will sit up. He started to lift his legs, and a moan escaped him before he could catch it between clenched teeth. His legs slid from under the blanket and his feet rested on the floor.

"Father, he is ready to faint," Marie cried as she came into the room with a large glass of water.

"He is tougher than that," Morissot said.

Maybe not, thought Tim, the darkness deepening in the room and seeping into his head, threatening to fill it with blackness. Then, to his amazement, as he sat very still, the darkness began

82

to recede. The pain dropped to an endurable level. By God, he wasn't going to faint, after all.

Marie hurried to Tim's side. "Drink some cold water. That will help."

He reached for the glass. His fingers caught her hand. She aided him to lift the glass to his lips and hold it there. Tim could not decide which was the more enjoyable, her cool fingers under his or the delicious water.

"Now, you can walk to the table and eat," said Morissot. "Marie, set out the food for Timothy."

"First a pair of pants and a shirt," said Tim.

"I'll get some clothes for you," agreed Morissot.

Tim saw a satisfied smile in the back of Morissot's black eyes.

Fannin arrived at the law office of Gilbert Rosiere promptly at nine A.M. The dark-skinned law clerk led him immediately back to the inner office of the lawyer.

"Welcome, Mr. Wollfolk. Welcome to New Orleans." Rosiere climbed erect, a tall bony man, and came around his desk. He clasped Lew's hand in a hard grip.

"Thank you, sir," replied Lew, matching the lawyer's grip.

"Please be seated," said Rosiere. He retreated back behind his desk.

Lew sat down in the overstuffed leather chair before the desk. Now the test began. Could he fool this sharp-eyed lawyer?

"My condolences to you for the death of your uncle," Rosiere said.

"I've heard that my Uncle Albert was murdered. Do you think that is true?"

Rosiere looked surprised. His sharp eyes locked on Fannin. "Who told you that?"

"Who told me isn't important. Is it true? If so, someone will pay."

"The police investigated his death. It has been classified as an accidental drowning."

"You are being paid to attend to my uncle's affairs, aren't you? Part of those duties would be to tell his nephew what you know. Also what you only suspect. Am I also in danger?"

"Has something happened that makes you think you are in danger?"

"You answer my questions with questions. But this one time I'll reply. I was attacked last night by two men with blackjacks. They seemed to be looking for me."

"What happened?"

"No more answers from me. It is your turn. Did my uncle have enemies?"

Rosiere hunched his shoulders. "Business on the waterfront is obtained by bidding for army, navy, and private contracts. Your uncle was a shrewd businessman. He underbid many competitors. Also he was easy to anger, and he fought several duels. Men were killed or wounded by him. He bought a placée, a quadroon mistress desired by other men. He kept raising his bid until all others had fallen aside. Yes, he had ene-mies. Probably many enemies."

Rosiere sat back in his chair. "You do not look injured. What happened to the two men who as-saulted you?"

Fannin laughed low, and rough. "I shall con-sider you my lawyer as well as my uncle's, so I'll tell you." He moved the flap of his jacket to the side to show the Colt pistol in his waistband. "Like my uncle, I won't be crowded. So I shot the hell out of both men, not killing them, just putting some holes in them."

Rosiere fastened his eyes on the gray-eyed young man before him. He did not much resemble Albert Wollfolk, but the challenging glint in the eyes, the hint of iron just below the surface, ran through both men. This Wollfolk would also make ene-mies, and very quickly. And probably also die.

"Shall we now get to your inheritance?" said the lawyer. "I assume you brought identification."

"Yes, I have letters telling who I am from the pastor of our church, one from a banker who knew me, and a third from my boss at the Lynch and Lynch Steamboat Company." Fannin pulled the papers from his pocket and handed them across the desk. He sat back and, keeping his face impas-sive, watched the lawyer quickly scan the docu-ments. Lew thought the man had already made up his mind that he was Wollfolk.

Rosiere handed back the identification papers. "Thank you." He picked up a document from his desk. "Your Uncle Albert has directed by means of his will that you are to receive sole possession of his property known as the A. Wollfolk Warehouse and Dockage, the clipper ship *Honest Traveler*, his personal residence on Washington Avenue, and the total sum of his money in the Mechanics and Traders Bank on Canal Street. There are two accounts, a business fund and a private one. You are a wealthy young man."

"My uncle has been very generous to me," Lew said. "In your letter, you said there are some bequests that must be carried out. What are they?"

"Albert Wollfolk also owns a five-room cottage on Rampart Street. He has a friend living there, her name is Cécile Pereaux. She is a placée, as I mentioned before, a quadroon." Rosiere hesitated, watching Lew. "Does that mean anything to you?"

"Only that the friend is a woman."

"She is one-quarter Negro, and his mistress. Mr. Wollfolk began the arrangement three or four years ago. He saw her at one of the Bals de Cordon, also called Quadroon Balls. That is the grand occasion where the young quadroon girls, always virgins, are shown off by their mothers to the white men. No black men are allowed. For one to show up would mean the worst whipping and possibly death. The girls are educated from a very tender age in music, verse, languages, and are quite beautiful. Often they go overseas to Europe to study.

"I have been to the balls. The girls are dressed most elegantly. The white men select the young women they find most appealing. Then they make arrangements with the mothers of the girls, usually a cash payment of several thousand dollars and always a house and an allowance for living expenses."

Lew wondered if the laywer had a placée of his own. "Is this a common thing with the men of New Orleans?" he asked.

"There are probably three thousand placées on the Ramparts, that's a section of town centered around Rampart Street."

"My uncle seems to have found a way to enjoy himself. What is to happen to Cécile Pereaux?"

"You are to see to her comfort and needs in a manner befitting a longtime friend of your uncle's. He suggests you visit her and see if you want to continue the same relationship he had."

Lew laughed. "Albert Wollfolk was a man who saw things in a simple light. But suppose I don't want the same arrangement?"

"Then Miss Pereaux is to receive the house on Rampart Street in her name, and free and clear of any mortgages. Also she is to be given the annual allowance that I just mentioned. Should she marry or take another man without marriage, the allowance may be stopped. Your uncle states that Miss Pereaux is a very honest and trustworthy person. He adds, and these are his words, 'In all matters of being a woman, Cécile is most splendid.' "

"I wish I'd known my uncle better. I think we would have gotten along nicely."

"He had many good qualities. But he was stubborn. Here is his will duly witnessed and legal.

Read it thoroughly. Take your time. Then tell me if you agree to the terms. Then I'll draw up the necessary papers, have the probate judge approve them, and see that they are filed in the public records."

Lew took the document written on two pages. "Before I read this, tell me about the various properties."

"All right. The warehouse and dockage company owns eight hundred feet of docks along the Mississippi, one of the largest single ownerships on the river. Also there is a big warehouse containing thirty-five thousand square feet of space and eighty drays and two hundred mules. All told, there are nearly one hundred employees. The business office is on Front Street just east of Toulouse. Your bookkeepers, and sometimes your white foreman, can be found there. The foreman is a new man hired a couple of weeks ago after the previous one did not show up for work. He seems to have simply vanished. See Tom Spandling, the head bookkeeper, for the details you want about the company.

"Mr. Wollfolk's private residence is one of the nicest in the city. You will enjoy living there. I'll give you the address."

Lew read the will slowly and carefully. Finishing, he looked up at the lawyer. "I accept my uncle's property and agree to the conditions."

"Very well, Mr. Wollfolk, come by tomorrow and I'll have the papers drawn up. I see no reason why you should not occupy your new home at once. Here is the address and also the address of the cottage on Rampart Street. Legally you can't take any business actions or write drafts on the bank account until all the papers have been signed by you, approved by the judge, and made a part of the public records. But if you need some money, I can advance you some from my personal funds."

"No need for that. What time should we meet tomorrow?"

"I'll need a few hours to draft the documents and the necessary copies. Is three P.M. all right?"

"That's fine." Lew stood up. "Until tomorrow."

Lew left the private office of Rosiere and went through the outer room. He scanned the two law clerks. Both were watching him. The dark-skinned man pulled his eyes away and looked down at the papers on his desk.

Fannin caught a hack and gave the black driver the address of the house on Washington Street. He settled back on the leather seat of the vehicle and relaxed, listening to the thud of the shod hooves of the trotting horse striking the ground. The first hurdle had been safely made. Rosiere had accepted the identification Lew had presented. But each step he moved deeper into the impersonation of Wollfolk made the situation more dangerous. Many things could go wrong to brand him as a fraud and thief. But the game was worth the gamble.

Lew watched the houses pass by the open window of the hackney. He thought the grim fact existed that unknown foes had struck down Albert Wollfolk. Now they could be watching Lew, waiting to strike at him. He might have to kill again to earn the inheritance.

8

THE hackney driver pulled his vehicle to a halt and turned to Fannin. "Here you be, sir, the address you said."

Lew paid the man and turned to survey his new home. The house, a pale yellow with snow-white trim set on three acres or so of land, was surrounded by a wrought-iron fence. It was two-storied with a garret floor and dormer windows above. Stately round columns reached to the top of the second floor. There were many tall windows to allow the cool night air to enter. He judged the house would contain at least twenty rooms. Protecting all from the frequent coastal rain was a durable gray slate roof.

Lew entered through the carriageway gate and walked in the shade of a row of large trees along the stone-paved lane to the rear of the house. Setting back from the main structure was a carriage house with space for three vehicles. A highly polished buggy with the top up was nearest Lew, then came a surrey, and third was a light spring wagon. To the right was a line of covered stables that could accommodate eight to ten horses.

On the rear of the property was a long brick

building with a steeply pitched roof and seven doors opening out toward the main house. Several black children, boys and girls, played in the yard under a huge pecan tree. Lew judged this the slave quarters.

"May I help you, sir?" asked a man's voice.

Lew turned. A black man stood on the back stoop.

"Yes, I'm Timothy Wollfolk. Albert Wollfolk's nephew. I have come to live here."

The man laughed pleasantly. "I'm Jacob. I'm what sees that the work gets done around here. I'm right glad to see you, Mr. Timothy. Mr. Rosiere said you might come. It's been hard on all of us without Mr. Albert."

"Jacob, would you show me around inside?"

"With pleasure, sir. Please come in."

Jacob guided Lew about the richly furnished home. Their feet made no sound as they walked on the thick wool carpet. The rooms with their high ceilings were cool. He was introduced to three black women and two men. All immediately broke into smiles when Jacob introduced him. Albert Wollfolk must have treated his slaves very kindly.

In the kitchen, Lew stopped. "What do you have left from breakfast? I missed mine and am hungry."

"Rosalee, you hear Mr. Timothy. Answer him," Jacob called out to a smiling fat black woman standing near the wood burning cooking stove.

"Sausage, strawberries with cream, bread, butter, or I can cook you something in a jiffy," Rosalee said.

"Just what you have ready will be plenty." Lew seated himself at the long kitchen table.

The big woman seemed to float back and forth across the kitchen, placing a clean cloth on the table before Lew and the food a few seconds later. "Will there be anything else you want?" she asked.

"Not one thing," Lew replied. "There's enough food here for three of me."

He began to eat. Jacob and the cook backed away and sat down at a small table near the wall. The woman said something Lew could not hear. The man nodded and both smiled.

Lew finished eating and spoke to Jacob. "Would you find someone to drive me into town? I want to pick up my belongings and bring them here."

"May I drive you, Mr. Timothy? It'd be a great pleasure."

"Certainly. I'd be pleased that you did."

"I'll be ready out at the side entrance in a minute, just as soon as I can harness a horse for the buggy." Jacob hastened from the kitchen by the rear door.

Lew ambled through the house, arriving finally at the door opening onto the carriageway. He had been wrong. There were twenty-four rooms, and that did not include the garret. How could a poor ex–Texas Ranger adjust to such luxury? Very easily, Lew told himself.

Then a frown crossed Lew's face. He was an impostor. All of this really belonged to a dead man floating in the Mississippi River. Fellow, I'm sorry about what happened to you. I hope my luck is better.

In the dark before the dawn, when man's vitality is at its lowest, Tim awoke from a deep pit of sleep. His wounds throbbed and ached. When he tested his muscles, they felt like wet strings. He gave up the idea of rising and searching for water to quench his deep thirst. Instead, he lay in the darkness and listened to a restless wind moaning about the eaves of the house, hating the men who had shot him.

Morning twilight gradually beat back the darkness in the glass of the window. Tim heard someone rise, stir about a little in the kitchen, and then leave. By the sound of the steps on the outside stairway, Tim guessed it was Lezin Morissot.

Tim climbed from his bed and dressed. Wobbly legged, he made his way to the kitchen. He drank a tall glass of water. At the washstand, he rinsed his face and combed his tousled hair.

He went out onto the balcony and, leaning on one of the iron pillars, stared out over the countryside. A light fog was lifting up from the trees and drifting slowly off on the slow breeze. Far off to the east, the ropy smoke of a cooking fire in a neighbor's house climbed sluggishly into the air. He heard the distant crow of a cock. A dog barked in a short staccato that died quickly among the trees.

Holding carefully to the railing, Tim made his

way down the stairway and into the rear yard. Once, and then twice, he circled the house near the tall protective wall. He felt better than yesterday; the damage to his body was receding and his strength returning. He started a third trip around the house.

A lone black butterfly fluttered down from the tree ahead. It did a solo dance, diving and tumbling in the air. A most alluring dancer, but one without a partner. The butterfly wandered up and over the wall and out of view.

"Father, Tim, is anyone here?" Marie called from the balcony.

"I'm here," replied Tim. "But your father left before daylight."

Marie came to the railing of the balcony and looked down at Tim. "He's probably gone fishing. What are you doing?"

"Walking. I believe your father is correct. Injuries heal fastest when the person gets up rather than lays in bed. I've set myself the task of walking five times around the house."

"May I walk with you? We can talk."

"There's no one I'd rather walk and talk with," said Tim. He knew he truly meant it.

Marie ran down the steps, her blue gingham dress hiked up to her knees. Suddenly at the last step, she caught herself up short and glanced at Tim. She dropped her dress and it fell to her shoe tops. She came demurely onward, her eyes on the ground.

Tim watched her approach. He allowed his eyes

to trace the contour of her body, the swell of her hips and the firm young breasts. She flashed a look up at him with her green eyes and smiled in a companionable way. Tim felt as if he was betraying her with his thoughts.

She fell in beside him and they walked together. Neither spoke as they wound a course among the many aged trees within the high walls. They completed the fifth trip, but Tim led on. Her presence had given him new strength.

"Oh, look," cried Marie. "There's a red bird. That means we will have a visitor before the day is over."

Tim glanced at her. She grinned with a little mischievous lift to her eyes as if questioning him whether he believed in that old saying about the red bird.

He answered the unvoiced query. "If that is true, what does the presence of that blue bird mean?" He pointed at the small flyer resting on the top of the wall.

"I have never heard that a blue bird has any special meaning," Marie said.

"Neither have I, but I have heard the one about the red bird."

They laughed together for no reason, except the pleasure of being in each other's company.

Tim's legs were trembling at the end of the eighth circuit of the house, and he recognized how little strength he possessed. He seated himself on a bench beneath a huge walnut tree. Marie sat beside him as he rested.

Tim felt unsettled and troubled, an emotion that even the nearness of Marie could not dispel. He should soon leave the home of the kind Morissots. He must claim his inheritance. Then he would search for the men who had shot him. They would think him dead and, feeling safe, would move openly about. Tim would find them. His anger at his enemies rose. He would buy a pistol and carry it with him. He might never prove the guilt of the men. But he could kill them.

Marie studied the face of this man who had appeared so unexpectedly into her life. His blue eyes moved restlessly about. Something greatly bothered him. She broke the quietness and said in a shy voice, "I thought we were going to talk."

"What would you like to talk about?"

"You said you have come to New Orleans from Cincinnati. Why did you come? If you don't mind telling me."

"I don't mind at all. My uncle, Albert Wollfolk, lived here in New Orleans for many years. He recently died. A lawyer, Gilbert Rosiere, wrote and told me I was the main beneficiary of his will. So I came down from Cincinnati to see the will and probably claim his properties. I don't know what he owned, but will find out when I meet the lawyer."

"My father may know of Albert Wollfolk. When do you plan to go to see the lawyer?"

"Very soon. A day or two. But I'll have a problem in identifying myself. All my papers were lost when I was robbed and shot. I will have to

96

send back to Ohio for statements of who I am from people who know me. That could take several days."

"You can stay here. I think my father likes you."

"Do you think he would make me a loan? I need clothes and some money to spend for other things."

"I believe he would. Ask him. He is a kind and gentle man."

Lezin listened without comment to Tim's description of his purpose for coming to New Orleans. He believed the young man's story.

"With the loss of my identification, I can't prove who I am," Tim concluded.

"I knew of Albert Wollfolk," Lezin said. "I've seen him a few times." He fell quiet, mulling what he had been told, what it might mean to his plans.

He sat with Marie and Tim on the balcony of his home. The night was deepening and he watched the fireflies wink on and off among the trees. The plague of mosquitoes was growing. Soon they would crowd the fireflies for sky room to fly. The blood-sucking pests made the summer a miserable time.

"You have not asked for help in straightening all this matter out," Lezin said.

"I do need help, and that is certain. I need money. Also I must write to people in Cincinnati who can vouch for my identity."

"I have money that you may have. Tomorrow

we will drive into the city and buy clothing that fits you. Write your requests to your friends up north and we can mail the letters while we are in town."

"I'm much in your debt," Tim said.

"Perhaps you would like to see some of the properties owned by Albert Wollfolk. I've seen his name on a warehouse along the river. Also I have a friend who can find out if he had other properties."

"I'd like to see all that he owned," Tim said. "I'll never be able to repay you for all your kindness."

Yes, you can, thought Lezin. I have a plan that deeply involves you.

9

CLOUDS were gathering and the day had already begun to grow dim as Lew rode his gray horse slowly along Rampart Street. He checked the numbers painted in neat, precise lettering on the stucco walls of the cottages. He wondered what Wollfolk's mistress Cécile Pereaux would be like.

He halted at the address given to him by Rosiere, a gray stucco two-story house with a delicate iron-railed balcony overhanging the sidewalk. All the homes along the entire block were very similar, the main difference the varied colors with which they were painted. The gate to the carriageway was open.

Lew debated whether to tie his mount to the iron post set in the edge of the sidewalk in front of the cottage, or to ride into the inner courtyard. But the debate with himself was short-lived. He reined the gray into the carriageway. After all, he owned the place.

He rode along the cool, tunnellike flagstone passageway. Halfway back appeared an arched opening into the house with a wooden stair lifting in a swift curve to the upstairs. The building was deep in relation to its width.

In the curtained light of the evening there was the peace of settled age about the large courtyard. Raised flower beds bordered by crumbling red brick surrounded a fountain, where a bronze figure of a child was sprayed by jetting water. Lew saw the source of the water: a raised cistern attached to rainspouts coming from the roof. A banana tree guarded a bunch of unripe fruit with its sheathlike leaves. A huge magnolia tree cast deep shadow near the rear wall. Vines sketched a lacelike tracery of leaves against the stucco and climbed higher to enjoy the daytime sun on the tile rooftop.

Tall French windows, bordered by green shutters, were set into the walls of both the lower and upper floors. Just for an instant, Lew thought there was movement behind one of the upstairs window curtains.

He swung down, and after tying the gray so it could not eat the flowers, he stepped to the door and rapped with the iron knocker. Almost immediately the door was opened by a middle-aged mulatto woman.

"Yes?" said the woman.

"I'd like to speak with Cécile Pereaux," Lew said.

The woman smiled and nodded quickly. "May I tell her your name?"

"Tell her Timothy Wollfolk wants to see her."

The woman did not evidence any surprise at his identity. Miss Pereaux must be aware of his arrival in New Orleans.

"Please come inside."

The woman closed the door behind Lew. "Take a seat, if you like, and I'll inform Miss Pereaux you are here." She left with a whisper of shoes on the carpet.

Lew wandered around the room. He was amazed by the height of the ceiling, at least fourteen feet. That would help make them cool in the warm summers. A beautiful tapestry hung on one wall. There were several quite attractive original paintings on the remaining walls. Overstuffed chairs and a sofa, all dark wood and velvet, were spaced about. Diagonal across one corner was a polished piano, mahogany case and ivory keys. The lid was open, and there was sheet music in the upright music board, as if someone had recently played the instrument. He wondered if Miss Pereaux had been the musician.

"Do you like music, Mr. Wollfolk?" The woman spoke from the inner doorway.

Lew pivoted around. He felt his heart lift at the

beauty of the woman. Her skin was dusky silk. Long hair, black and slightly curly, was piled in a mound on top of her head. Her eyes were black obsidian, set far apart. She was nearly as tall as Lew. He easily understood why Albert Wollfolk had bid so strongly against other men for this lovely female.

Without waiting for his answer, Cécile crossed the room to him and extended her hand. It was cool to Lew's touch. He held it, feeling the bone and muscle beneath the smooth skin.

Lew tried to read her thoughts, but her eyes held a look of remoteness, as if the meeting had no significance to her. Yet he knew the death of Wollfolk had changed her future to a very great extent. And what his nephew thought of her was important.

"Yes, I like music. Do you play?"

"But of course." Her voice was cold, carrying a tone of being wounded.

"What kind of music do you prefer?"

"I've never heard a tune that I didn't like."

Cécile stepped away from Lew. She seated herself at the piano and began to play.

Lew sank into the big chair and listened to the delightful tune springing from under the woman's nimble fingers. He watched her as she became caught up in her music. Her body swayed with a supple grace as she reached for a note. Her fingers sometimes became almost invisible in the faster section of the piece.

The selection of music ended, and Cécile began

another. The piece was slow, almost a lullaby. Lew had never heard it before, but found it enjoyable and relaxing. He laid his head back on the velvet of the chair and closed his eyes, so that the sight of the beautiful woman would not detract from the music.

The tune ceased. Lew opened his eyes and looked at Cécile. She stood up and came to the center of the room.

He quickly stood up. He realized the particular pieces of music selected were not accidental, but rather had been very carefully chosen to create some desired effect upon him. He believed he knew what it was. The woman was intelligent. He liked that.

"Very lovely," Lew said. He moved closer to her.

She gazed back at him, her eyes still holding that cold, faraway expression. "Why did you come to see me, Mr. Wollfolk?"

Lew saw a pulse beating visibly in the small hollow at the left base of her throat, like a tiny trapped animal trying to escape. She was human, very human, and the tension was great within her as she waited for his answer. The piano recital had been an exhibition of one of the skills she possessed, skills of pleasure that she had to give to a man. She was on the stage of reality, where the harshness of life was acted out. And she knew what the reality was.

He extended his hand and placed his index finger on the throbbing spot in the hollow of her throat. He felt the rapid pulses of blood rushing past beneath his fingertip. The cold, unemotional aloofness was but an act.

"My uncle was very fond of you. I came to see why," Lew answered. He removed his hand and lowered it to his side.

"He was a very gentle man, and good to me," Cécile replied. She was taken aback by his manner of touching her, as if reading her inner thoughts through the contact of his fingers.

"Yet he had men who hated him," Lew said.

"He did not treat men as kindly as he did women."

Lew thought he detected a twinkle in the black eyes. He smiled. "Few men do," he said.

"Mr. Wollfolk, would you be kind and have dinner with a lonely woman?"

Lew's smile broadened. And suddenly she was smiling with him. Without waiting for an answer, she clapped her hands together.

Almost instantly the mulatto woman came to the door of the room. "Yes, Miss Cécile?"

"Dinner for two, Titine." Cécile turned to Lew. "Do you like fish, Mr. Wollfolk? I have pompano fresh from the docks. Its flesh is firm and white. Or would you like meat?"

"The fish," said Lew. "I've had only red meat for a very long time."

"Then we shall have the pompano. And, Titine, serve it with your delicious sauce, richly seasoned with spices, and at least three kinds of fruits. Serve my favorite wine. Have the bread hot from

103

the oven with lots of butter." She cast an inquiring look at Lew. "Is that satisfactory?"

"Sounds like a wonderful meal to me."

"Titine, please see to it," Cécile told the woman.

"Yes, Miss Cécile." The woman hurried from the room.

"Now, Mr. Wollfolk, I know you want to talk with me, but can't it wait until after dinner?"

"Yes, I'd prefer that myself." Lew felt a strong desire to touch the woman again.

"Then I have a suggestion. Do you dance?"

"Yes, but likely not the same steps that you dance."

"We shall see. Come with me."

Cécile guided Lew to an adjoining room. The rug had been removed from the center of the space and the wooden floor was smooth and waxed. A divan, two padded chairs, and a small table with straight-back chairs sat near the walls. Five large music boxes some two feet across sat on the table.

"Albert Wollfolk loved to dance." A momentary shadow of sorrow cloaked Cécile's face, then she spoke to Lew again. "He had those boxes made to play his favorite tunes. Perhaps you would like to also dance to them?"

"I would like to try."

"We can listen to them and you can select the one you like. Or maybe we could start with a waltz."

"A waltz would be fine," Lew said.

Cécile walked to a domed silver music box and raised the lid. She wound it tightly.

"Are you ready?" she asked.

"I'm always ready for an easy waltz."

Cécile closed the lid and came to Lew. He caught her hand and waist. Her hand was no longer cold, but rather like a little warm animal cuddling against his palm. The music started. They moved off in the fluid steps of the waltz.

Lew thought of his predecessor to this room. Albert, you were a lucky man. Until someone killed you. As the hours had passed, Lew had become ever more certain that murder had been committed.

He shoved aside the thoughts of Wollfolk and concentrated on this time and the girl Cécile in his arms. She was a mere wraith instantly responding to his slightest movement, even if offbeat, making him feel very skilled. He knew he could create an entirely new dance and still her steps would have been in complete harmony with his.

They danced to the tunes of the music boxes, one after the other. Titine's announcement that the food was prepared was an intrusion to Lew. But Cécile led him off to the dining room.

They ate at a small table, one that could accommodate but two. Wollfolk must not have liked visitors. Neither did Lew, and more and more he wished he had known the man. He felt a sadness, as if he had lost a good friend. Strange thoughts. How many of them were because of the woman and this place?

Lew finished his food. Quietly sipping his glass of wine, he looked at the woman across the table

105

from him. Evening dusk had come early because of the gathering clouds, and her eyes had dimmed to large pools of darkness. He wondered what she was thinking as she gazed back at him.

Cécile studied the young Wollfolk. She felt her deep loss at the death of Albert Wollfolk. Her use of the words "lonely woman" to Timothy were true. Could he lift some of her loneliness? He seemed to like her.

A hard brittle burst of rain rattled on the glass panes of the window. Cécile jumped at the sudden sound. She turned to stare out through the window, watching the new rain swiftly increase to a driving downpour.

"I hope the dreaded *vomito* doesn't come," she said.

"What do you mean?"

"Often a wet spring and summer bring the *vomito*, the yellow fever." Cécile continued to stare out the window.

"Why is that?"

"No one knows. Even our best doctors are mystified. Sometimes many people die, hundreds in a week. Then, gradually, the dying stops and the fever is gone. Over the years New Orleans has seen many plagues."

"I have heard of the fever," Lew said.

Cécile turned her dark eyes upon Lew. "The rain is hard and will most likely continue until morning. Would you want to remain here tonight?"

"I would like that," Lew replied.

"Good. I'll have Titine prepare for your stay."

"I'll take care of my horse."

"There are stalls and feed at the end of the courtyard. You may use the raincoat by the rear door. It should fit you."

Lew left the house. He hardly felt the rain beating down and pouring inside the raincoat, for the thoughts of the woman filled his mind. Swiftly he untied the gray horse and led it across the dark courtyard to the stables. He gave the animal a ration of grain and hay and hurried back to the house.

Titine met him at the door with a candle. She helped him out of his rain gear. "I'll show you to your room, Mr. Wollfolk. Please come this way."

She guided him up a stairs to the second floor and down a hallway containing three doors. "This room is yours, sir," she said, and pushed open a door. "If you wish to bathe, the water is drawn and warm." She gestured at another door.

"Thank you, Titine," Lew said.

"There are several candles and an oil lamp in the room. You can light them with this." She handed him the candle.

A large double bed occupied one side of the room. There was a dresser, two chairs, a writing table, a brassbound trunk, and a closet door standing open to show a long rack of clothing: shirts, coats and trousers. Hats filled the top shelf. A complete outfit of dry clothing had been placed on the bed.

"Well, I'll be damned," Lew said under his breath. Cécile was telling him that he was master

107

of the house. What he wanted was his merely for the asking. And he would indeed ask.

He bathed leisurely, luxuriating in the feel of the water on his skin and the pleasant surroundings. He had stepped into a ready-made world. The properties and pleasures that had taken Wollfolk many years to accumulate were now Lew's. And all because he had come to help a man being murdered and then killing those men who had committed the terrible deed.

He dried himself, donned the fresh clothing, and went out of the bath. The house had become quite dark. His candle cast but a faint glow in the hallway. The doorway at the end of the passageway stood open and full of bright-yellow light. Inviting light.

He went along the passageway to the door and knocked lightly on the wooden jamb.

Someone stirred in the room. Cécile came to the door. She looked him up and down. "Everything fits," she said.

"Everything fits," agreed Lew. "Would you like to talk now?"

She took him by the hand and pulled gently. "Please come in and we will talk. And then we shall entertain ourselves while it rains outside."

10

LEZIN watched Tim come down the stairway from the balcony of the house and climb up into the wagon beside him. The white man moved stiffly, favoring his left side. Still, he was much improved, healing cleanly and quickly, as young healthy animals do.

Marie waved from the balcony. Tim waved back and smiled up at her.

Lezin saw the happy expression on his daughter's face. Soon it would be time to speak to her about Tim.

He slapped the horse with the reins and drove out of the carriageway and toward New Orleans. Once they settled down on the main road, Lezin let the horse have its head.

He extracted five twenty-dollar gold pieces from his pocket and held them out to Tim. "This should be enough to buy what you need in the way of clothing. How much additional money do you want?"

"No more. That will be plenty," Tim said. For a fisherman, Lezin seemed to have considerable money, and he handled it in a casual manner. His house was well-furnished. Marie had been sent away to school for several years. Lezin himself appeared to be an educated man. Probably self-taught, thought Tim.

They entered New Orleans and Lezin began to point out the important and interesting places of the city. He drove through the Garden District and then into the Vieux Carré. They halted at stores Lezin knew, and Tim purchased new clothing. He put the garments on as they were acquired, and he placed the items borrowed from

Lezin in the rear of the wagon. Tim's letters to Cincinnati were mailed at the U.S. post office.

Morissot halted the wagon at a small law office. "Earl Kidder is a black lawyer," Lezin told Tim. "He does legal work for me now and then; he can find out what properties Albert Wollfolk owns— at least those that are recorded in the public records. Let's go in and see him."

"It might be best if nobody knew who I am until I get the identification back from up north," said Tim.

"You may be right. Wait here. I'll just be a minute. Then we can drive down to the waterfront and take a look at the warehouse and docks that have the Wollfolk name on them."

Lew read the documents, one attesting to his identity as Timothy Wollfolk and a second formally accepting the conditions of the inheritance. He signed both papers with a flourish and handed them back to Rosiere. He hoped the lawyer did not possess a letter or some other paper containing the dead man's signature with which to make a comparison.

Rosiere took the papers. He evaluated the young Wollfolk and the expensive clothing he wore. Today he resembled the older Wollfolk more.

"I have an appointment with the district probate judge at four P.M.," Rosiere said. "I'm certain he'll find everything is proper and will sign an order legally making you the beneficiary of your

110

uncle's estate. By evening, all of the properties will be for your use and enjoyment."

I have already enjoyed some of Wollfolk's possessions, thought Lew. He spoke to the lawyer. "I appreciate your help in handling my uncle's will. I hope you will continue as the Wollfolk lawyer and give me advice."

"It would be my pleasure to do that," said Rosiere. "What do you plan to do now?"

"It's time I get involved in the business. I will stop by the office and talk with Spandling and find out how everything is going. Then I'll go down to the docks and warehouse."

"I should warn you again that competition for business of the waterfront is very cutthroat. Trust nobody."

"Not even the men my uncle hired?"

"He must have thought they were honest men. But he has been dead for a month. Men change as the situation changes. Who knows how they will act to a new owner of the company? The new white foreman came well-recommended, but I personally know nothing about him."

"I may need money. When can I draw from the bank?"

"I'll record the probate papers in the public records today after the judge signs them. Then I'll stop by the bank and give them copies so that they will be informed that you are now the legal owner of the Wollfolk accounts. By tomorrow, the funds will be at your disposal."

"All right. If you want to get in touch with me,

leave a message at the big house. Jacob will hunt me down."

Lew entered the ground-floor office of A. Wollfolk, Warehouse & Dockage Company. The space was quite large. A vacant desk and chair sat on the right back near the wall and facing the entrance. A door stood ajar and Lew saw three men perched on stools drawn up to a long desk. Ledgers and papers were scattered about each worker. On the left, a hallway led off to the rear.

Lew walked to the open door and called inside. "Where's Tom Spandling?"

"Back in his office," the nearest man said. "I'll get him for you." He came out the door and went down the hallway.

A moment later he returned with an elderly man, quite spindly with a pair of tiny glasses perched upon the bridge of his nose. The man looked closely at Lew. "I'm Tom Spandling," he said.

"And I'm Timothy Wollfolk."

Abruptly the man smiled, as brightly as a young boy's smile. He held out his hand. "Glad to meet you, Timothy. I saw Mr. Rosiere on the street earlier this morning and he said you were in town."

"Hello, Tom." Lew shook the man's hand. "I'd like a rundown on the business."

"Certainly, come into my office."

"That was Mr. Wollfolk's office," Spandling said, pointing as they neared the rear of the building. "Do you plan to continue with a private office here?"

"For now, yes. Let's talk in there instead of your office."

Lew went immediately behind the large walnut desk and sat in the tall-backed leather-upholstered chair. The floor was covered with a thick-pile wool carpet. The walls were of stucco and painted white. The painting of a graceful three-masted clipper ship hung on a wall. Directly below it were framed architectural drawings that Lew thought could be of the same ship.

He gestured at the painting. "I would guess that's the ship *Honest Traveler* that's being built in Algiers. When is it scheduled for completion?"

"On September thirty this year. Or I should say it was until I stopped construction immediately upon Mr. Wollfolk's death."

"Why did you do that?"

"I had told Mr. Wollfolk that shipping was a hazardous business, much more a gamble than a business such as we have with the docks and warehouse. I recommended to him that if he insisted on building a ship it should be a steamship. I decided to hold up the construction until the new owner could decide what he wanted to do."

"Then go tell the shipbuilder to begin work at once. Tell him to make up for the lost time. I want the *Honest Traveler* completed and ready for sea on the original schedule."

"But don't you want time to reconsider Mr. Wollfolk's plans and make your own decision? I can advise you on the current conditions of shipping and waterfront business."

"Does the company have enough money in the bank to pay for the ship and meet other operating costs?"

"Yes. Also we are profitable month to month, but expenses are high, and because of the accelerated war effort, they are going even higher."

"Tom, I appreciate what you did, but I'll trust my uncle's judgment until I have solid information to the contrary. We will proceed with his plan."

"Certainly, Tim."

"Then restart the building of the ship at once."

"I'll go across the river and speak to the shipyard-owner tomorrow."

"Please go today, just as soon as we finish here. Tell the builder that I'll be over tomorrow to talk with him about the ship."

"I'll do that."

"Tell me about the work we have now and what contracts are coming up in the future. How full is the warehouse?"

"The warehouse is about three-quarters full. The dock space is about the same. But the contracts for storing and transporting cargo are drawing to an end. We have no bids out for new business."

Lew looked sharply at Spandling. "Why are there no bids on army and navy contracts? There must be dozens open and waiting for bidders."

"True. There are nearly two dozen contracts of varying sizes open for bids. Nearly all of them will be closing in less than four weeks."

"Then why aren't you bidding?"

"Mr. Wollfolk always made the bids personally. He trusted no one to do that for him. He was ready to prepare bids on all of the open military and private contracts when he died. We have missed some very large ones."

"How about the eighty drays? How busy are they?"

"The drays are mostly used for hauling and moving the cargo we have contracts for. Nearly all are busy."

Lew considered what Spandling had said. With the existing contracts about finished, the business would soon be grinding to a halt. Lew groaned inwardly, for he had little knowledge of bidding on a contract, merely some idle conversation with the supply officer of the Texas Rangers.

"Tomorrow morning at six, I want copies of all the invitations to bid that the military has, and also all that the private companies have that are still open. Have all your bookkeepers here to help us. Work them tonight to gather our cost figures. We are going to bid."

"Yes, sir."

"Who's boss at the docks?"

"Karl Gunnard is boss of the docks, drays, and warehouse. Julius Ruffier works under Gunnard and is the boss of the blacks."

"All right. Now start planning how we will bid for cargo to haul on our new ship."

Spandling smiled his pleasant smile. "I like the way you think. Here is something else for you to consider. Much of the army equipment that goes to Mexico to fight the war must come back to the States. We need our piece of that business also."

"Good. Tell me about the contracts the company is working on now."

They talked for several minutes. Lew asked many questions to round out the information Spandling gave him. Every contract was quite profitable. Wollfolk had made no mistakes. Lew doubted he could do as well.

"Thanks for all you have told me," Lew said.

He walked past Spandling and left the office. He was worried. He was in over his head, and he knew it. The company could be destroyed by a few low bids. Tomorrow very early he must find out how much money was in the company and private bank accounts.

The war would not last long, a year, perhaps a year and a half. The big money must be made now. Wollfolk had known that, and that was why he had ordered the building of the ship. Docks, warehouses, and ships made a proper business combination.

Lew halted at the top of the levee and stood staring down at the river. The great hubbub of noise and activity on the river's edge still amazed him.

Hundreds upon hundreds of men and drays pulled by mules hurried about on the waterfront. Ship's officers came and went to their vessels in preparation to put to sea or up the Mississippi. The long boom arms of the ships swung cargo

116

nets bulging with war goods onto the decks. Army officers watched with zealous eyes the loading of their fighting equipment to see that it was not damaged by rough or careless hands. Scores of craftsmen of many kinds scurried about the docks and the decks of the ships to sell an item or repair something broken.

Smoke billowed from the stacks of some of the steamships as they built steam to pull away from the docks. Two harbor boats, with eight strong oarsmen and a coxswain at the tiller of each, were warping a clipper ship away from the shore and out into the river current, where the ship could scud away on the power of the wind. Half a dozen ships at anchor in the river were cranking in their anchor chains so that they could beat their competitors into the vacant berths.

Lew thought the river had stopped rising. However, he had noted that the ships' captains paid little attention to the water level. The Mississippi was either rising or falling every hour of the day.

He dropped down the side of the levee and walked along the river's edge to the Wollfolk section of the wharf. A steamship was tied up and loading. A line of drays was bringing goods down from the cavernous warehouse to the aft gangway. A chugging steam engine drove a windlass to hoist the goods aboard. Stevedores were carrying crated cargo from a long mound on the dock to the forward gangway. The crates appeared quite heavy with two stevedores working at each container.

117

Lew drew close to the navy ensign checking the cargo being loaded against a written invoice.

"How's the loading going?" Lew asked the officer.

"Damn poorly," replied the ensign, turning an aggravated face to Lew. "The captain wants to leave at daylight tomorrow. The stevedores could do it if they worked hard. But at the rate these men are working, it'll take another day."

He gestured at the black stevedores. "Look. They're doubled up on that crate and it doesn't weigh much more than a hundred pounds. One man should be able to carry that with no problem at all. And look over there at those drays bringing supplies from the warehouse. They are hardly moving. I've seen this thing before. Wollfolk has a slowdown by his men. Unless he fixes this quick, he'll not get another navy contract."

Lew checked the slow lazy pace of the stevedores and the drays. "It'll be fixed pronto," Lew said.

"Who are you?" questioned the ensign.

"I'm Wollfolk. You'll be loaded on time."

Lew went swiftly across the wharf and up the slope to the warehouse. The structure was four hundred feet long and high-ceilinged. Wide double doors stood open in all four walls, and the river breeze blew through.

In the end, where the wind entered, a white man sat with his chair hiked back against the wall and his feet thrown up on a battered wooden desk. A giant black man was near the center of the

118

warehouse. He held a piece of paper fastened to a board and was checking off items as they were being loaded by other blacks into the drays.

Lew crossed to the white man. "You Gunnard?" he asked.

"Yes, I'm Gunnard. Who are you?"

"I'm Wollfolk."

Gunnard slowly dropped his legs one by one from the desk to the dirt floor. He climbed erect. "Howdy, Mr. Wollfolk. Welcome to New Orleans." He hooked his thumbs in his front pants pockets.

Lew measured the man. Muscles bulged his cotton shirt. His head seemed overlarge and heavy-boned, especially the eyebrow ridges. His eyes were deeply socketed beneath the ridges, like the eyes in a skull. The man would be immensely strong, and from the scars on his face, he was a brawler.

"Julius, Wollfolk's here," Gunnard called out to the black boss. His voice was loud enough that all the other men in the warehouse could hear him. He ran his sight up and down Lew's expensive clothing. A smirk stretched his lips.

Lew heard the scuff of the bare feet of the black men on the dirt floor. They halted close behind him.

"That warehouse has Wollfolk's name on it," Lezin told Tim. He pulled the wagon to a stop and chucked a thumb at the building on the levee. "I asked around some, and the people I talked with said it still belongs to Wollfolk."

"Let's take a look," Tim said.

"Right by me," said Lezin.

They climbed down from the vehicle and entered the building. Two white men were facing each other and talking. Several Negroes quit their work and gathered near the white men.

Tim heard the bigger white man, dressed in a workingman's clothing, speak to the second white man. "Mr. Wollfolk, meet Julius Ruffier. He's the boss nigger. He keeps all of the other niggers in line."

Tim was stunned for a moment. He was the last Wollfolk. So who could this man be? Then an icy anger ran through Tim as he realized what the presence of the man meant.

Lezin saw the stricken expression on Tim's face and then the surge of anger. "This explains the attack on you at the river, he said in a low tone. "It was not just a robbery. It was to be a killing so that this impostor could take your place." But he can be easily removed, thought Lezin.

"You are right," Tim said, his voice a rough whisper. "Now I'll need more proof of who I am than ever before. Say nothing. We'll take all my uncle's property back from this man and he'll pay dearly for trying to have me killed."

Tim moved forward toward the false Wollfolk.

11

LEW pointed down at the steamship tied to the wharf. "Gunnard, I want that ship loaded by dark. There's still four or five hours of daylight left. That should be more than enough time."

"The men are working as fast as they can," said Gunnard. There was a mocking tone in his voice.

Tim had drawn nearer to better hear the conversation and examine the impostor. Now, at the words of the white overseer, the face of the impostor changed, the anger flashing cold and bright like a flame suddenly ignited.

"You're a liar, Gunnard. Load the ship like I said." Lew's words were sharp, like pieces of metal hitting.

"To hell with you," Gunnard snarled. He had taken money from Stanton Shattuck to see that the ship was not loaded on schedule. To fail to accomplish that task would be to sign his own death warrant. He looked Lew over for the second time. This fancy-dressed Wollfolk would be easy to handle. "These men won't work for you. They know that you probably killed Albert Wollfolk so that you could inherit his property." Gunnard licked his slack lips and a foxy look came into his eyes. "They might work faster if you whipped the boss."

Lew was surprised at Gunnard's charge that he had harmed Wollfolk. His desire to smash that grinning face to a bloody lump soared within him. "Gunnard, I'm going to beat the hell out of you." Lew slid out of his jacket. "Get ready to fight," he warned.

Gunnard smiled craftily. "Not me. You've got to whip Julius. And there ain't a man in all New Orleans who can do that. Many have tried, but everyone ends up with broken bones, or with a brain so addled that they're not men anymore."

For the first time Lew really looked at the giant black man. He was nearly a foot taller than Lew and twice his weight. He was the strongest-appearing man Lew had ever seen. There was a keen intelligence behind his black eyes. He was not some dumb ox that Lew could outmaneuver.

Lew pivoted slowly, letting his view wash over the thirty or so other black men intently watching. He smelled their hostility. Farther away toward the door, a white man, three or so years younger than Lew, and a mulatto were approaching. The white man walked stiffly, as if crippled or injured. Both men had hard unfriendly expressions. Lew had seen that type of look before upon outlaws he had fought. The mulatto looked especially ready and willing to do murder. Why was that?

"You!" Lew pointed at the young white man. "Are you with Gunnard?"

"No."

"Can you use a pistol?"

"I can hit a reasonable target," Tim said.

Lew pulled his Colt from his belt and turned it buttfirst toward Tim. "Then come here and take this gun. It seems I'm going to have to fight. Don't let a second man jump me while I'm busy."

Lew saw the man's eyes sharpen with some thought, then they became hooded, hiding his feelings completely.

A cold tickle ran up Tim's spine at the offer of the pistol. He could accidentally—yes, quite accidentally shoot the impostor. Then a better plan came full-blown to him, jelling quickly in his mind. Something strange and dangerous was happening here. It was deeper than a mere fight over loading a ship. He knew it at some primal level. Why not let the impostor take the brunt of the unknown peril? Let the giant black kill him if he could. If that did not happen, then wait and see what followed. Tim stepped forward and took the pistol in his hand.

Tim backed away a few paces as the impostor stripped off his shirt. Muscles rippled and flowed like steel wires across his back and deep chest. His wrists were thick and the fists broad and heavy-boned. He glanced at Julius.

The Negro said not a word. He motioned with his hands for his workers to stand back and give him room for the battle.

The impostor uttered a savage growl and spun away from Julius. He leapt, his body moving with unnatural speed and formidable strength, upon

Gunnard. He struck the man a mighty wallop to the face. Tim heard the crushing sound of a fist striking forcibly against flesh and bone.

Gunnard staggered backward. He twisted to the side, trying to draw away from the unexpected assault and catch his balance.

But Lew pressed his attack, boring in, striking the half-dazed man a second blow to the face. Then he swiftly sprang to Gunnard's side and flung out his arm to catch the man around the neck.

Lew jerked Gunnard down into a half-bent position. At the same time he brought up his right fist. A sickening crunch echoed throughout the warehouse. Three times, almost too fast for Tim to see, the impostor's fist pistoned up to crash into Gunnard's face.

Gunnard hung unconscious on Lew's arm. Blood spouted from his broken nose and mouth. Lew flung him aside as so much offal.

Lew shook himself as some great wolf might do upon coming out of a cold, drenching rain. The rims of his nostrils were ice-white and his eyes burned with a fury barely controlled. The veins in his neck were thick blue cords. He whirled to face the giant black man.

"One bastard down, and you're next. Come and fight," Lew exclaimed with furious impatience. He flicked the dripping blood from his torn knuckles. "I did not harm Albert Wollfolk. But believe that I did if you want. Come show me how good a man you are." His mouth shut with a grim snap.

Julius hesitated, but not from fear. There was the ring of truth in the white man's voice. He knew Gunnard was a liar and trickster. If there was a choice to be made between the two men, Julius would choose the word of a Wollfolk over Gunnard's.

"Come on and let's fight," Lew challenged. "You are a dead man either way. If you kill a Wollfolk, then other white men will come and hang you. If you don't kill but merely cripple me, then I'll come back with my pistol and kill you. Either way you die."

"It is not because I'm afraid that I don't fight you," Julius responded. "I believe what you say, that you didn't kill Mr. Albert."

"Well, so you're smart enough to know the truth when you hear it," Lew jeered.

"Yes," Julius replied simply.

Lew examined the black man's face, searching for the falseness in him, for the deception.

"So what is next?" Lew asked.

"We'll load the ship as you ordered."

"Good. But first throw that son of a bitch off Wollfolk property." Lew stabbed a finger at the unconscious Gunnard.

"Take him to the hospital," Julius directed two of his men. "If you are questioned by the police, tell them the truth, that he fought Mr. Wollfolk and lost. That it was a fair fight."

The two men lifted Gunnard's loose-jointed body and lugged it off to an empty dray.

Lew spoke to Julius. "Can you handle Gunnard's job and your own?"

"He did very little."

"Then you are the boss of the warehouse and docks. And your pay is doubled."

Julius nodded his agreement. He stepped forward and held out his hand. Lew felt the strength of the man, like a vise close to crushing the bones in his hand.

Julius released his powerful hold on Lew and turned to his men. "You heard Mr. Wollfolk. That ship gets loaded before the sun goes down."

The men hastened off. Lew saw pleased grins on some of their faces. He looked at the white man who held his pistol.

"You did not have to shoot anybody. Could you have done it?"

"I can kill a man, in the right circumstances."

"I believe you could," Lew said. He spoke to the mulatto. "I know you could too. I hope neither of you plan to kill me."

Neither man replied. The outcome of Lew's battle had not changed their thoughts about him at all.

"So why are you two here?" queried Lew. "Are you looking for work?"

Morissot shook his head in the negative. Tim's mind raced. What better way to know what was happening to his properties than to work for the impostor?

"I could use a job," Tim said.

"What can you do?"

"I'm an accountant."

"Where did you learn that?"

"In Saint Louis," Tim lied.

"Do you know anything about ships and cargo?"

"Not oceangoing ships, but I do about river steamboats and contracting."

Lew concentrated his attention on the man. "What is your name?"

"Sam Datson," Tim replied, making a quick decision to use his grandfather's name on his mother's side of the family.

"I need an accountant. How about working for me? I'll pay twenty dollars a week."

"Twenty-five," Tim said. Twenty was more than a fair salary, but the impostor seemed generous . . . with someone else's money.

"Twenty-five it is," agreed Lew. He put out his hand and shook Tim's. "Meet me at my office at Front Street and Toulouse tomorrow at six A.M. We have much work to do."

"I'll be there," replied Tim. He nodded at Morissot and both men walked toward the wagon.

Lew stared after the two men until they were out of sight. A very odd pair. And they did not like him. He would have to be on his guard.

The old huntress placed the bait in the trap and leaned back. Her breathing became shallow and slow, and she moved not at all. The prey were about, but they were very wary.

127

She ignored the flow of time past her. After seventy years she knew it could be neither slowed nor hurried. A breeze came over the levee from the river, carrying the sound of men and equipment working. She culled out the obnoxious human noise and sensed only the breeze.

One of the prey she sought landed with a flutter of wings on the ground a few feet distant. Another one came down beside the first. They clucked their bird talk back and forth. Hesitantly they began to draw closer, pulled by the sight of the bait. The heads of the birds flicked from side to side as first one sharp eye and then the other peered hard at the woman near the tempting food.

The huntress dreamed of the evening meal, which would consist of one of the birds. She would pluck it carefully and then light a piece of paper to singe off the hairlike feathers that remained. The bird would be tough—they usually were—so she would cook it for a long time. Then, toward the end, potatoes and butter and many spices would be added. She had been carefully hoarding tiny amounts of these things until today. All would be simmered until a thick broth remained and the flesh tender and falling off the bones. Her old mouth moistened at the anticipated meal.

One of the birds hopped upon the end of the huntress's seat. It struggled to overcome the instinctive fear that it had of these large, two-legged creatures. Suddenly it fluttered its wings, trying to startle the human into movement.

The huntress peered out through a slit between

her eyelids. The prey was less than a foot from the bait. She prepared to spring the trap.

The second bird came up on the seat with a flap of its wings. At the encroachment, the first bird darted for the bait.

Morissot found Old Ella on the park bench in a remote corner of Jackson Square. He halted and stood quietly observing her. She did not stir, slumped against the back of the bench. Her left hand lay on the torn dress of her lap while her right hand, with fingers spread wide, was outstretched on the seat. A broken crust of moldy bread lay on the palm of her hand. Two gray and brown pigeons were drawing close to her in short, nervous stop and gos.

One of the pigeons sprang ahead of its partner, and its head dived down to grab the bread.

Ella's hand suddenly convulsed, her long fingers closing on the bird's head. The left hand swung across to clamp the back of the bird and smother the fluttering wings. Ella gave a twist to the head of the bird and then another turn, and immediately covered the dead bird inside a fold of her dress.

She swept a hasty look around to see if anyone had noticed her killing the park pigeon. No one was in front of her. She turned to check to the rear.

"Lezin Morissot, why are you spying on an old woman?" she asked angrily. "Go watch the young women who can do you some good."

Morissot smiled. "Today you are the woman I want to see."

Ella laughed, her toothless old mouth opening in a dark pink-lined pit. "A lie is better than nothing. I need some money. I hope you want me to do some work for you."

Lezin sat down beside Ella. "There is something you can do for me. I want to know all you can find out about a man who calls himself Timothy Wollfolk. He has an office near the waterfront at Toulouse and Front Street. Follow him for the next few days. Tell me everything he does."

Ella was one of the beggars common in New Orleans. She lived in the loft of an abandoned building on the east side of Vieux Carré. She was gaunt and stooped, and dressed in her raggedy clothing, she could go anywhere without arousing suspicion.

Her face was nothing but crinkled black parchment, black to the point that it seemed to have a purple cast to it. However, inside her slightly bulging forehead was a mind that noted everything and forgot nothing.

Lezin took several silver coins from his pocket and handed two dollars to Ella. "Here is your pay." He gave her a third coin. "This man may have a buggy or horse, you may have to hire a coach to keep up."

It would be unlikely that she would ever ride. She could walk nearly as fast as one of the Chickasaw Indians.

"I'll bring you good information," Ella promised.

"I know you will. You have never failed me." Lezin reached out and petted the back of her black hand. "Be careful of this man. Don't do something that will get you hurt."

"Is he dangerous?"

"I only know that he is a savage fighter."

"I shall be watchful of him. Where is he now?"

"Just a short way from here at the waterfront warehouse of A. Wollfolk. That's opposite Toulouse Street." Lezin described Lew to Ella.

"I'll find him."

"Good. Two days from now at this time, meet me right here. If for some reason you can't meet me then, come to my home as soon as you can."

"I'll do exactly as you say."

"Remember, be careful and take no chances with this man." Lezin turned and walked from the square.

Ella rubbed the back of her hand where Lezin had petted her. That was the first time another human had touched her in many days, oh, so many days. That caring kindness from Lezin, a strong man afraid of nothing, was worth more than his money. But the money was good too, she thought, not wanting to belittle it and somehow bring bad luck and thus lose the coins.

At the corner of Exchange Alley and Conti Street, the little boy with the wooden sword pranced about the sidewalk thrusting and parrying against an invisible opponent. He halted and peeked for a moment through the open door to the inside at the men in the fencing school, then he recommenced his own battle against an imaginary foe.

Lew watched the tyke for a minute and then headed down Exchange Alley. He wanted to see this place where the use of sword and pistol was taught. He read the names of the famous dueling masters on the side of the buildings: L'Alouette, Montiasse, Croquère, and many others. He had heard that there were more than fifty *maîtres d' armes* on this street.

Someone cursed in French from within one of the open doors. Lew, drawn by curiosity, turned and entered.

A slightly built man in a white shirt and trousers closely contoured to his body stood facing a second man. Both held rapiers—thin, two-edged swords—in their hands. Blood seeped slowly from the upper arm of the younger man and formed a growing red stain on his shirt.

"Edmond, I could have killed you just as easily as I pricked your arm," said the older man. "I have told you before how to hold your defense. Just so." The fencing master took the stance. "But you always forget in the excitement of the contest. So this time I teach you a harsher lesson. Hereafter I think you will remember. I do not want you to die on the end of someone's sword."

"Yes, Monsieur Baudoin. I shall not forget this lesson," said the student with a wry smile.

"The wound is but a tiny thing. Continue your

lesson to the end and then see a doctor. Go and practice with Emile."

Baudoin walked to Lew. "Do you wish to obtain the skill to fight the duel, *monsieur?*"

"I've been thinking about that," Lew said. "But I haven't yet made up my mind."

"What is your name?"

"Timothy Wollfolk."

"You are related to Albert Wollfolk?"

"Yes, he was my uncle."

"My name is Yves Baudoin. I'm sorry about his death. He often practiced here. He was a very good fencer."

"Do you teach the use of the pistol?"

"I certainly do. I have a shooting hall on the outskirts of town. We practice there, where the sound will not disturb others."

"Pistols are more to my liking," Lew said.

"You have dueled with pistols?"

"Yes," Lew replied shortly.

Baudoin held Lew's eyes for a moment. Often the bravery of a man could be read there. Then he spoke. "I don't encourage spectators. But observe what goes on here for a little if you wish. I must return to my students." Baudoin strode away down the long hall.

Lew watched the master duelist give his instructions to the men, young and middle-aged and one who appeared quite old. His blade would move with amazing swiftness when he demonstrated an attack or defensive movement, then he would do it in slow motion and again rapidly. His students copied his actions with varying degrees of skill.

Lew left the practice gymnasium. He hailed a hackney and directed the driver to take him to Rampart Street. He did not think he would spend much time in the big house in the Garden District. His appetite for Cécile would not soon be satisfied.

Lew, his eyes upon Cécile, leaned against the corner of the cottage wall near the carriageway. She was standing on a worn marble bench near the rear of the courtyard, reaching out for the red flower on the top of a climber rose. She caught the blossom, broke it free, and jumped down to the ground.

She raised her hand to put the flower in her hair, but froze there with it lifted. She became alert, listening like some wild creature of the forest. Abruptly she twisted, to stare directly at Lew.

They looked at each other through the shadows under the old trees. Suddenly she laughed, a wholesome sound. The melody of it filled the walled courtyard. She ran toward him like a strong wind, full of vibrant energy.

She came straight to him and threw her arms around his neck. She rubbed her cheek against his and then reared back to look at him. "Do you ever make love before it's dark?" she asked.

Lew hugged her for an answer and she gave a little sigh of pleasure.

12

"WE have our cost of operation calculated," Lew said. "Now we need to decide how much profit to add to come up with a final bid offer." He looked intently at Datson and Spandling. "What amount do you two recommend?"

Spandling had written on a large blackboard the daily cost to operate the docks, warehouse, drays, and the workers' wages. A separate array of numbers—the estimated time required to do the bid items on the several contracts—had been prepared by Datson and Ruffier. The Negro boss had returned to the docks.

"By examining your uncle's last bid, it appears he added in a thirty-percent profit margin," Spandling said.

"That seems like a fair profit," Lew said. "But how much can we really bid and still get enough of those contracts to keep our men and equipment busy?"

Lew spoke to Tim. "What do you recommend, Sam?" The man had said almost nothing since his arrival early in the morning.

Tim shrugged. "Thirty percent should get us contracts. Perhaps a one-hundred-percent profit would also. That difference means many thousands of dollars."

"Is that the best answers you men have?" Lew said.

"We don't know the cost of our competitors, or how they will bid," Tim said.

Lew climbed to his feet. "You two prepare all the necessary papers. Just leave off the final dollar amounts. Sam, when that work is finished, come down to the docks. I'll meet you there in an hour. I have a plan." He strode from the office and into the street.

Lew silently read the two numbers on the piece of paper the president of the Mechanics and Traders Bank on Canal Street had handed to him. The A. Wollfolk Warehouse and Dockage Company account had a balance of one hundred and seventy thousand dollars. The Wollfolk private deposits totalled one hundred and eighty-three thousand dollars. Either sum was a huge fortune, much greater than Lew had ever thought possible that he would control.

He could withdraw the money from both accounts and leave New Orleans at this very minute and travel to Europe and live like a king, or go back to Texas and build an empire. Should he remain here, something could happen at any moment to expose his false claim to the Wollfolk fortune.

But even as Lew thought of grabbing the money and running, he knew he would not, regardless of

136

the very real danger to him. He liked the challenge to him of keeping the Wollfolk company operating and profitable. But more than that, if murder had been committed in the death of Albert Wollfolk, Lew wanted to find those responsible for it. That would be further payment for the fortune that had suddenly fallen into his hands. And it would be justice. The lawman in Lew felt good about that.

Lew brought his attention back to the bank official. "Thank you for your help. My uncle trusted you and your bank. I shall do the same."

"Thank you, Mr. Wollfolk. We are pleased that you have decided to leave your accounts with us."

"Good day, sir," Lew said.

"Walk with me along the waterfront," Lew said to Tim. "As we do that, check the amount of unused docks, if any, and also how much warehouse space is empty."

"I understand what you are doing," Tim said, moving off in step with Lew. "The capacity of the waterfront owned by your competitors that is not being used should give us a very good idea of how closely they will bid on contracts. However, we can merely look up and down the river and see that there is little space not being used."

"True. Also I've walked part of the waterfront before. I can see that there are just as many ships waiting to get into the shore to unload or load as there was three days ago. However, few of them are contracted to us. But mainly I asked you to meet me here so I'd have a chance to talk with you alone."

"What about?"

"Spandling is very old. He could become ill and be unable to work. I want you to go over the books with him. Be prepared to take over his job as head bookkeeper. In fact, be my head book-keeper without saying anything at this moment."

"I'll do that," Tim said.

"Good." Lew lengthened his stride, swerving around a line of men rolling barrels of molasses from a long shed and toward a berthed ship.

Tim stared frankly at the man who had falsely taken his place. He seemed cocksure of himself. What kind of conspiracy had he devised to take over the Wollfolk properties? Who else was in-volved? Where were the men who had shot Tim? He would find out those things and then there would come a reckoning for all the wrongs done him.

As Lew and Tim completed their tour of the waterfront, the wind began to blow in damp gusts, sweeping in from the forested swampland south of the river. The dampness congealed to rain, the drops pitting the surface of the river in millions of tiny craters and peppering the docks and ships.

"Let's find shelter in the warehouse," Lew called to Tim, and broke into a run for the building.

Julius raised his hand in acknowledgment of the presence of the two men as they ran into the end of the warehouse. They seated themselves at the battered wooden desk. The big black boss continued to direct the loading of the drays as they dashed in and gathered in the dryness of the building.

"What do you think?" Lew asked, sweeping his arm to indicate the docks below them.

"I'd say less than five percent of the available capacity of the waterfront is not being used," Tim replied. "And that five percent is probably unused because of scheduling problems. Some awfully big profits can be made here." Tim could not help but add, "Your uncle was a smart businessman to own such valuable property."

Lew looked closely at Tim, his eyes sharp and probing.

Tim tried to keep his expression noncommittal. Had he said too much? He would have to be careful when around the impostor. He must not become suspicious of who Tim was.

"I agree," Lew said. He looked out into the rain.

An old black woman, soaked through by the cold rain, was edging toward the door of the warehouse. Lew saw her shiver. He motioned to her. "Come into the dry," he called.

The woman bobbed her head and scuttled in under the roof of the building. She watched Lew with quick black eyes as she came to a stop.

"Wrap yourself in one of those and get warm." Lew pointed at a pile of large cotton sacks nearby.

The woman did as suggested, folding one of the sacks about her. She sat down on the floor against the wall. She became absolutely motionless, only her eyes rolling now and then to check Lew.

Tim roamed his sight out across the docks to the berthed ships, and beyond them to the indistinct shapes of the vessels at anchor in the river. The stevedores and deckhands of the ships had vanished as if melted away by the rain. Tim knew they were still there hunkered down under the dry tarpaulins covering the cargo stored on the docks, or in the cabins or holds of ships. But for the moment, the deserted wet waterfront seemed a dismal place. A dark pall of anger fell upon Tim as he considered his recent bad luck and the false Wollfolk so close to him. The ache of his wounds seemed to increase. He moved in his chair to a more comfortable position.

Lew noted the grimace on the accountant's face. "You have been hurt?"

"Yes. A horse fell with me. I'll soon be well."

Lew turned his attention to the outside. "It rains too damn much here. I've been told that a lot of rain brings a plague to the city."

"I've heard the same thing from the steamboat men that run the river. Sometimes they refuse to bring cargo to New Orleans when the fever hits here."

The two men fell silent. The storm grew more boisterous, whipping sprays of water in the open doors. Thunder rumbled off to the south. The rain drummed on the rooftop and cascaded down in noisy waterfalls to the ground.

Gradually the rain slackened to a drizzle. Julius ordered the drays back to work.

Lew stood up. "We'll get a little wet, but let's go on to the office."

"All right," Tim said.

They left at a rapid walk toward Toulouse Street. Behind them the black woman rose with a groan. Cold rain made her old bones ache. She moved off in a shuffle after the white men.

Upon arrival at his office, Lew went directly to his desk. Spandling had placed the contracts in a neat pile. Lew began to fill in the final bid offer. The first contained an estimated 30-percent profit. For each contract thereafter, the bid contained a profit 10 percent larger than the previous one. His offer on the last contract would give him more than a 200-percent gain.

Lew recorded his bids on a sheet of paper and put it in his pocket. He sealed each bid offering. He would deliver them himself. When the results of the bidding became known, he would know how his competitors bid, for at some point in his graduated series of profit margins, the contract would go to someone else.

The skeleton of the large clipper ship *Honest Traveler* was held upright by long wooden beams anchored against the out-bowing ribs and the sides of the dry dock. Her keel rested on several round wooden rollers prevented from moving by angular chock blocks driven in tightly. Three tall masts and various piles of ships timbers lay nearby.

"Are you sure the ship can be ready in four months?" Lew asked Cue Sorensen, the shipbuilder in Algiers.

"Most certainly. The hardest part is over. And that is getting all the necessary materials on hand. We have it all, the hard oak for the hull and even the choice spruce from Maine for the masts. I've got a sailmaker cutting the sails. If you give me the word, I can have her ready for sea in three months."

"You have that word. Get her ready. But I'm surprised that the month you lost wouldn't have delayed completion."

"I've had no lost time. Within an hour after Albert Wollfolk was found dead in the river, another man came to me and offered to take the ship at the same terms."

"Who was that man?"

"Stanton Shattuck. Do you know him?"

"No. Who is he?"

"He's one of your competitors on the docks."

"So he thought to buy my ship. Well, he'll not get her. Build her sound. I'll start looking for a captain."

"With every ship that is seaworthy, and some that aren't, busy carrying cargo to Mexico for the military, you'll not find a good captain without a berth," Sorensen said. "I'd suggest you look at the best first officers around and make one of them your captain."

"Good idea. I'll check them over. I'll come back

across the river every day or so to see how things are going."

"Come in workclothes someday and do some work on her yourself. You might like that. You should surely step the masts."

Lew swept his view over the ship's strong wooden ribs and internal framing etched against the sky. "I'd like that."

Lew walked down the bank and climbed into the hired riverboat. "Back to New Orleans," he told the coxswain.

"Yes, sir," said the man. He cast off from the mooring. The river current pulled them away from the shore. The two oarsmen dropped their blades into the oarlocks with a rattle of wood on wood.

"Heave away," said the coxswain.

The oars dipped water and the coxswain swung the tiller to head the boat toward the opposite side of the Mississippi.

Lew stared west out over the river and across the bayou lands toward Texas. His job as a Ranger had been dangerous. However, he believed there was more danger here in New Orleans. Somewhere out there in the teeming population of the city, the same men that had killed Albert Wollfolk now waited the opportunity to strike at him.

13

OLD ELLA was very late, more than two hours, and the day was drawing to an end. Morissot was

143

worried. He had given her a dangerous task. He rose from the bench in the corner of Jackson Square and walked across to the intersection of Decatur and Saint Peter streets.

A black woman with a coffeepot in a basket halted and offered to pour Morissot a cup. He waved her away and looked down both Decatur and Saint Peter. Pedestrians and vehicles flowed along the streets. Four soldiers leaned against a nearby wall. They ogled the passing women and talked and laughed among themselves. A block away a band of slaves was paving a section of Front Street with square blocks of granite. There was no sign of Ella.

Morissot returned to the square and looked about in all directions. As he drew near to the bench once again, he saw Ella at the base of one of the large oaks.

"Lezin," Ella called in a voice barely loud enough to be heard. She beckoned for him to come. She caught Morissot by the arm and drew him behind the tree. Her eyes swept the open avenues between the trees.

"Oh, my! Oh, my," she moaned, and looked up at Morissot with wide, frightened eyes.

"Ella, what is wrong?"

"Lezin, you should have told me," Ella said with a tremble in her voice.

"Told you what?"

"About Kelty, the assassin," she said accusingly.

"You saw Kelty? What happened? Tell me all, and from the beginning."

Ella gripped Morissot's hand. "I did as you said. I followed the man Wollfolk. The first evening and night he spent with his placée on Rampart Street. The following day he traveled around, but mostly was at his office and the warehouse. Then the night again with his placée. The second morning I followed along behind as he went to the warehouse on the waterfront.

"As I'm watching Wollfolk talk with that giant Julius, a man comes up beside me." Ella shuddered. "He grabbed me by the arm. Oh, God! Lezin, he hurt me terribly. I thought he was going to crush my very bones."

Morissot spoke softly to Ella. "It's all right now. You are safe."

Ella had known of the Irish assassin for a long time. Lezin also thought she knew what he did. But never had she given a sign to indicate it.

"How did you know this man was Kelty? You never told me you knew what he looked like."

"I didn't until today. I've seen men I thought could be Kelty, but I wasn't ever sure. Now I know. The minute I looked into his face, I knew. There was murder in him. He would kill me without a second thought."

"Describe him to me."

"Broad and strong, with black beard and eyes."

Ella was correct. Morissot and Kelty had come to know each other in their world of murder for pay. Never had a word passed between them, just a locking of eyes for a brief moment in those rare encounters on the street.

"I knew it was Kelty," Ella said, reading Morissot's expression.

"What did Kelty say?"

"He said, 'Why are you following that white man?' I said I wasn't. That's when he hurt me again."

Ella stared into Morissot's eyes. "He knows what I look like. I'll never be safe again."

"Yes you will. He only kills white people." That was the story told by those who knew that a killer named Kelty existed. However, Morissot believed Kelty had also killed blacks.

Morissot had never slain a white man. Now he may have to kill the false Wollfolk. He would also kill Kelty if he harmed Ella. The immediate question was why was Kelty spying on the man he most probably thought was Wollfolk.

"How did you get away from Kelty?"

"I fainted. The very first time in my life. When I came to my senses, he was gone. But I thought he was just hiding someplace near and would follow me. I didn't want him to see you. So I wondered around as if I was fuddled. Then, when I thought it safe, I came here."

Morissot knew Ella would have been safer if Kelty had learned who she was spying for. "You can tell me the rest of what you learned about Wollfolk later. Where did you last see Kelty?"

"There on the downriver side of Wollfolk's warehouse," Ella pointed.

146

"Go home, Ella," Morissot said. He would like to have more information about the impostor, but Ella must not be the one to gather it. He gave her five silver dollars.

Ella clutched the coins in her old hand. She hastened away, her eyes darting here and there like a doe that had once been mauled by the savage wolf.

Only pure luck allowed Morissot to spot Kelty driving the buggy heading north on Dumaine Street. Two little black boys were jigging in the street for pennies. A few people were standing and watching, and calling encouragement to the lively stepping lads. The killer Irishman drove through the gathering, scattering them and causing the boys to spring aside. The crowd's angry shouts drew Morissot's attention.

He fell in behind the assassin's vehicle and trailed it north toward Lake Pontchartrain. As the number of people on the street thinned, he slowed and fell farther to the rear. Morissot hoped Kelty was heading home because he wanted to know where the Irishman lived and could be found when the need arose.

Kelty looked to the rear now and then as he traveled. There was nothing out of the ordinary to arouse his suspicions.

He wondered about the old Negro woman he had discovered spying on the young Wollfolk. Why was she doing that, and for whom? Shattuck and the Ring would sooner or later hire Kelty to kill the man as he had killed Albert Wollfolk. For that reason, Kelty had decided to spend a few hours following the nephew. He was glad that he had. The knowledge that someone else was also interested in the man was very valuable information. Too bad the old hag had fainted before he could force her to tell what she knew. He had frightened her so badly that her brains were scattered, for when she had come to, she had wandered about like a crazy woman.

On a straight stretch of road and on one of the rises of land seldom found on the flat delta land, Kelty stopped the buggy and sat for several minutes. He watched to the rear as the day waned and the dusk came. He saw one man on foot. The fellow turned off on a side road at a distance. In the growing murk, Kelty went on.

Morissot slipped through the woods which were filling swiftly with night. He had observed Kelty stop for a time and then continue on for a mile or so before veering right onto a lane running easterly. Morissot now moved parallel to that narrow way.

The lane ended at a house set in among large trees. Kelty's buggy, barely visible, sat by the front stoop. Morissot saw no sign of the man. The windows remained dark. No family waited for the assassin, or were they merely absent for the evening?

The house remained dark as the minutes passed. Morissot started to move closer, then abruptly halted. He shivered as if someone had drawn a feather along his spine. He looked to the right at the dark trees and slightly lighter shades of darkness between them. Kelty was in the woods with him. And he was creeping nearer.

Morissot stole to the left, placing his feet with no sound. He had uncovered what he had hoped to, where the man lived. He had no reason to fight Kelty. Not yet.

He came out onto the main road and broke into a fast walk to the south. He would remember that Kelty was a wary animal, one that would not be taken easily.

When the rain ended, Tim made his way along the muddy road toward the Morissot home. He walked swiftly, enjoying the strength that had increased every day. He slapped at the mosquitoes that swarmed about him, and he wished he was more like the natives of New Orleans, who seemed to ignore the biting pests.

Marie met him with a smile at the gate and walked along the carriageway with him. "Father wants to talk with you. He learned something yesterday that should interest you."

"What is it?"

"Something about the impostor." She turned her green eyes on him. "You are in danger as long as he exists. Please be careful. Should he learn who you are, he would try to kill you."

"He's the one that's in danger," Tim said. "I'll

soon take my revenge for what he has done to me."

Lezin called out from the kitchen as Tim and Marie entered the house. "Tim, come have a cool glass of wine with me. You must be hot from your walk and I want to talk with you."

Lezin poured both Marie and Tim a glass of red wine. He refilled his own glass. "A friend of mine told me some news about the false Wollfolk. It appears that a man named Kelty has been following him around, at least for a day or so."

"Who is Kelty?" asked Tim.

"A paid killer, an assassin."

"Why does he follow the impostor? Is it to protect him?"

"I don't think so. He trails at a distance. I think Kelty might be planning to kill him."

"Who told you about this? Is it the truth?"

"A friend told me, a very reliable friend."

Tim almost asked how the friend would know to tell Lezin such a thing. However, he held his tongue. Lezin would tell him only what he wanted to. The man seemed protective of Tim. He wondered why.

"There is something in all this that I can't fathom," Tim said. "I felt the same way when the fight at the warehouse happened."

"I agree the situation is taking strange twists."

"Anything else?" Tim asked.

"The impostor spends his nights with a placée on Rampart Street."

Tim cocked a questioning eye at Lezin. "A placée?"

"A quadroon mistress, a woman who is one-quarter Negro. It is common in New Orleans for a white man to take a light-skinned mulatto woman and set her up in a house on the Ramparts. This placée has been there for a few years, as Albert Wollfolk's mistress."

"So my replacement has taken that over also?"

"It seems he is very thorough."

"I'll worry about the placée later. Right now we need more information. How do we get it?"

"I can have my friends try to find out things about the impostor." Lezin meant to continue his surveillance of the man with or without Tim's approval. However, it would best fit his plans if Tim knew what he was doing.

"Yes, please do that."

"I will. Now something more pleasant. Would you and Marie like to go froggin' with me this evening? The sky is clearing and it's going to be a nice night for a change."

"Oh, yes, Father! I'd like that," cried Marie.

"I like frog legs too," Tim said.

"Good. Then it's settled. Tim, harness the horse, for we must travel a couple of miles from here. Marie and I will make up the mixture of spices and meal to cook the frog legs in. We'll eat what we catch right on the spot."

"That's a deal," Tim said. He left the room and went off to the stables.

Marie hurried into the kitchen. She began to hum happily.

Lezin followed his daughter. "Marie, you like Tim, isn't that so?" he asked.

She blushed brightly as she raised her face to Lezin. "Yes, very much."

"He would make an excellent father for your children."

Marie blushed even redder. "He would never ask me to marry him. A white man can't marry a woman with Negro blood in her veins."

"I know. But I wasn't thinking of marriage."

Marie's eyes opened wide in great surprise. "But, Father?"

Lezin plunged ahead with his plan. "The Morissots have been free men for a hundred years. Your great-grandfather was one-half white, for his father was a white man. He paid a white woman to have his child. Therefore, your grandfather was three-quarters white. I'm seven-eighths white. You are almost white. Look at your skin and eyes, very much like your mother's."

"I wish I could have known my mother," Marie said. "It's too bad she died of the fever."

"Yes, it is," Lezin said. He recalled that year the yellow fever struck New Orleans so devastatingly. Thousands died during the weeks the disease ran rampant on every street. He had stayed clear of the city. However, one day as he traveled to the river to fish, he heard the cry for help from the house of a white man. He could not deny the call and entered the home.

The man and his two children were dead. The wife, though too weak to rise and filthy from her own vomit and waste, had survived the worse symptoms of the disease. Lezin had loaded her into his wagon and took her to his home, the very one where Marie and he now lived.

The white woman had great stamina, and under Lezin's care she had recovered. Her body recovered its strength and the roses came to her cheeks.

When Lezin came to her bed in the dark, she had welcomed him. Over the next several months she remained in the house, rarely venturing outside. For a white woman to be seen in Lezin's house, especially carrying his child, would mean his death—and perhaps her own as well—at the hands of white men.

A healthy baby girl was born to the woman. She nursed and cared for the infant for three days. On the fourth day when Lezin returned home, the woman was gone. A note stated simply that she was leaving and going to her people in the north. She asked that he not try to find her.

The woman had left the baby. For that Lezin had thanked her a thousand times as the years passed. He hired a wet nurse and began the long pleasant task of raising and educating his delightful daughter.

Lezin spoke to Marie. "White men rule the world and enjoy all the privileges as rulers. Now the Morissots have the opportunity to become white. Children born from you and Tim could go where they wished and do what they wanted without fear, for they would have passed into the white world. For three generations we have strived to accomplish that. Now you can complete the task.

"Remember, daughter, it is better to be a bastard than to be black." Lezin's voice was full of rancor.

"I understand, Father. But how do I make him want me?"

Lezin's face cleared, and he laughed lightly. He caught Marie by the chin and kissed her tenderly on the cheek. "You are a beautiful young woman. You could have any man you wished. I'm sure you will think of a way. Now hurry and get things ready for tonight. I'll get my frog gig and torches."

14

"You owe me, Shattuck," Gunard growled. "I did your crooked work. I slowed Wollfolk's niggers down for several days. Maybe you don't owe me the whole five hundred dollars, but sure part of it."

"Gunnard, I owe you nothing. Your reputation as a fighter is pure horseshit. You let a kid from Ohio whip you and you didn't lay a knuckle on him." Shattuck threw a contemptuous look at Gunnard's face with its swollen lips, his nose broken and knocked off to one side by Wollfolk's fists.

Shattuck stood by the wall of the Flatboat Saloon. It was located in a section of New Orleans

154

with no formal name, but called the Swamp by the pirates, rogues, muggers, and cheap killers who lived, fought, and often died there. He looked along the main street of the Swamp; it was lined with crudely constructed buildings, single-story and made from the lumber of broken-up flatboats that had come down the river over many years.

A few people carrying candle lanterns moved through the evening dusk on the muddy street. There were no sidewalks, only the wet black dirt, now stirred to mud by rolling wheels and the feet of men and horses. A light reflected a weak glint of silver as one of the lantern people veered around a water puddle. A streetwalker was propositioning a man in the light coming from the open door of the gambling shack. Three richly dressed young Creoles with swords buckled to their waists entered the saloon. Nobody paid Shattuck and Gunnard as much as a glance.

"I want two hundred dollars and I'll go on my way," Gunnard said. "That amount of money don't mean anything to a rich man like you."

"You'll get not one penny from me." Shattuck's temper rose and his voice was brittle. He should never had come to meet with the man. But there had been a threatening tone in the note delivered by the Negro boy at Shattuck's office.

"Two hundred dollars, Shattuck, and I'll not tell what happened to the white foreman who worked for the Wollfolk Company before I did."

"What do you know, Gunnard?" Shattuck's

voice was flat. The son of a bitch actually had the gall to threaten him. Stupid man.

"I know he was murdered and slipped into the river," Gunnard replied. He pressed his arm against the butt of the knife on his belt. The weapon felt reassuring, for Shattuck was a dangerous man. But without doubt, he would have a large sum of money on him. Gunnard needed money. The beating Wollfolk had given him had finished him in New Orleans. Two hundred dollars would take him to Saint Louis and get him started there.

"You know nothing," Shattuck said. Gunnard was guessing, but his guess was on the mark. Kelty had killed the foreman and thrown his body into the deep, wet grave of the Mississippi. It made no difference what Gunnard told in the Swamp, for there was no law in that godforsaken place. But he must not be allowed to come uptown and tell his tales.

"We can't talk out here," Shattuck said. "Let's get out of sight." He walked down the side of the building toward the adjacent alley.

Gunnard hesitated, then followed behind Shattuck's broad back. Shattuck was not to be trusted, but why not put a knife into his spine once he was in the dark alley? Then Gunnard could have all the money the man carried. Gunnard pulled his knife and moved quickly upon Shattuck.

The ex-prizefighter sensed the man closing on him. He stepped swiftly into the shadowy alley and whirled. He found a somewhat solid spot in the sloppy mud and set his feet. His fists balled into bony hammers. He felt the familiar rush of hot blood of the fighting ring. Then Gunnard came around the corner and was outlined against the brighter light of the street.

Shattuck struck Gunnard a savage blow to the face. Instantly he hit the man twice more, left and right.

Gunnard's forward momentum made the blow doubly damaging to him. He staggered, stunned. Only one thought remained: cut Shattuck with the knife. Gunnard swung a roundhouse swipe with the sharp blade.

The knife missed as Shattuck sprang clear. Then, before Gunnard could strike again, Shattuck plunged in, both fists swinging, cruelly smashing Gunnard's face.

Gunnard fell against the wall of the building. He dropped his knife. " 'Nough," he gasped.

"Like hell." Shattuck's voice was merciless. His brutal fists pounded Gunnard to the ground.

Gunnard lay on his back. He feebly raised an arm to ward off further blows.

Shattuck kicked the man onto his stomach. He jammed his boot down on the back of Gunnard's head and stomped his face into the sloppy mud.

He held the fallen man's face buried in the mud until the man ceased struggling.

"You weren't worth two cents, let alone two hundred dollars," Shattuck said to the corpse.

He left the alley by the far end. Gunnard's death would not even be reported. He would eventually be picked up and thrown into the river with other broken and useless things found lying on the streets of the Swamp.

"Damnation, this place is dead as a Bronze John hospital," said Leandre, staring around the bar-room. It was nearly empty of patrons, and the bartender was leaning half-asleep on the bar.

"A man could die from lack of excitement," agreed Maurice. "Let's do something other than sit here and get drunk on rum."

"The Swamp is always a rollicking place after dark," Gustave said. "And it's been dark for hours."

Leandre straightened quickly. "Now, why didn't I think of that? Gustave, you're always ahead of Maurice and me. Down there in the Swamp, we may even run into some of the Live Oak Boys and have a little practice with our swords."

"Now, Leandre, don't start a fight in the Swamp," said Maurice. "There are too many tough men for us to handle."

"You've got your pistol, haven't you?"

"Yes."

"So do I, and also Gustave has his. We'll shoot our way out if we find more trouble than we can handle. Come on along." Leandre was chuckling happily as he left the barroom and struck off down the street.

"I wish we could see a hackney to hire," Maurice said as he fell in beside his comrades.

"We can walk to the Swamp in less than half an

hour," Leandre said. He lengthened his stride and began to tell his friends a new joke he had heard.

They reached the bayou, full of the fetid stench of human waste, and crossed over on a rickety wooden bridge into the Swamp. They passed two blocks of poorly built and ill-kept buildings, and then they drew close to a saloon. The rumbling, growling voices of many men drifted through the open door and into the street.

Leandre peered at the faded sign hanging over the door. "How does the Flatboat Saloon strike you fellows?" he asked.

"From the sounds, it must be a lively place," said Maurice.

"Sounds more like a cave full of bears," Gustave said.

"Be damned if it doesn't," Leandre said. "Let's go inside and see what the bears look like." He led into the saloon.

The structure was quite deep, with a long wooden bar on the left. A score of crude tables with empty wine casks as seats sat in a row on the right. Three card tables and a craps table were crowded with players. A young whore was working the crowd, moving from table to table and propositioning the men. The odor of stale beer, rum, and whiskey and the sour smell of nearly a hundred unwashed human bodies filled the air with a scent that seemed to have weight.

Several of the rough-looking men halted their conversation to stare at the expensively dressed young Creoles making their way toward an empty table near the wall. A big, burly fellow pointed at the swords on the sides of the three and said something to the men near him. They all laughed.

Leandre noticed the gesture at him and his friends, and the laugh. He halted and started to turn.

"Not now, Leandre," Gustave said. "I haven't had my rum yet."

"Right as usual," Leandre said. He turned from the men and continued on to the table.

The bartender left his station behind the bar and crossed the room to the new arrivals. "What'll it be, gents?"

"Some of your very best rum," Leandre told the barkeep. "This much." He measured off a goodly height with his fingers. "And bring my friends the same." Leandre caught himself. "No. Bring the bottle unopened, and clean glasses." It was not unknown for Mickey Finns, drinks heavily laced with opium, being served to men from uptown. They woke up naked in alleys. Sometimes they did not wake up at all.

The bartender nodded and moved away. Leandre looked back at the men who had laughed at him. They had resumed their conversation and were paying him no attention.

The young Creoles drank their first rum and talked. Gustave poured another round and picked up his glass. He looked at the gathering of muggers, pirates without ships, and men with a dozen other unlawful, mean occupations.

The young whore saw Gustave looking about

and started across the room in his direction. As she passed the table where the burly man sat, he reached out and caught her by the waist and pulled her onto his lap. She wiggled free and, making a few quick steps to elude his reaching arms, ended up near the Creoles' table.

A little teasing smile came to her painted face as she leaned close to Gustave. "I'll let you tumble me for a quarter," she said.

Gustave studied the girl through the thick rouge she wore. She appeared to be thirteen or so. She could have been pretty, but her whiskey breath, dirty teeth, and soiled dress robbed her of that possibility.

"No, thanks," Gustave said.

"You don't like me." Her lips curved down in a pout.

"But I do. Where are you from?"

"From Kentucky. I came down the river on a flatboat."

Gustave thought she spoke as if proud of making such a long journey. She had most likely started that trip as a fresh hill girl. Now, like the battered and short-lived flatboats whose timbers and planks ended up in the shacks in the Swamp, the girl had also ended up in this hellhole section of New Orleans.

"I don't like that look on your face," said the young whore. "What are you thinking?"

"Oh, nothing," Gustave said. He had allowed his thoughts to show. He straightened his face. "I have never been upriver and was wondering what the trip would be like. How was it for you?"

"Part of the trip was fun. But the men were even dirtier and uglier than those here."

The girl looked into Gustave's young and handsome face and smiled wistfully. "Come and give me a tumble. If you don't, I'll have to let that dirty fellow there do it to me."

Gustave glanced at the man, who was stonily watching across the room at him. Then he looked back at the girl. "I don't want any loving tonight, but"—he reached into his pocket and brought out a handful of silver coins—"here is some money so that you don't have to bother with that man."

The child whore giggled and snatched the money from Gustave's hand. She brushed his cheek with her lips and danced away.

The burly man grabbed at the whore as she passed. But jingling the coins in her closed hand, she dodged out of his reach. She scampered out the door like a small girl.

Leandre chuckled. "Gustave, my good friend, one moment you talk me out of the foolishness of starting a fight, then the next minute you give your money away. That little whore will be back here tomorrow night, and she'll be tumbling the men, as she calls it."

"You're probably right," Gustave said. "However, I wanted to do it, and it was only a little money."

"Trouble's coming," Maurice said, looking past his two comrades.

The man who had missed catching the girl was coming toward the Creoles. "Why did you give her money?" he asked in a belligerent voice. "Now I'll miss out on a little frolic with her."

"I didn't mean to take away your pleasure," said Gustave. "The poor girl needed a little rest. So I gave her some coins." He smiled good-naturedly.

"You rich young bastards think you can do whatever you want. Maybe uptown you can. But not down here in the Swamp."

"You call us bastards," exclaimed Leandre, his face tightening. He started to rise to his feet.

Gustave caught Leandre by the arm. "This is my game," he said.

"Are you sure? I'd like to run my blade through this ass."

"I'm sure."

The man stepped forward. His hand rose to touch the knife on his belt. "Did you call me an ass?"

Gustave climbed swiftly erect. His sword gave out a sibilant whisper as he pulled it from its scabbard. The sharp point darted out to touch the man's chest. The man halted abruptly to keep from being impaled on the weapon.

"Easy does it," Gustave said. "That knife isn't a match for my sword."

Lucien Custus turned his big red head and watched the developing argument between his man Spradley and the Creoles. Spradley was a rough, dangerous man. However, Custus did not think it

163

would be an easy matter to beat the Creoles, even the youngest one. That fellow's face had lost its good-natured smile. His arm was cocked to run the thin sword through Spradley.

Custus had seen duels fought with rapiers. Deadly affairs with much blood flowing. The dueling academies for the rich produced tough, skilled fighters.

"Spradley, let it go," Custus called. "The Creole gamecock can cut out your guts before you can sneeze."

Spradley looked down at the sharp double-edged blade. He tensed, ready to try to knock the weapon aside.

Gustave saw the man's intention. He pushed the rapier forward to pierce the thin fabric of the man's shirt and pricking his skin with the cold point. The insult had rankled him the same as it had Leandre. If the man wanted to fight, then let it begin now.

Leandre cast a short look at Gustave. He recognized the temper building behind the young man's wide-eyed look. And a spot of red was growing on Spradley's shirt where the sword point pressed even harder.

Spradley glared at Gustave. "Put that sword away and I'll teach you a lesson."

"With pistols?" suggested Gustave.

"With pistols," Spradley said.

"The length of the saloon should be short enough range for even you to hit a man. Does that suit you?"

"Yeh," Spradley grunted. His eyes ground into the remaining Creoles. "You two will be next."

Leandre and Maurice both laughed. "You joke when you are near death," said Leandre.

"Spradley, I don't think you should be so quick to fight this young gamecock," Custus said. "Let the matter drop."

"Stay out of this, Custus," snapped Spradley. "He's not tough enough to beat me."

"It's your funeral," Custus said. "But the least I can do for you is to loan you a good pistol." He pulled his weapon and handed it to Spradley. "It's in good working order and has fresh loads."

Custus turned and called out toward the rear of the room. "Clear a line of fire."

Men hastily jumped to their feet and shoved aside the tables and casks. They moved to stand tightly around the wall or bar.

Leandre spoke to Gustave in a low voice. "Take the position near the door. Maurice and I will help you shoot the hell out of anybody who tries to stop us from leaving after this is over."

Gustave nodded and slid the rapier back into its scabbard. He drew his pistol as he walked to stand near the entrance.

Leandre spoke to Custus. "Why don't you be the judge and give the signal to fire?"

"Is that all right with you?" Custus asked Spradley.

"Sure, Custus. I'll show you how this dueling is done." He examined Custus' pistol as he walked to the rear of the saloon.

165

"Guns at your side," directed Custus. "Stand ready to fire."

Gustave smiled at his comrades and then faced around to lock his eyes on his opponent. This was his first duel with a pistol. Even so, his heart was beating quite nicely, slow and easy.

"Fire," Custus cried.

Gustave's hand flashed up, his pistol thundered.

In the opposite end of the room, Spradley staggered. He dropped his pistol and clutched at his chest. His mouth fell open, howling soundlessly. He crumpled to the floor.

The man nearest Spradley went to kneel by the body. He glanced up at Custus. "Dead. Hit plumb center."

Several of the men looked at Custus, as if awaiting some signal from him.

Custus stretched a tight smile across his mouth. "I warned the dumb son of a bitch." He faced the young Creoles. "Spradley was wrong. You're tough bastards, all right. That's the kind of men that are welcome in the Swamp."

"In that case, I'm buying," Gustave said. He extracted a leather pouch from a pocket and tossed it upon the bar. It landed with a ring of coins.

"That's enough gold to buy drinks for everybody. And then some more rounds."

15

THE black wave of the night came stalking as Lezin stopped the wagon at the edge of the swamp. He jumped down and in a minute had removed the tree branches covering a pirogue, a boat that had been hollowed from a cypress tree. He shoved it halfway into the water of the bayou.

"Load the boat," Lezin said to Marie and Tim. "Watch the sharp prongs on the gig."

The two young people transferred the gear from the wagon to the boat. Lezin arranged the provisions to his satisfaction. He took up a broad-bladed paddle.

"This is going to be a fine night for giggin' frogs," Lezin said. "And I know just the right place. Hop in, Marie. Shove us off, Tim."

As Lezin propelled them noiselessly through the black water of the swamp, Tim examined the craft. It was at least fourteen feet long, broad-bottomed, and stable in the water. The tree that had made the boat had been a giant. The walls of the vessel had been scraped to a thin shell. Old cracks were liberally sealed with tar. Many days of labor had gone into creating the craft.

The pirogue followed the twisting, bending bayou. The only sound was the soft swish of the water past the hull and the momentary drip of water from the paddle as Lezin swung it forward for the next stroke. The air was still and heavy with memories of the heat of the day. On the banks, cane, buckvine, cypress, and gum crowded the water and elbowed one another for room to grow.

The swamp filled with the purplish black shadows of night. The narrow bayous, overhung by the limbs of the trees, became black tunnels. Still Lezin paddled them on, seemingly having eyes of a night-seeing animal. Tim was certain Lezin knew the swamp; however, some light could not but help to ensure they did not become lost in the maze of watercourses.

The pirogue left the sluggish water of the bayou and entered the still water of a small lake. Lezin rested his paddle. The boat drifted to stop in the darkness.

The sounds of the swamp came alive. Now that the boat was not moving, the mosquitoes closed in with their buzzing; finding an unprotected arm or face, they dived in to land and sink their long snouts deeply into the warm bodies until they tasted the rich blood.

Tim waved the pests away. He felt a deep calm as he sat with Marie and Lezin on the lake with the dark swamp surrounding them. The attempt on his life and the impostor controlling his rightful inheritance seemed of less importance.

He heard the croaks of frogs and the calls of a hundred other night creatures. A savage bellow rumbled out from a far bank. Instantly a second came rolling over the water. The blackness seemed to ripple to the hoarse sounds.

"What was that?" Tim asked.

"A bull alligator," replied Lezin. "He's getting ready for his night hunt. There's many of them in the swamp." He picked up his paddle and checked the location of the stars. "Now to find the frogs," he said. He dipped the paddle and sent the pirogue off through the murk.

Trees took shape ahead. Tim judged them oak and ash from the pattern of their black branches against the sky. That probably meant slightly higher ground, for those trees did not like their feet in too much water. The boat came to a sliding stop, its bow rising slightly as it rode up on the shore of the lake.

Lezin sorted among the items in the boat and found a torch made of a tar-soaked cloth fastened to the end of a stick. He lit it with a lucifer. A yellow flame burst to life, lighting the fringe of meadow along the shore of the lake and the edge of the woods farther back.

"Oh, look," exclaimed Marie. "A deer."

A huge stag stood at the edge of the meadow near the woods. Its large ears were spread in an intent, listening attitude. Its nostrils quivered and sucked at the air, questing for the scent of these intruders into its domain. The great sweep of antlers on its head caught the light of the torch and reflected it back ivory-white.

The deer caught the human scent. It snorted

and stomped the ground. The sharp rack of antlers were lowered for a moment as if the beast would charge the intruders.

Abruptly the ghostly gray animal pivoted toward the woods. It exploded into a smoky blur of frantic flight, its great horns laid along its back as it fled in a series of long, lithe bounds, disappearing in the woods so swiftly it seemed it had been only a fantasy.

"A beautiful animal," Tim said.

"The swamp has many animals," Lezin said. He inserted the butt end of the torch into a hole made for it in the bow of the boat. He stepped out into the waist-high grass and dragged the craft more than halfway out of the water.

"This is the place where the biggest frogs are," he said. "You two wait for me here. It's better if one man goes giggin' by himself."

Using his hands, Lezin made a thick pat of mud in the bottom of the boat. He built a fire on the mud and then added a handful of green grass to the flames.

"The fire and smoke should help keep the mosquitoes away," he said.

Lezin took his ten-foot frog gig from the boat. He examined the two steel points and the barbs that prevented the prey from escaping. "Good and sharp," he said.

He hung a burlap sack over his shoulder. Into it he placed three torches. Picking up his gig and taking the lit torch from the boat, he moved off along the shore of the lake.

Tim sat with Marie and watched Lezin's flickering yellow light until it vanished among the trees. "Do you often come with your father when he goes out to gig or fish?" Tim asked.

"I used to. But then, after I became older, he stopped asking me to come with him. There have been times when I wished I was a boy."

"I'm glad you're not," Tim said.

Marie did not know how to respond to that, so she remained silent. She watched Tim's face in the firelight, then looked out across the swamp to where her father had gone. She remembered his words that a woman could make a man want her. She only wanted Tim to love her. Should she try? Suddenly she could feel the throb of her heart in her bosom.

A knot of wood, superheated by the fire, exploded with a pop. A jet of sparks rose straight up in the perfectly still air. Marie jerked at the sound, then became motionless again.

Tim studied the young woman, tracing the planes and curves of her face with his eyes. So beautiful. And so near, only an arm's length away. It seemed to him that sitting with Marie by the fire of branches in the immense cave of the black night, they were the only two humans in the entire universe.

Tim batted at the mosquitoes. Now that they no longer were moving in the boat, the insects were much worse.

"The smoke is not keeping the mosquitoes away," Marie said. "I have a piece of netting that will keep them out. Would you want to share it with me?"

"Yes. Where is it? I'll get it."

"I can find it easily." Marie dug the netting from among the items in the bottom of the boat. "You'll have to sit closer to me, for the netting is small," she said. She moved slightly to the side to provide room for Tim.

He sat down in the bottom of the boat near Marie. He felt her hip pressing against him. The feel of her flesh stirred him pleasantly.

Together they lifted the net and draped it over their heads. It hung to touch the bottom of the boat.

"This should keep us from getting bit," Marie said.

"I think so too," Tim said. Marie's shoulder and hip both pressed against him now. His breath quickened and his blood hurried more swiftly through his veins.

"The fire is dying and I'm afraid of the dark. Would you hold my hand?" Marie timidly put out her hand.

The flames were indeed weaker, but Tim recognized the fib. She was not afraid of the dark. He caught her hand in his.

Marie looked at Tim, her eyes luminous as jewels. She was too close, too alluring. He pulled her to him and kissed her gently on the lips. God! How sweet was the taste of her. He kissed her again . . . and again.

Of one accord they lay back in the bottom of the boat.

The last flame of the fire flickered out. The darkness came into the hollow of the pirogue. It began to rock, and small waves ran out across the lake, chasing one another and whispering as if telling secrets.

The big bull alligator raised its head and bellowed, warning any trespassers of the danger lying in its mighty strength. It bellowed once again and then closed its toothy jaws with a rattle of ivory.

It slid out of its den under the bank and into the lake. It swam effortlessly, its fourteen-foot, four-hundred-pound body gliding through the water with but a tiny wake. It knew exactly where it was headed.

The alligator left the deep water and made its way through the cane grass in the shallows. It stopped when its feet on the short legs touched the muddy bottom. It raised its head, staring with its one good eye into the darkness, and sniffed the air.

It smelled the scent of deer, the prey it sought. But it was old scent. The alligator would wait. It was extremely good at that. Sometimes it had to wait days between meals.

The alligator crawled up from the water and onto the game trail. In a slight depression, it lowered itself to lie flat on its stomach. When the deer finally came to drink, it would catch it by the leg and drag it into the lake. There it would roll with its prey, breaking its bones and drowning it. The alligator always liked that last battle. No matter how much the deer might struggle, the alligator always won.

The alligator closed its one good eye. Its nose and ears would alert it to the presence of something coming that could be eaten.

As it lay in its ambush, it felt the pain in the empty eye socket. A very powerful enemy had put out that eye. At the remembrance, an angry rumbling growl arose in the beast's chest.

The bullfrog heard the heavy animal crushing the grass as it came along the edge of the water. The frog hunkered lower and tensed, ready to spring away. The night turned suddenly to day. The frog became blinded by the brightness.

Lezin spotted the big frog squatting at the edge of the water and facing the lake. He held his blazing torch steady and extended the spear slowly. Two feet from the green body, Lezin stabbed out.

The frog sensed the impending strike and tried to leap to safety. The double-pronged gig straddled its spine and pierced it from back to front. With its powerful rear legs kicking in a wild, futile motion, the frog was hoisted into the air on the end of the gig.

Lezin grabbed the big hind legs of the struggling amphibian and jerked it from the iron barbs that held it. He whacked its head on the hard wooden shaft of the gig. The animal went limp in his hand. Opening his sack, he dropped the dead frog in with the score or more of them he had already speared.

Lezin entered a finger of woods that extended down to the water's edge. The torch, almost burned out, cast a feeble light among the trees. Lezin would soon have to light the last one. Then he would return to the pirogue. But first there was one more place he wanted to check for frogs. Big ones could usually be found there. He stepped up on a log lying across the path.

The log suddenly rose, hoisting Lezin into the air. Just for an instant, he thought the log had simply rolled. But a rolling log did not lift a man.

Gator! Lezin leapt frantically as the mammoth beast's back jerked from under his feet and the gaping jaws flashed back for him.

The long teeth snapped shut on one of Lezin's pant legs. The stout cloth held, throwing him to the ground. He dropped the frog spear. But he saved the precious light. In the darkness the beast would have all the advantages. Lezin whirled and lay on his back.

He saw the alligator gathering itself to drive toward him. He began kicking the broad snout with his free foot and yanking with all his strength on his pant leg. The cloth ripped free.

Lezin rolled, came to his feet, and sprang clear. He calmed his pounding heart. That was a near thing. He held his torch up to better see the alligator. One glistening yellow eye glared at him.

So we meet again, old man gator. I speared you in the head the last time we met and you tried to eat me. I thought you would die, but you only lost an eye. You are a tough one, and now two feet longer and a hundred pounds heavier. But can you live with no eyes?

Lezin cautiously stepped closer to the big alligator. The beast lay partly on the handle of his gig. Lezin caught hold of the end and yanked the gig loose.

The alligator ran forward a few quick steps. Lezin swiftly retreated.

Lezin inched slowly back toward the beast. He reached out with the head of the gig. There would only be time for one thrust. It had to be good, and the shorter the range, the more likely the iron barb would hit the mark.

The alligator saw the man creeping closer. The smell of the thing stirred almost forgotten memories. This was the foe that had hurt it so badly that long time past. The alligator charged.

Lezin drove the left-hand prong of the gig into the yellow eye of the alligator, just as the beast rushed forward with open jaw. He sprang backward, wrenching at the gig. The point ripped loose from the shaft and remained behind, sunk deeply in the eye socket of the alligator.

The beast bolted blindly onward to the very spot where Lezin had stood a moment before. Then suddenly it felt the pain of its wound. It bellowed, and bellowed again, the roar shattering the night for a mile in every direction. The alligator whipped around, trying to see its hated foe. But impenetrable blackness lay everywhere. The animal sensed the danger in such total blindness. When threatened, it always found safety in the water. It tore through the brush and trees toward the lake like some low-slung juggernaut.

Lezin lit his last torch from the weak flame of the old one. He followed the trail of the alligator to the shore of the lake. He lifted his torch as high as he could. Just barely far out in the water, he could make out the back of the animal. The beast, without its eyes, was helplessly swimming in circles and gradually drifting out toward the center of the black body of water.

Tim saw the light coming through the woods. It flicked on and off as trees blocked it from his view for a second. He fed sticks to the red coals on the pad of mud in the bottom of the boat. He wanted the fire burning when Lezin arrived.

A flame sprang to life, illuminating the interior of the boat. Tim looked at Marie. She smiled at him as she rearranged her clothing.

Tim smiled back. However, Lezin's return was not a pleasant event to him. He had taken advantage of the man's trust and made love to his daughter.

"The mud has mostly dried," Marie said. "The boat may burn."

She began to dip water with cupped hands from the lake and poured it on the floor of the boat so that it would run onto the clay and rewet it.

"Everyone all right?" asked Lezin as he placed

the shaft of the torch into the hole in the bow of the boat.

"Everything is fine," replied Marie. "Tim and I had a very pleasant time while you were gone."

Tim said nothing. The truth was in Marie's words. He hoped the father could not read the exact truth.

Lezin looked at his daughter. She smiled radiantly at him, and the smile could have healed a fever victim.

Lezin turned his back to the pair. Tim needed more time to compose himself. "Let's cook a meal fit for a king," he called over his shoulder. "Marie, heat the skillet."

He squatted on his haunches and dumped the frogs from the sack. Skillfully he severed the large hind legs from the torsos and began to strip the skin from them. He held a handful of the legs out for Tim to see. "Look at the beautiful white flesh," he said.

Tim nodded. "Should be delicious," he replied.

Lezin handed the frog legs to Marie. She rolled them in the corn meal and spices they had brought and dropped them in the hot, sputtering skillet. They added more pieces of meat until the skillet was full.

Lezin laid his empty sack and the shaft of his gig in the boat. He sat down on the bow.

"Father, did you know that you have lost the head of your gig?" Marie asked.

"Yes, I will add a new one."

"It must have been a big frog to tear off the point," Marie said.

"Not a frog. I had a little trouble with an alligator."

"Are you all right?" Marie asked in alarm.

"I'm fine."

Tim sat quietly listening to the conversation between Marie and Lezin. Her voice gave him great pleasure. He would never get tired of having her near him. How was he going to arrange that?

Marie brought out a bowl of salad, a loaf of bread, and three plates. She removed the skillet of frog legs from the fire and set it down next to the other dinner items.

"Both of you help yourself while I pour the wine," Marie said. Tim and Lezin filled their plates heaping full. Marie handed them their wine, then filled her own plate.

The three were quiet, eating and staring at the heart flame of the fire.

Lezin studied the radiant face of his daughter. He wanted to laugh and shout. He smiled gently and laughed inside his head.

16

"TWENTY-TWO soldiers and one sailor are dead," said Dr. Carstensen, his face strained and haggard.

"How many have died at Charity Hospital?" asked Honoré Savigne.

The two men moved down the long hallway

leading to the east wing of the Marine Hospital. That isolated area served as the quarantine section of the hospital. Eight days had passed since Savigne had watched the unloading of General Scott's wounded and ill fighting men returning from Mexico.

"Eighteen at Charity."

"Forty-one men dead of yellow fever, and you are only now reporting it." Savigne could not control the sarcasm and disapproval in his voice. He hoped none of the heroic and sacrificing Sisters of Charity had contracted the deadly disease.

"I've kept the board of health informed, and they in turn kept Mayor Crossman and the city council members alerted. Several times, as more and more men died, I requested permission to release the news. Today they finally agreed; the board is posting bulletins at the official places and giving copies to the newspapers. I wanted to tell you personally and to apologize for my untruths to you that day at the docks."

"There's more to this than just the number of deaths," Savigne said, his reporter's keen instinct for sensing the unspoken vibrating rapidly. "What's changed?"

"I have fourteen new cases, men who were not in Mexico," the doctor said.

"Then the disease is spreading. The epidemic has started."

"God! I'm afraid so. How I wished I knew how the disease was transmitted from one patient to another, or if it really is. But we haven't the slightest idea. I had hoped isolating the infected men would prevent others from catching it. But, as in the past, that has had absolutely no benefit. These new sick came from the docks and the hospital itself. Charity Hospital is experiencing the same thing. They have seven new cases."

Savigne looked ahead at the double doors that opened into the quarantine ward. The goose pimples rose on his skin. Most of the men confined there would leave as corpses. Only the strongest would have any chance to survive. In a few days there would be no quarantine areas, for every bed would be full of those sick with the terrible scourge. Thousands would die in the dark bedrooms of their homes. Then later, as the disease spread even wider, many dead and dying would be found in the streets, falling there too weak to walk as they tried to flee the city.

The rich would attempt to ward off the fever by drinking lime water, dosing themselves with quinine and opium. The poor would put onions in their shoes. Savigne had observed that the onions were just as effective in preventing the disease as the more exotic and expensive methods. Not one of them worked.

New Orleans was familiar with death. Over the city's life more than a hundred thousand people, a number equal to the current population, had died in epidemics of yellow fever and cholera.

Dr. Carstensen shoved the door open. Though it was but midafternoon, the ward was dimly lit, for rain poured down from the dark heavens. A double row of beds containing at least fifty patients stretched along both sides of the ward. Several mosquitoes that had found holes in the netting that covered the open windows buzzed about the sick.

A man lay covered by several blankets. Still he was shivering. He spoke to Carstensen, "Doctor, I'm so very cold. May I have another cover?"

"I'll have the nurse bring you one," Dr. Carstensen replied.

"One of the new cases?" Savigne asked in a low voice. A bursting headache was the first symptom. Then came a teeth-chattering chill. Then the hellish fever.

"Yes," Carstensen said. "Look and make your report for the paper."

A patient thrashed about on his bed in a feverish delirium. He shouted out in an undecipherable babble of words. His bloodshot eyes fell upon Savigne, but they did not see him. The man began to cry as if from some great sorrow.

Another patient, a large, powerfully built man, his face a dark bronze, began to retch. He lay on his back, and the black vomit boiled out of his mouth and spread across his face. He began to strangle in his own vomit.

Carstensen sprang to the man's bed and swiftly turned him on his side. The doctor began to pound the man on the back. "Nurse! Come and help," he shouted.

Savigne's bile rose bitter in his throat. He remembered the horrible black vomit from that time as a boy when his mother and father had died. He pivoted and hastily left the quarantine ward. He hurried down the long passageway and out into the street.

He stood in the rain on the sidewalk and looked at the people passing by, examining the unsuspecting faces. He extended his view to observe the people riding beneath the raised tops of the vehicles rolling by on the street. His eyes were met only by a placid expression of men and women enduring another rain. Soon those faces would be filled with fear as death struck thousands of times around them. And then they too would fall and die.

Savigne walked slowly toward the newspaper office. This was one story he dreaded writing. The thought came to him that he should leave the city. But he knew he could not.

He slapped at a stinging mosquito as he recalled the epidemics he had survived. The disease would pass him by as it had every time before.

The rains had come again, beating down steadily during the night and into the afternoon. Though the hard rain had now ceased, fine mist settled out of the dreary overcast. Lew thought it a day well-suited for a quiet game of poker.

The Saint Charles Hotel was just ahead. He had heard of the huge four-story building with its dome of beautiful proportions soaring one hundred and eighty-five feet into the sky. It contained three hundred and fifty rooms and fourteen baths with cold and hot running water. The Saint Charles was noted for its palatial dining room and fabulous bar and saloon.

Lew would have liked to bring Cécile to the Saint Charles. But that could never be. Negroes and mulattos were not entertained here; they were bought and sold on the auction block in the center of the open space beneath the dome.

He guided the gray horse through the sloppy mud and the puddles of water and up to the row of iron tie posts at the entrance of the hotel. He glanced up at the low-hanging clouds, so close to the earth that they half-obscured the high dome of the structure. Rain would soon fall hard again. Lew dismounted and tied his slicker over the saddle to keep it dry.

A funeral procession came around the corner and into the street where Lew stood. He turned to watch it move slowly past. There were many deaths these days—victims of yellow fever, the newspapers reported. Both of the caskets were marked with lampblack, as was the custom to indicate Bronze John had killed again. Lew could hear the wailing of the women trailing along behind in the mud. The men were mute in their sadness.

A horseman came splashing around the end of the funeral procession and up to the adjoining tie ring. He stepped down, careful to place his booted foot on the brick sidewalk.

Almost immediately a buggy spun along the street. A young woman called out to the man and reined the trotting horse close to him.

The man's face twisted with anger as he looked at the woman. He went quickly to the buggy. The woman said something that Lew could not hear.

"Go home, bitch," the man growled.

"Not unless you come with me," snapped the woman.

"Go home and stay there," the man repeated, his voice rising.

"No," shouted the woman in a shrill voice.

The man's hand shot out and he slapped her, rocking her head savagely back and forth. "Do it now, before I beat you."

The woman dropped the horse's reins and both her hands came up to her face. "Goddamn you to hell," she screamed, her pretty face a mask of fury.

The man turned from her. He seemed to see Lew for the first time. "She's crazy jealous, you know. I should've locked her up before I left the house." He brushed past Lew and entered the lobby of the Saint Charles.

A sob came from the woman. She wiped at the flow of blood coming from her cut lips, smearing it over her chin.

Lew took his handkerchief from his pocket. He stepped to the woman and gently began to wipe the blood from her cut lips. The blood continued to flow from one bad split at the corner of her mouth, and he pressed the cloth firmly over it.

"I'm sorry, ma'am, that he hit you," Lew said. "Are you all right?"

The woman clasped his hand that held the handkerchief. She stared steadily into his eyes with an intense, penetrating look. She did not reply.

Lew removed the handkerchief. The bleeding seemed to have ceased. "There, that should do it. But take this." He offered the piece of cloth to the woman.

"Thank you," the woman said, and took the handkerchief. She looked at the red stain. "He's beat me worse than this. He's going to kill me someday. I think it'll be very soon, unless somebody stops him. He only married me for my land and slaves."

She seemed on the verge of saying something else to Lew. Instead, she flung her sight quickly at the entrance of the hotel. Fear came to her eyes. She dropped the handkerchief on the floor of the buggy and jerked the buggy whip from its holder. She lashed the horse into a dead run along the muddy street.

Lew turned and entered the Saint Charles. He was disturbed by the beating of the woman. A man should never do that.

He asked a hotel steward the location of the gaming room and, following the directions, climbed the stairs to the second floor. The room was large with several tables and many players already at their game. The man who had slapped the woman had just seated himself at the only partially filled table. One seat remained.

Lew did not want to be at the same game as the man, but he had no choice if he was to play cards without waiting for a seat at a new table of players. He crossed the room to the empty chair.

"Is this a private game or may a stranger sit in?" Lew asked the men at the table.

Two military men—a naval captain and a marine colonel—sat across from each other. On the captain's right was a thin man, who examined Lew with a hard stare. A heavy cane with a thick butt hung on the edge of the table near him. The fellow who had struck the woman was the fourth and last player.

"You are no more a stranger than the colonel and I are," said the captain. "Our ship just arrived in port yesterday from Norfolk. This is our first shore leave in many days. I'm Captain Tolbert. This is Colonel Bullock."

The colonel impatiently riffled the cards in his hands. "Sit down," he said. "The game's poker, with table stakes."

"If you have money, you can play," said the man with the cane. "What is your name?"

"Timothy Wollfolk," Lew replied.

He saw the eyes of the man come to a quick, intense focus on him.

"The nephew of Albert Wollfolk?" asked Farr Rawlins.

"Yes."

"Then I would judge you have plenty of money to cover about any size bet." Rawlins pointed at the empty chair. "Join us. My name is Rawlins. That is Enos Grivot." He nodded at the man. "He won't mind, he'll play cards with anyone."

Grivot looked sullenly at Lew.

Bastard wife-beater, Lew thought.

Rawlins noted the silent, unfriendly interchange between Grivot and the young Wollfolk. There was some sort of ill will here. It showed plainly on Wollfolk.

"Let's play poker," said the marine.

"Patience, Colonel," said the captain. "These gentlemen of New Orleans will take your money soon enough.'

"Like hell they will," the colonel said.

Lew pulled out his wallet and placed a stack of bills in front of him. He picked up the cards dealt him.

Several hands were played with Lew ending up just about where he had started. Then Rawlins dealt him a high set of cards. After a couple of rounds of betting, the two military men and Rawlins had dropped out, and Lew found himself alone with Grivot. He still felt his anger at the man. Now, wife-beater, let's see how brave you are.

Lew raised Grivot's bet. The man came back with a raise of his own. This continued for three rounds of raises, then Grivot called Lew even.

Both men had full houses, Lew's was slightly larger. He raked in the pile of money, more than $1,500.

Rawlins smiled slightly. He had deliberately cheated to give Wollfolk the winning hand. At the same time he had given Grivot a strong hand to keep him in the game. The fact that the military men and he had lost their opening bets did not bother him at all. He hated all military officers, ever since he had fought with General Jackson against the British. That bloody battle on the Plains of Chalmette had been fought days after the war had ended.

Rawlins, a young lieutenant in the cavalry at the time, had lain severely wounded on the battlefield for a day and a night before he had finally been found and his injuries treated. He had only partially recovered, limping through life with a bad leg for more than thirty years. To hell with all military officers.

Rawlins saw that his ploy was working and that the hostility between Grivot and Wollfolk was growing. He would aggravate it even more. He had the skill at cards to easily bring it off. For the first few years while recovering slowly from his war injury, he had been a professional gambler on several of the great river steamboats that sailed up and down the Mississippi. Few men could match him with skill at cards.

Lew began to win. And the strong hands came often. He bet aggressively, especially against Grivot, taking the man's money with relish and piling it up in front of himself.

Lew picked up his next hand and spread the cards so that he could see them. He expected good cards, and they were extremely good. Why had he been so certain of them?

It came to Lew that he knew why: because Rawlins had dealt the cards, as he had dealt most of Lew's other winning hands. The discovery jolted Lew. He looked across the table at the man. Rawlins' face was unreadable as he studied his cards.

Lew slowly shuffled his hand as his mind raced to evaluate the situation. A stranger was cheating, dealing Lew high cards so that he would win. Lew had no friends, so therefore Rawlins was an enemy. Enemies did not help a man to acquire money without a motive. What did Rawlins hope to gain? One thing for certain, the man was very good with the pasteboards.

Lew glanced at Grivot. The man was watching him with an angry expression. He had lost several thousand dollars.

"I open for five hundred dollars," Grivot said. Lew covered the bet. The two military officers dropped out. They were barely holding in the game, anteing up and hoping for a turn in their luck.

"I'll stay," Rawlins said, placing his money in the center of the table.

Grivot discarded. "Give me one card," he told Rawlins.

"Two cards," said Lew. He would play the game as the hand indicated, drawing to the three jacks he held. He picked up the cards as Rawlins dealt and slipped them unread in among the others.

Grivot looked at his cards and then folded them into his hand. "I bet a thousand dollars." He tossed several bills into the pot.

"I'm out," Rawlins said, and laid his hand down.

Lew pondered the situation. Had Rawlins purposely helped him to win to build up his confidence only to now begin to deal him losing hands? Let's take a look. Lew unfolded his cards.

The three jacks had become four. A powerful hand. Still, it could be beaten in several ways. Lew checked Grivot's remaining funds. The man had three, maybe four thousand dollars left. Lew could match that and, even if he lost, come out winning several thousand dollars. He reached for his money.

"Your thousand and a thousand more," Lew said.

Grivot counted the bills before him. "Your thousand and twenty-five hundred more," he said. Grivot's face was flushed, but his hands and eyes were steady as he pushed all his money into the center of the table.

Grivot had no more money with which to bet again. With table stakes he could not leave to obtain more. Lew could win by merely betting more than twenty-five hundred dollars.

Lew glanced at Rawlins. Just for an instant he caught the cunning look in the man's unblinking eyes. Before they slid away.

Lew began to smile. Rawlins did have a trick and it was simple. In fact, so simple that Lew had almost missed it. He wanted trouble between Grivot and Lew. Perhaps a fight. Grivot must be very good with weapons.

"What should I do, Rawlins?" asked Lew in a

quiet voice. "You dealt me the cards. Are mine larger than Grivot's or did you give him the best hand this time?"

Rawlins stared back without expression. "I don't know what you mean."

"Sure you do. You fed me good cards so I could beat Grivot."

"I did nothing of the sort."

"Wollfolk, you cheated. You admit it," exclaimed Grivot. "I knew it had to be that. Now you try to blame it on Rawlins. I've played many games with him and he's an honest man."

Lew ignored the ranting man. He counted out the amount of his original sum of money and shoved it into his pocket. The remainder he pushed away. "All of you, take back what is yours," he said.

"You are a goddamned cheat." Grivot's voice rose to a roar. His angry flush had deepened to purple. "And now you play the coward." He leaned across the table and struck at Lew with an open hand.

Lew knocked the blow aside. He did not like the man, but he did not want to kill him.

The military officers and Rawlins began to back away from the table. Lew heard chairs scraping behind him and the scuff of feet as other players hurried to get out of the line of fire.

"Easy, Grivot, don't play into Rawlins' hand. He wants us to fight."

"You are a coward. But I'm not. You're going to fight."

He plunged his hand inside his clothing.

"Don't do it." Lew flipped aside the tail of his coat to expose the butt of his Colt. He hoped Grivot would pull only a knife. There Lew could control the situation without shooting him.

Grivot snatched a pistol from a shoulder holster. He swung it toward Lew.

Lew jerked his pistol from his belt. Grivot was amazingly fast. He would also be very accurate. It would be dangerous to only wound him when he stood close. He could still kill. And should Grivot live, he would try again.

Lew shot the Frenchman directly through the heart.

Grivot pitched forward. As he fell, his pistol thundered into the table, blasting the paper money away in a blizzard. The gunpowder smoke of the two pistols blended together, rolling and tumbling, engulfing the dead and the living.

Lew stepped back, holding his pistol ready, watching Rawlins and the other men in the gaming hall as the smoke rose and thinned.

"Captain, and you, Colonel, I gave back the money when I knew Rawlins had cheated, and you saw that I did not want to fight. Will you tell the police that?"

"That is the truth and I will so inform the authorities," said the captain.

"So will I," said the marine colonel.

Lew put the pistol back into his belt. Abruptly he whirled upon Rawlins. "You have caused me to shoot a man. If you were a whole man, I'd kill you for that."

Lew moved quickly forward. The open palm of his hand smacked Rawlins in the face, knocking him to the floor. "Crippled or not, don't cause me trouble again." He spun and strode from the room with long strides.

Rawlins pulled himself to his one good leg. His head rang and blood flowed from his paper-thin mouth. His eyes burned with fury. He hopped to the card table and grabbed his cane. Watching Lew's retreating back, he propped himself up.

His hand slid inside his jacket just as Lew stepped through the door and was gone.

Rawlins removed his hand from his clothing. He glared at the men watching him.

Then he turned and, leaning heavily on the cane, made his way from the gaming hall.

—————————17—————————

TIM had little pain from his old wounds as he worked with the black stevedores on the dock. He selected his loads from the mound of stacked cargo and fell in line with the string of men moving to the ships. When he had shouldered his first load, the men had cocked their eyes in deep surprise. Now they simply made room for him as he lugged his burden.

The men hummed as they trod back and forth bent under their loads. The hum was no special tune, just a low undulation of their deep voices, like the drone of a hive of worker bees. Tim hummed with the black men, and it did seem to lighten the weight of his load.

He was lathered with sweat from the very beginning of the morning. Often he had to rest, hunkered down by the piles of boxes or crates out of the reach of the hot sun. His legs were wobbly with fatigue by the time Julius called a halt for the noon meal. He reflected upon Lezin's words: that Jonathan sewed a tight stitch. The statement was correct. Not one of the injuries had ruptured under the strenuous labor.

Tim stumbled to one of the drinking buckets sitting in the shade of the warehouse. He lifted it and poured it all down over his head. Using the tail of his shirt, he wiped at the water coursing down his face.

He was exhausted by the morning labor, but only hard physical work would fully restore his strength. In a week or so he would be recovered. But first he had to get through this day.

The slow wind cooled Tim as he leaned on the warehouse wall and gazed down at the river. Seabirds soared and hung in the air, their sharp eyes searching downward. Now and then one would fold its wings, dive down, and snatch something edible from the water. Two oystermen had found a few feet of open pier and had rowed in to tie their boat. Now they sat shucking their catch of oysters. In the center of the river, a tall-masted naval war ship had cranked up its anchor, hoisted its acres of white sails, and was gliding off on the current like a giant swan. Several other ships still hung at anchor waiting to find space at the docks. None of them was contracted to the Wollfolk Company.

Two ships were tied up at the Wollfolk docks. One of the ships was the result of the impostor's ingenuity. He had hired a fast boat powered by four skilled oarsmen. When an oceangoing ship appeared coming up the river, or a river steamboat or flat boat came down from the north, he would spring into the rowboat and the oarsmen would speed him off to intercept the new arrival. If the vessel had no contract for dock space, he would negotiate one on the spot. Tim had to admit the man was hustling to find work for the men and keep the company busy until new contracts could be won.

Tim worried how he would take his property away from the impostor. He was the toughest man Tim had ever encountered. In a few seconds he had beaten the large German to a senseless lump. Then he had killed the Frenchman over a game of cards in the Saint Charles. He always carried that Colt revolver, though now it was in a holster under his arm. Tim knew he could not beat the man in a face-to-face fight with either fists or guns. If the law did not give him his inheritance, then he would have to simply kill the man without warning.

Tim walked to the place where Julius rested during the noontime period. He wanted to talk with him. But the man was curled up asleep in the shade like a big black dog.

Tim lay down beside Julius. His head felt light and woolly with his fatigue. He straightened out flat on his back. Ah! The pleasure of a moment of rest.

Sometime later he awoke and glanced around. Julius was gone. The drays and stevedores were streaming back and forth from the ship to the dock or to the warehouse.

"Julius, why didn't you wake me?" Tim called out.

"You worked hard enough for a man with those bad wounds. So I let you rest."

Tim looked down. His unbuttoned shirt had fallen apart and the red and purple of the healing flesh of the bullet wounds on his ribs and shoulder showed plainly. He pulled the garment together and rebuttoned it. He had not wanted anyone to find out he had been shot.

"You should have wakened me," Tim said.

Julius pointed up at the sky. "Old sun is still high in the heavens. There's plenty of daylight left for you."

Tim climbed erect. Every muscle in his body felt bruised and strained. He went back to work on the docks.

"Timothy Wollfolk, come and ride with me."

Lew had just left his office and turned toward Rampart Street. He looked in the direction of the call. An exceptionally pretty woman sat in a canary-yellow buggy. She was dressed in blue silk. She smiled brightly and waved at him.

"Good evening, Mrs. Grivot," Lew said, removing his hat.

"My name is Annette. Come ride with me a little."

Lew hesitated. How did she know his name? The fact that she did meant that she most likely knew he had killed her husband. So why was she here?

"All right." Lew was deeply curious. He crossed the street, stepped up in the buggy, and sat down. As he turned to speak to Annette, she leaned quickly toward him and kissed him soundly on the lips. She pulled away from Lew and, laughing gaily, cracked the whip a foot above the horse's ears. The buggy moved off smartly along the street.

Lew studied the woman. He was much surprised by her greeting, almost like a woman greeting her lover. The gay smile remained on her lips. That was a complete reversal from the frightened expression she wore when he had seen her in front of the Saint Charles. Grivot's death had surely not saddened her.

"Are you well, Timothy?" Annette asked.

"Very well. And you?"

"I've never felt better, or freer, in my life." She spoke to the horse and it speeded its pacing step, whisking the vehicle across Canal Street and into the Garden District on a street of white seashells.

Annette fastened her attention on Lew. "I learned only today who you were. That the man who spoke so kindly to me at the hotel was Timothy Wollfolk."

"Who told you that?"

"Farr Rawlins. He was a friend of my husband, Enos. Farr told me a man named Timothy Wollfolk had fought and killed Enos. He described that man. I knew immediately that it was the same man I had seen." Annette looked deeply into Lew's eyes. "Farr thought I would be mad at you for killing Enos. But he would have soon killed me in one of his rages. You have saved my life."

Lew wondered about the accuracy of Annette's statement. And Farr Rawlins, why had he lied about Lew forcing the fight?

"Who is Rawlins?"

"He's a waterfront businessman."

"What else do you know about him?"

"He's rich and has rich friends. They call themselves the Ring. I heard him tell Enos that once when they were drinking."

"This Ring, is it a secret group?"

"Yes, I suppose so. When I asked Enos about it, he laughed and said they were a mean bunch of bastards and that he would not want to be one of their competitors. He told me not to talk about them."

"How many members are there?"

"Enos told me there were four members, and all are powerful men."

"Do you know any of their names?"

"Only one. Stanton Shattuck."

Shattuck again. That was the second time the

man's name had cropped up in some connection to events that affected Lew. He would like to know the names of the other two men.

The trotting horse suddenly shied to the side as a little white dog ran out barking from the manicured lawn of one of the big houses on the street. The dog dived in, nipping at the heels of the horse. Annette reached out swiftly with her whip and cut the little white animal sharply across the back. With a series of hurt yipes, the dog scurried away, its tail between its legs.

"Damn little nuisance. It's always there running out and scaring the horse." Annette's face was furious. Then she smiled warmly at Lew. She reined the horse into a lane leading up to a large three-story house.

"I'm glad Farr told me about you. No man has ever killed for me before."

Lew was startled by the woman's remark. "Kill for you? I tried not to fight with your husband. It was Rawlins who tricked him."

Annette continued to smile at Lew. "I know that you must say that. To kill a woman's husband so that you could have her would be murder. But you can admit the truth to me."

"I told you the truth. I didn't want trouble with Grivot. I was angry at him for hitting you, but I tried to talk him out of the fight."

Annette's smile vanished. Her lips compressed to mere red lines and twisted strangely. Her eyes flattened. "Don't joke with me," she said in a high, tight voice.

"I'm not joking," Lew replied. "I didn't want to fight your husband."

Annette laughed, a strained, contorted laugh. Her countenance changed, all the prettiness washing away and her features sharpening threateningly. She spoke in a furious voice. "You lie! Yesterday in front of the Saint Charles, I read your thoughts. You wanted me. Then you followed my husband into the hotel and killed him."

Lew grabbed the reins and jerked the horse to a quick stop. "I felt sorry for you when your husband hit you. That was all. I told you I did not want to fight him."

Annette clasped Lew's hand tightly in both of hers. "I don't believe you."

"You must, because I didn't want your husband dead." Lew sprang out of the buggy. He hurried back along the lane toward the street.

"Damn you to hell," Annette screamed at Lew's back. "You can't just walk away from me."

Lew ignored Annette's shrill cry. He turned onto the street. He wanted to put a very great distance between him and the confused woman. He hastened his step down the white shell road.

Lew heard the crunch of iron-rimmed wheels on the hard surface of the road. He looked to the rear. A man in a surrey was overtaking him. So involved had Lew been in trying to make some sense out of the Grivot woman's odd actions that he had not heard the vehicle until it was very close.

"Fellow, it's getting ready to shower again. Do you want a lift down town?" asked the driver of the surrey.

Lew saw the sky was darkening under a lowering overcast. "Yes, I'd appreciate a ride," he told the man. He swung aboard as the surrey stopped, and took a seat beside the driver.

"I saw you come out of the Grivot lane. Are you a friend of the family?"

"I knew Grivot slightly."

"Too bad he's dead. He had a big plantation to operate and a lot of slaves to boss. It'll be difficult to find a good overseer."

"Can't Mrs. Grivot run the place? Didn't she before she married Grivot?"

"You must not know much about the Grivots. I grew up with Enos right here in New Orleans. He inherited land and slaves. He was a shrewd man and increased both several times over. Four or five years ago, he met Annette Hachard in Baton Rouge and married her."

"She told me that she had the property before she married Grivot."

"She's one of the prettiest women you'd ever hope to find. But she's a liar, and about half-mad. She was insanely jealous of Enos. Once she took a knife to him, cut him twice before he could get it away from her. Most men would've divorced her. Not Enos. He was a hard and violent man. I think he enjoyed hitting the woman to control her. He would beat her half-unconscious when she became wild. Sometimes he locked her up to keep her

202

from following him around town. Now that he's dead, it's hard to tell what crazy things she might do."

Lew did not respond to the man. He would stay far away from the woman. He watched the carriages and people on foot and horseback hurrying past.

Overhead, lightning flared, sulkily trapped within the dark cloud masses and lighting them internally with a smoldering purplish glow. Thunder rumbled over the town. An ill-tempered wind forced the tall trees lining the road to buck and bow.

"Drop me off here," Lew said.

The man halted the carriage. He looked at the street sign stating Rampart Street. "Have a pleasant evening," said the man.

"I plan to," Lew replied.

Cécile stood in the upstairs window and watched the windswept street. The pedestrians were thinning rapidly. The buggies and surreys all had their tops up in preparation to ward off the imminent rain.

Tim came into sight and her heart lifted in several quick beats. She smiled to herself at the stir he caused in her.

On the street a gust of wind whipped Lew's hat from his head. He caught it in midair. She was amazed at the swiftness of his reflex. He passed under the window and entered the carriageway of the house.

Cécile almost turned away from the window

when a bright-yellow buggy stopped on the street in front of the cottage. A white woman stared down the carriageway after Tim. Then she seemed to sense Cécile watching, and her sight darted up to the window above.

Annette recognized the cottage of a placée. And the brown-skinned nigger wench stood there in the window gloating, humiliating her by stealing Timothy's love. Black, brown, or white, damn any woman to hell that kept Timothy from her. He had killed for her. She knew it was true regardless of what he said. She had the corpse of her husband to prove it. That made Timothy hers.

She stood up in the buggy to be more on the level with the brown woman. She raised her fist and shook it angrily at the window. "You god-damned nigger whore!"

At the shout from the white woman, Cécile backed away from the window and into the shadowy room so that she could not be seen from the outside. The white woman continued to stare for a moment at the place where Cécile had been. Then she dropped into the seat of the buggy and slashed the horse savagely with the whip.

Cécile watched until the yellow buggy turned a corner and was lost to view. She walked fearfully down the stairs to meet Tim. It was very bad for a placée to have a white woman as a foe.

"Do you know a woman who rides in a yellow

buggy," Cécile asked Lew as she dipped him a portion of crab soup from the tureen.

Lew took the bowl from her and set it carefully on the table before he answered. "Enos Grivot's widow has a yellow buggy. Why do you ask?"

"Such a woman followed you here."

"Stay away from her, as I will, for she is unpredictable. She may be half-mad and could be dangerous. She thinks I killed her husband so that I might have her. That is not true."

"I'm glad," Cécile said. "I shall be careful of her."

"The soup is very good," Lew said, deliberately taking the conversation off on a different tack.

Cécile followed Lew's lead and they talked of many things as they ate.

"May I go downtown and do some shopping tomorrow?" she asked. "It has been weeks since I have gone out."

Lew looked at her in surprise. "You never have to ask my permission. Go when you please."

He extracted several bills from his wallet. "Here is some money. Buy yourself something pretty."

Cécile smiled at Lew. "Not for me. I'm going to get you something."

"What?"

"I'll not tell you now."

Lew let his eyes feast on the woman's beautiful face. He recalled the smoothness of the brown, burned-honey skin against his, but there was more to the woman than the soft female body. There was an internal strength in her, and a directness and clarity of thought that greatly pleased him. She was very precious to him.

"Then, as a penalty for keeping secrets, you must play some music for me."

"And you might think of some other penalties later." Cécile laughed.

"I'm sure I will," agreed Lew.

18

As the days passed, Lew often had his hired rivermen in their sleek, fast boat row him across the Mississippi to the drydocks of Algiers. While the oarsmen lounged in the shade waiting for a ship to appear on the river, Lew worked with the skilled craftsmen under the guidance of the master builder, Sorensen, and watched the clipper ship take form. Sometimes he would accompany Sorensen and they would talk about shipbuilding as they inspected the timbers and joints before the decks and passageways were closed in.

He learned much from the sailmaker about the shaping of the sails. He had thought that the canvas was simply cut into rectangles or triangles, depending upon where the sail was to be used. Instead, there was an art to the shaping of the thousands of square feet of sail. The sailmaker would unroll the bolts of material on his wide table. Then, as he cut the canvas, he told Lew what sail he was making, and his reasoning for the particular shape and size.

The day arrived when Sorensen sent a special messenger to Lew and had him cross the river to the shipyard. When Lew arrived, he found Sorensen had mounted a tall tripod of stout timbers to bridge the ship. The main mast had been hoisted up on the tripod by a block and tackle hooked to a windlass. The butt of the mast hung directly over the strongly reinforced well that extended to the keel of the ship.

Sorensen called down from the deck of the ship. "Tim, come aboard. The main mast is ready to be stepped."

"Thank you, Sorensen," Lew called back. He climbed the gangway and crossed to the mast. He put his hands on the long, slender timber that had once been a living tree and now was about to become part of a clipper ship, the fastest vessel in the world. It would be even faster than the noisy, smoky steamships.

"Stand ready to lower," Sorensen directed the workers at the windlass. "Tim, give your orders to the men."

"Lower away slowly," Lew called. He gripped the thick butt of the mast and clasped it firmly against his chest. He twisted so that the mast rotated a fraction of a turn and came into perfect alignment with the opening of the well.

"Down! Keep it coming down," Lew shouted to the men cranking the windlass.

The mast entered the well, slid downward with a heavy rasp of wood on wood, and stopped abruptly with a thump on the keel of the ship.

"Mast stepped," Lew shouted. He continued to stand by the great wooden spar. It still had to be wedged tightly into place and shrouds, stays, and sails rigged to it. Yet the placement of the mast sent a chill through him. He felt as if he had helped put the heart into the clipper ship.

He stared upward. From his angle of view, the tall mast appeared infinitely long, reaching to punch a hole in the sky, where the strong winds of the earth blew never-ending. Soon the wide white sails would be set and would fill with those robust winds. The sails would hum under the power of the wind. The ship would be truly alive then.

Sorensen drew close and spoke to Lew. "The owner of a ship, or the captain, should always be the man to have his hands and shoulder on the main mast when it drops into its final resting place. That makes a bond between man and ship. It brings good luck."

"A man can always use good luck," Lew said.

"Do you want to help set the remaining two masts?"

"No. I have several things that I must do in New Orleans before it gets dark."

"Then come again when you can."

"I'll surely do that."

Lew ran his hands up the smooth wood of the mast. At that moment he decided that he would go to sea when the *Honest Traveler* made its maiden voyage. In the meantime, he would watch the construction of the beautiful clipper ship. He wondered if Albert Wollfolk had decided to build a sailing ship rather than a squat, ungainly steam-ship merely for the beauty of the one over the other.

The rainwater lay in broad pools where it had fallen. The pools were warming as the clouds parted and the sun shone through to strike the ground. A green scum that looked like velvet and stank dreadfully covered the surface of the water. The slops and garbage of the past day added their fermenting ugliness, for the slave brigade of street cleaners had not yet come by this extreme end of Decatur Street.

Mosquitoes rose up by the thousands from the foul liquid mixture on the ground. They swarmed about Lew and Baudoin as the two men traveled in the dueling master's buggy east toward his private shooting range.

"Someday I shall have a *baire*—a netting you would call it—sewed and fitted to my carriage to keep the pesky things away," Baudoin said as he slapped at the mosquitoes.

"Sounds like a great idea to me," Lew said. He had been constantly battling the blood-sucking in-sects since leaving Exchange Alley. Everywhere around New Orleans, netting was coming out of storage and being hung. Spandling had enclosed all the desks at the company office. Cécile had covered the windows of the cottage and hung a large envelope of netting over their bed.

"This is my training hall," Baudoin said. He halted the horse beside a long building with open sides. It was the only structure on the rather large lot. Immediately adjacent to the rear of the plot of ground, the swamp began, with its tangle of brush and streets.

"I have never enclosed the building. I want the students to practice by the natural light, whether it be bright sunlight or the dim grayness of a storm. A duel will in almost all cases be fought outside. But we need the roof because of the frequent rains. Come let us sharpen our skill with pistols."

Baudoin gathered up a wooden box containing his dueling pistols from the buggy seat. Lew took the pouch holding his powder, balls, and caps and followed Baudoin. The structure, some sixty feet long, was narrow and had a dirt floor. Targets hung on thick wooden backstops at one end. The opposite end had a crudely made table.

"We shall shoot from behind the table," Baudoin said. "You begin."

"If I do something that can be changed to improve my accuracy don't hesitate to tell me," Lew said to the dueling master. "I'm not used to a shoulder holster," he remarked as he drew his pistol. "Usually I have carried my gun in a hip holster."

"I was not aware that men in Ohio commonly carried guns on their sides."

"Some do," Lew replied. He must be more careful of speaking of past things. Texas was a place far different from Ohio.

Baudoin watched the young Wollfolk raise his pistol and shoot. The movement was smooth and the shot was squeezed off without a flinch at the very moment it came level. Wollfolk's strong arm controlled the kick of the revolver to but a slight upward bounce. The second shot came instantly upon the sound of the first. Both bullets had struck the center of one of the smallest bull's-eyes.

"Well done. Well done," Baudoin said. The pistol seemed to be a natural appendage of Wollfolk's arm. He was one of the very rare instinctive shooters.

"The range seems short," Lew said. "Why is that?"

"This distance is the approximate range two opponents would stand during a duel. But we can set targets at other ranges. What would you like?"

"Twice that distance, or even longer. If a man can hit a distant target, then surely he can hit a close one."

"Come, let us set one up outside," Baudoin said. "Step off the paces you would like. I'll bring a target."

The two men practiced for more than an hour, until nearly all of their powder and balls were spent. Then they sat together at the table and, while meticulously cleaning the handguns, discussed the finer points of shooting.

The throng of people blocked Decatur Street in front of the Cabildo. Vehicles were backed up. Drivers and passengers were climbing down and walking forward.

"What's happening?" Lew asked.

Baudoin stood up in the buggy and looked over the heads of the people on the ground. "Looks like a public flogging is being readied. The whipping stand and post have been brought out of the Cabildo and set up, and a policeman is bringing a prisoner toward it."

"Why a flogging here?" Lew asked.

"The Cabildo, that large building on the right, is the seat of city government. Court is held there. The punishment for certain crimes is to be whipped in public. It appears a fancy-dressed mulatto is the unfortunate person today. Probably a placée that some white woman is taking her revenge on."

Lew climbed erect and shaded his eyes against the westering sun to look ahead. "What do you mean about revenge?"

"A white woman can swear that she saw a placée flaunting herself before a white man. That brings an immediate arrest of the placée by the police. Then there is a short discussion with a judge. The verdict is always the same, for the judge takes the word of the white woman over that of the Negress. That assumes the white woman is known and reputable. The punishment is ten lashes in public with a whip well laid on. The flogger of the court likes his work and does indeed lay it on very well."

Lew watched the mulatto woman being dragged upon the whipping stand. She struggled fiercely as they forced her arms up to be tied to the iron ring fastened to the top of the post. For an instant as she fought the policeman, her face was turned toward Lew.

A shiver shook Lew as he recognized the woman. Then rage poured through his veins like molten lead. "Goddamn, it's Cécile." He leapt from the buggy and hurtled forward.

Two men walking closer to view the spectacle were knocked apart. Lew hardly saw them for his eyes were locked on Cécile. He drove at the wall of people ringing the whipping post.

The policeman swiftly finished tying Cécile's hands. He nodded at the flogger and backed away to the edge of the crowd.

The flogger raised the whip, a four-foor leather strap attached to a handle of about the same length. He was smiling as he struck with the whip, a whistling, cutting stroke upon the woman's back.

Lew saw Cécile cringe under the blow. Then she straightened. She pressed her forehead against the post and stiffened, awaiting the next slash of the whip.

Lew yanked people roughly out of his path. He heard their curses. A man hit him. He felt the sting of the fist. But he ignored everything, except the hateful fall of the second cut of the whip on Cécile's back. Then he was through the press of people and rushing across the opening at the man with the whip.

The whip rose and fell. A silent sob shook Cécile's body. The arm drew back again.

The flogger found his hand caught abruptly in midswing. A powerful grip crushed his fingers against the wooden handle of the whip. A face with gray eyes hard as granite was thrust within a foot of his own. "If you hit her again, I'll kill you," the man growled at him in a ferocious voice.

The flogger tried to wrench free. But the man held him solid as iron.

"Did you hear me?" Lew squeezed harder.

The man winced. "I'm an officer of the court. The judge ordered me to give the wench ten lashes. I'm going to do exactly that. You'd better let me go."

"I don't give a damn who ordered you to whip this woman. I know her, and she would do nothing to warrant such punishment."

"Mister, she may be your nigger, but a white woman saw her showing herself to tempt a white man. That means she gets a whipping."

"What woman? Whoever she is, she's a liar. Show me."

"There. Standing over there at the edge of the crowd." The man pointed with his free hand.

Annette Grivot smiled wickedly at Lew when his eyes fell upon her. Damn you, Lew thought.

"She's a crazy woman," Lew said. "You can't believe what she says."

"I don't give a fart about that. Let me go or you'll be up here and I'll be laying this whip on your hide. Here comes the policeman now."

Lew saw the lawman hurrying towards him. He turned back to the man with the whip. He leaned very close. "If you hit her again, I'll call you out on the dueling ground and shoot out both your eyes. Believe me, I can do it. Now go ahead and give the rest of your licks. Make it look good, but damn you, don't you hit her."

Lew released his grip on the man's hand and stepped down from the platform. The policeman moved straight at him. Lew held up his left palm to the lawman.

"Hold it," Lew said. "It's all over. Just a little discussion to find out what was happening." If it was necessary, he would fight the whole town to protect Cécile.

The policeman waited for the flogger to voice a complaint against the man who had stopped the punishment. But the man said nothing. He raised his arm and struck at Cécile.

The swift air current thrown out by the speeding end of the whip rippled the cloth covering Cécile's back. Lew saw the leather itself had not touched her flesh. The man was very practiced. He struck six times more, rapidly, one after another.

The flogger hung the whip over his shoulder. "Turn her loose," he ordered the policeman in a curt tone.

The policeman stepped close to Cécile and hastily released the thongs that bound her to the iron ring of the post. "You may go," he said.

Cécile lowered her arms. She turned, her black eyes snapping with anger, and stared directly at Annette. Then Cécile's head came up, and she walked toward the entrance of the Cabildo.

'Where are you going?" asked Lew, taking up a position beside her.

"They have my purchases inside the Cabildo. I'll not leave without them."

The crowd gave way before Lew and Cécile as they entered the building. She gathered up her possessions from the desk in the front office of the judge's chambers. Hugging them to her breast, she pivoted around and left.

"I'll hire a carriage," Lew said.

"No. Don't do that. A placée can't ride in a carriage in the streets of New Orleans. She must always walk where ever she goes."

Lew saw the three splotches of blood, each large as his hand and growing, on the cloth covering her back. The whip had cut lasting marks. "Are you all right?" he asked.

"They can't hurt me," Cécile said.

She looked at Lew.

His eyes were filled with pain for her. And there too was an anger like she had never seen before in a human.

Lew's jaws clenched at the unfairness of a law that allowed an innocent dark-skinned woman to be whipped merely on the word of a white woman. "If the Grivot woman was a man, I'd kill him before nightfall," he said.

"But you can't." She was worried about him. He was taking her whipping harder than she did. And that was very bad. Revenge would not do, for it would only bring trouble.

Cécile reached out and touched Lew's arm. She

216

had to chase the hot hate from him. Her lips bowed upward in a bright smile. "Truly, I'm not hurt."

Lew knew she was trying to draw him away from his thoughts of revenge for her public flogging. He looked into the depths of her black eyes. She was not only a beautiful mistress, but an excellent companion. A man could travel a very long journey with this woman and never become disappointed or grow weary of her.

19

THE four companies of Missouri Volunteer Riflemen marched grim-faced across the muddy drill field of the U.S. Barracks. The captains and their lieutenants marched at the head of the columns. The soldiers looked straight ahead. The right guards lifted the company guidons and shook the pennants and tried to make them flare, but the damp cloths hung limp and lifeless against the wooden staffs.

Lew and Tim halted at the entrance of the military compound to allow the departing soldiers to pass.

"The Missourians don't seem very happy about leaving for Mexico," Lew said to Tim.

"They've probably seen the funerals and read the articles in the papers about the yellow-fever epidemic here in New Orleans—and in Vera Cruz, where they'll be landing in Mexico. The disease

217

scares them much more than the Mexican army does. Ten men are being knocked out of action by disease to every one wounded or killed in battle."

Lew did not reply. His thoughts had shifted from the departing soldiers to the request of Colonel Hays of the Army Quartermasters Corps. The colonel had asked Lew to come to the U.S. Barracks and discuss military contracts with him.

The last company of departing soldiers passed through the gate. Lew and Tim moved into the compound.

The U.S. Barracks encompassed an area three hundred feet along the river and nine hundred feet deep to the north. It was designed for a garrison of four companies but held twice that number. The commandant's building, flanked by the offices of his staff officers, was located in midfront. A large parade ground—handsome in dry weather, but now a field of mud and water—occupied the center. The soldiers' quarters and base hospital were behind the parade ground. Farther to the rear were the storehouses and powder magazine, and a wagon park filled with ammunition carriers, ambulances, field kitchens, and ferrier carts.

"I was told Colonel Hays' office is in the building on the right of the headquarters," Lew said to Tim. He led, striking out over the sodden ground, trying to pick the more-solid-appearing earth.

They were halted by an armed guard at the entance of the quartermasters' office, then allowed to pass after identification was made and the purpose of their visit stated. They crossed a large room where several men in civilian clothing lounged about talking, or sitting silently waiting. Lew and Tim went directly to the door marked Colonel J. T. Hays.

"My name is Wollfolk," Lew told the corporal at the door. "Colonel Hays has asked me to come and talk with him."

"Yes, sir. He told me to send you straight in," said the corporal.

Colonel Hays stood up behind his desk as Lew and Tim came into the room. "Welcome, gentlemen," he said. "Thank you for coming so promptly. Which one of you is Timothy Wollfolk?"

"I'm Wollfolk," said Lew, stepping forward and shaking the officer's hand. "This is my chief accountant, Sam Datson."

The colonel shook Tim's hand and reseated himself at the desk. "Time is short. Shall we get directly to the reason I sent for you?"

"How can we help you, Colonel?" Lew asked.

"It has to do with your bids on the military contracts. You were the low bidder on many of them."

Lew glanced at Tim. Then he looked back at the officer. "That is good, Colonel."

"Maybe so, and then maybe not so good from my point of view. I have some concerns. New Orleans is the chief military depot and staging area for the war against Mexico. During the next few months, hundreds of chartered merchantmen loaded with soldiers and war supplies will be arriving from the East Coast. An even greater number of river steamboats will be coming downriver from Cincinnati and Saint Louis and half a hundred other cities carrying men and supplies.

"The soldiers will go to Fort Jesup or come here to the Barracks for a few days to be completely outfitted. The army will take care of that. However, all of those army supplies that will be arriving will be handled by private contractors like yourself. The very outcome of the war depends upon the temporary storing and swift repacking and shipping of the vehicles, clothing, medicine supplies, and other goods according to the quartermasters' plans."

"We understand all of that, Colonel," Lew said.

The colonel leaned over his desk. "Mr. Wollfolk, your company has eight hundred feet of dock space. Now, tell me frankly, can you handle all of these contracts you are low bidder on?" The colonel handed Lew a sheet of paper containing a list of contracts.

"The Wollfolk Company is low bidder on all of these?"

"Yes."

Lew hitched his chair closer to Tim's and held the papers so that both of them could read it. They quietly studied the listing, recalling and discussing the contents of the contracts.

Finally, Lew said, "What do you think, Sam?"

"Two large ships or three smaller ones can berth at our dock at one time. By tying other ships to the first ones, we can handle four, maybe six at a time."

Lew nodded in agreement. "We have one crew of stevedores and drivers working twelve hours a day. We can put on another crew for a twelve-hour night shift."

"We may need another bookkeeper," Tim said.

The two men looked at each other. There was agreement in their eyes. Lew turned to the colonel. "We can handle the contracts."

Colonel Hays did not speak for a full minute, evaluating the two young men before him. Finally, he said, "The Wollfolk Company has always carried out every contract in an excellent manner. But that was under the management of Albert Wollfolk. I have reservations about you because of your lack of experience. Should you fail, I then have to immediately find another company to complete the contracts. That would surely cost the army a premium over the existing price. Would you put a cash performance bond to ensure your compliance with the provisions of the contracts?"

"How much bond?"

"One hundred thousand dollars."

Lew was staggered by the amount of the bond. The company funds would not be enough to cover the bond and also the purchase of the clipper ship. A portion of Albert Wollfolk's private bank account would have to be used. Still, the total profit from all the contracts would be nearly four hundred thousand dollars.

Lew spoke to Tim. "How do you feel about it, Sam?"

"That's a very large sum of money, but we can do it."

Lew faced the officer. "My answer is yes, we will post the bond."

"Then write the U.S. Army a bank draft for that amount," said the colonel. He slid pen and ink and a sheet of paper across the desk to Lew.

Lew shoved the writing material back. "Have your clerk properly draw the draft up and I'll sign it."

"Very good. What bank?"

"The Mechanics and Traders Bank."

"I know of it." The colonel stepped to a rear door and left the room.

Shortly the officer returned with a sergeant. The enlisted man handed Lew the bank draft. Lew signed it.

The colonel gave him a receipt for his check. He stared sternly at Lew and Tim. "I warn you that only an act of God or war in the city will exempt you from completing these contracts on the schedules that have been set."

The colonel gestured at the sergeant. "Post the full list of successful bidders outside. Then come back here, for I want you to go and make arrangements to cash this draft and have it deposited in the army funds."

"Yes, sir," said the sergeant. Carrying the paper, he went from the room.

"I wish you good luck, gentlemen," the officer said. "The official notifications and the signing of the contracts and bond will be within three days.

Work on the contracts will begin immediately after that. Prepare yourselves to carry them out."

Lew and Tim went out into the big outer room. The men who had been waiting crowded around the sergeant as he fastened the announcement to the bulletin board.

Lew spotted Farr Rawlins pushing to the front of the group of men. Rawlins glanced at Lew and then looked away.

"Let's watch a minute," Lew said in a quiet voice to Tim. "These men are our competitors. One or more of them are very likely responsible for Albert Wollfolk's death."

Tim was startled at the statement. In a surprised voice, he said, "Do you mean he was murdered?"

"I'm certain of it. Also I've been attacked. And Gunnard's action to slow operations at the warehouse must have been paid for by somebody. We have enemies. They have killed, and they will kill again."

Tim looked at the impostor, trying to read his thoughts as the man closely scrutinized the bidders clustered at the bulletin board. During the past days working with him, Tim had come to respect the man's quickness of thought and his generosity. Now this last pronouncement added further doubt to the impostor's true role in the events surrounding the attempted murder of Tim. But what justification did he have in making the false claim to the Wollfolk inheritance? Tim shook his head in puzzlement.

The unsuccessful bidders left. They looked at Lew as they passed. There was not one friendly face among them.

Lew heard Rawlins speak, his voice crackling with anger as he pointed at the list. "Stanton, we got very few contracts."

"Damn it, I can see," growled Stanton.

Lew heard Rawlins speak to the man named Stanton. That would be Stanton Shattuck. Now Lew had identified the two men Annette Grivot had named.

Lew spoke in a voice that only Tim could hear. "There is a group of four men that call themselves the Ring. Farr Rawlins, that man with the cane, is one of them. The tall man next to him is another. His name is Stanton Shattuck. I don't know who the remaining two are."

Tim only nodded. He would ask Lezin to help him find out more about the group.

Eight men were left at the bulletin board. Lew checked them, hoping to notice some word or gesture that would tie them to Rawlins and Shattuck. But nothing indicated connection, so he concentrated on their faces, wanting to remember every one.

Shattuck controlled his anger and looked steadily at Rawlins. "You wanted to wait and see what Wollfolk would do about bidding for the military contracts. Now you know. He has won most of them. Are you satisfied?"

Rawlins remained quiet. He sat in his usual

chair in the private office where the Ring often met. He fondled the head of his cane. Shattuck was not in a state to be argued with.

Shattuck raked his eyes over Loussat and Tarboll. "Nearly three hundred steamboats are coming down the river each month. About that same number of oceangoing ships arrive. Right now most of them are carrying war supplies. The military contracts to handle that cargo are the most lucrative in the city because the soldier boys have a war to fight and no time to argue about cost."

"I agree," said Lousset. "I don't want to handle only the low-profit private contracts. I'm also worried about the next round of military contracts. Wollfolk may well win those too."

"There's more than the military contracts to think about," Shattuck said. "There's the long-term future to plan for. New Orleans will double in size in ten years. The shipping will increase even faster, to many millions of dollars each year. There will be a need for three to four miles of new docks along the river. We must be the men who build those docks. Whoever controls the shipping controls New Orleans. Wollfolk must not be allowed to jeopardize that. Boom times are here now and will stay."

Tarboll rapped on the table. "I agree. Let's not gamble any more on what Wollfolk might do. It's time he died."

"Do you agree with Tarboll that Wollfolk should die?" Shattuck asked Rawlins in a sarcastic voice.

He remembered the bruise Rawlins carried for days after Wollfolk had knocked him down in the Saint Charles Hotel.

Rawlins glared stonily at Shattuck. He had about enough of the big man. "It's past time somebody should die," he said in a grating voice.

Shattuck's and Rawlins' eyes did battle. "Who did you mean?" asked Shattuck, his tone suddenly oily.

Rawlins smiled his thin-lipped smile. "Woll-folk."

Shattuck stared hard into Rawlins' face for a handful of seconds, then skimmed his attention to Lousatt. "What do you say?"

"Let's go to Paulaga at once and hire him to dispose of Wollfolk permanently," Loussat said matter-of-factly. "It should be an easy task for someone as skilled as he is with a sword and pistol to kill him."

"It'll be costly," said Tarboll. "But whatever the price, it'll be worth it."

"Loussat, you know Paulaga best," Shattuck said. "You make the arrangements."

"I'll do it today."

"We need fifty to sixty men for the night shift," Tim said. "They must be men used to hard work and not in the pay of our enemies."

"There are probably ten thousand free blacks in the city, but nearly everyone that wants to work is already working," Julius said.

"There are slaves in the city jails we can get,"

226

said Spandling. "They've been put there by their owners while they are traveling and away from their businesses or plantations. We can hire them on a temporary basis until we can find permanent laborers."

Lew sat in the end of the warehouse with the three men. As he listened to them discuss methods to handle the new contracts, he stared at the ships on the river riding higher than the city itself. The sailors on the decks of the ships could look over the levee and down into the town beyond at the women on the streets.

On the dock, a group of sick and destitute soldiers discharged from the army squatted in a group between two large piles of cargo. They had created a roof to keep off the frequent rain by stretching ropes and hanging a tarpaulin over them. When Julius had started to forcibly remove the soldiers, Lew had stopped him, telling him to let the men alone as long as they did not cause trouble. Cadwaller, the night watchman, complained loudly that the presence of the men made his job more difficult, for they were often coming and going from the dock and he could not tell if a thief had stolen in. Lew had told Cadwaller the ex-soldiers could stay for they had earned a little charity.

"We could buy enough slaves in a couple of hours to fill a second crew of workers," Spandling said.

"I don't want slaves working for us," Lew said.

"But we could give them credit for their work,

and when they had earned enough wages, we could then set them free," Spandling replied.

"That might work," Lew said. "When is the next auction?"

"There's one this afternoon at the Saint Charles," said Spandling.

"I'll take a look," Lew said. "Sam, come with me to the hotel."

Lew caught Tim by the arm and stopped him on the sidewalk. "Wait a minute." he said.

An old blind man sat on a rickety chair and played a fiddle. His fingers jumped nimbly from cord to cord and the bow stroked the strings with a bouncy flair.

Lew leaned against the wall of the nearby building and listened to the delightful tune. The old man bobbed and weaved in harmony with his music. He finished with an energetic flourish of his bow.

"Well done, fiddler man," Lew said. He stepped close and dropped a silver dollar into the metal cup at the feet of the man.

The fiddler cocked his head, blinked his blind eyes, and nodded. He recognized the dollar ring. "Thank you, sir, for your generosity," he said.

"I merely paid for a job expertly done."

A strange look flooded over the fiddler's face. Then he smiled. "No one has ever said that to me before. I thank you most heartily."

Tim moved off in step with the impostor. He wondered if the man was that free and easy with his own money. Somehow Tim thought he would be. That confused his feelings about the impostor even more.

They passed a funeral procession led by three open hearses carrying eight coffins. Four of the coffins were for small children. All the caskets were smeared with lampblack. Another funeral cortege was coming into sight ahead.

20

"GENTLEMEN, the auction shall begin in five minutes under the dome," said the hotel steward. He walked slowly among the men sitting at the tables of the large barroom of the Saint Charles Hotel. He turned and walked to the front, winding his way around the twenty-foot-tall columns that supported the hotel floor above.

Still intoning his message, the steward passed down the yards-long bar where absinthe, rum, and more potent drinks were being served.

Lew and Tim rose from their chairs and left the barroom with several other patrons. The men gathered under the great high dome arching over the center of the palatial inner court of the Hotel. They began to seat themselves on padded chairs ringing a raised, carpeted platform.

A line of black men came into view from a side room. Each was dressed in a pair of white cotton pants. They were barefoot and naked above the waist. The whites of their eyes showed as they

229

peered nervously around. The steward called out, directing them toward the auction block.

"Timothy, good to see you again," called Baudoin, making his way up to the assemblage of white men. "I see you have come to observe the auction."

"Hello, Yves," Lew said. The man smiled a lot, a pleasant fellow to be around. "I'd like to introduce you to Sam Datson."

"Sam Datson," said Baudoin, putting out his hand, "it is a pleasure to meet you. But I've heard that name before," Baudoin snapped his fingers. "I know where. Aren't you the new student of Black Austin, the mulatto duelling instructor?"

"Yes," Tim said.

"Austin tells me you are one of his most promising young duelists. Especially with the pistol. It seems you Americans like the firearm better than the sword."

"Sam, I did not know you were taking dueling lessons," Lew said.

"It seems that in New Orleans a man must often settle his own problems," Tim replied.

"Quite true," Baudoin said. "I estimate New Orleans averages ten duels a day. Thirty-two duels in one day were reported in the newspaper earlier this year. I'm certain some were missed, for they are not advertised. In fact, some are deliberately kept secret."

Lew watched the first group of slaves being herded up on the auction block for inspection. One of the black men stopped and refused to step up on the raised platform. The steward spoke sharply to him. Still the man did not move. The steward beckoned to the auctioneer standing nearby.

The auctioneer, a large man, came swiftly to the side of the platform. He grabbed the black man and roughly shoved him.

The Negro stubbornly resisted being moved.

"Goddamn black bastard," growled the auctioneer. He slugged the black man in the side with his fist. "Get up there before I take you outside and horsewhip you."

Baudoin watched the Negro climb reluctantly up on a block. He spoke. "There'll be no bid for that slave. He's too unruly. After this auction is over, he'll get a whipping that will peel his back and show his ribs."

"Was he unruly because of being a man and having too much pride to be a willing slave?" Lew said, scowling at the treatment of the man.

"Perhaps it is pride. But pride in a black man is dangerous to him. That one will have a mean and short life ahead of him." Baudoin changed the subject. "Do you plan to purchase some slaves to work your docks?"

"I did at first, but now I've changed my mind. I'll see you again, Yves."

"Are you ready to leave, Sam?" Lew asked.

Tim nodded, feeling ill-at-ease at the cruelty to the black.

As Lew and Tim turned to walk away, a man

called out loudly. "Wollfolk, I want to talk with you."

Lew looked in the direction of the voice. A richly dressed man was walking toward them, a second man following a step behind.

"It's Paulaga," Baudoin said. "He seems angry. What have you done to him?"

"Nothing. I don't even know him."

"Be careful of him. He is a dueling instructor and good with weapons. He sometimes fights for pay. Someone may have set him on you."

"Wollfolk, you are a scoundrel," Paulaga spoke again in a strong voice that could be heard throughout the broad space. "You cheated Enos Grivot at cards and then killed him when he caught you at it. Now you follow his widow and insult her with your amorous intentions."

Lew laughed coldly. He recognized the hand of Farr Rawlins in Paugala's false charge, and perhaps Annette Grivot was also involved. Paulaga wanted a fight. He would press the lie until Lew challenged him.

Lew heard the sudden silence around him. The preparations for the auction had ceased. He swept his sight over the watching men and then back to Paulaga.

"Paulaga, you are a fool. You have it all backward. She is the one who has what you call amorous intentions."

Tim surveyed the impostor, watching his reaction to the charges of Paulaga. He saw the gray eyes harden, like spheres of water suddenly freezing to ice, warning Paulaga off if only he could read the sign. There had been that same change in the impostor just before he had leapt upon Gunnard. Tim wondered if Paulaga wanted to kill the impostor, or did he really want to kill a Wollfolk?

"You lie," Paulaga said, continuing to advance.

"And you are a dumb bastard trying to force a fight."

Paulaga's stride almost broke at Lew's harsh retort. He had not expected such a quick, fearless reply.

"Make him give the challenge if there is to be a duel." Baudoin whispered. "Then you will have the choice of weapons."

Paulaga heard the whisper, but could not make out the words. "Baudoin, what did you say to him?" he demanded belligerently.

"Don't trifle with me, Paulaga," warned Baudoin, his ire rising swiftly at the tone of the voice. "You may overplay your hand."

Lew saw Paulaga blink at Baudoin's words. Then the man's attention focused back on Lew.

"I'll stop you from frightening Mrs. Grivot," Paulaga said, again using his loud tone.

"You can't stop something that's not happening," Lew said. He began to walk away.

Paulaga sprang across the distance that separated him from Lew. His arm reached out to catch Lew by the shoulder.

Lew heard Paulaga's booted feet on the floor. He spun and caught the outstretched hand. He twisted the arm sharply. Instantly he stepped forward and with his clenched fist struck Paulaga at a point where the man's arm attached to the shoulder.

Paulaga winced with pain.

Lew smiled inwardly. That hurt, didn't it. "Leave well enough alone, Paulaga," he snapped.

"I challenge you to a duel," Paulaga's voice grated like rock rubbing.

"I accept," Lew replied.

Paulaga saw the eagerness to fight in the young Wollfolk. A tingle of warning came to life in his mind. Something was wrong here. Had he been misled by Loussat about the bookkeeper from Ohio? Then he shrugged away his doubts, confident in his skill to slay the man. But that blow to the shoulder, though thrown only a short distance, had jarred him soundly.

"Russee Loussat is my second." Paulaga pointed at the Frenchman standing nearby. "Who is yours?"

"Baudoin, will you be my second?"

"It would be an honor," Baudoin replied.

"The seconds will agree upon the conditions of the duel," Paulaga said.

"Let's set them now," Lew said.

"Wait. We should talk first," Baudoin cautioned. He caught Lew by the arm and drew him aside.

Tim followed. He was taken aback by the quickness with which the violence had erupted.

Baudoin looked at Lew with respect. "Timothy,

that was skillfully done. I salute you. I know of no man, except perhaps myself, who could have so quickly increased his odds to survive a duel with someone who may be better with weapons."

"What do you mean?" Tim asked, mystified at the words.

"Didn't you see? He tricked Paulaga into showing whether he was left- or right-handed, then he twisted the arm and struck the shoulder. Paulaga will be sore and stiff in the morning."

Tim replayed the events that had just occurred. The impostor had, an instant after being confronted, devised a counterattack and carried it out. And Tim was planning to fight this man. A shivery doubt came to Tim that his plan to fight the impostor might be a deadly mistake.

"What range do you think Paulaga practices shooting at?" Lew asked.

"Probably twenty-four to thirty paces," Baudoin said. "That would be about twelve to fifteen paces each for him and his opponent in a duel. However, you can select any reasonable distance you want." Baudoin knew what the young Wollfolk was thinking.

"Make the distance twice that—say thirty paces for each of us. The weapons should be Colt revolvers. We will shoot until a man falls."

"A show of blood will not do?"

"No. You said Paulaga was good with weapons. Therefore, he must be killed or seriously wounded, for strong enemies should not be allowed a second chance at you."

"Do you feel that confident?" Tim asked.

"I will beat Paulaga," Lew said. "And eventually I'll find and kill the man that murdered Albert Wollfolk."

"What place would you like for the duel to take place?" Baudoin asked. "Les Chenes d'Allard, that is under the oaks in the city park, or in the field near the slaughterhouse beside the river."

"Under the oaks. I saw a duel there when I first arrived. A good place to die, if it comes to that."

"I agree. That is the most fitting place."

"Then please arrange it for tomorrow morning, my friend," Lew said.

Lew bought a quart of berries from the blackberry woman on Dauphine Street. He walked on, eating a few of the largest berries. He ate very slowly, savoring to the utmost the sweetness on his tongue, for he did admit to himself that he might die, come morning.

The fight bothered him, for it was a useless thing with nothing to be gained, and it contained much danger to him. It was obviously something contrived by his enemies. Even though he should kill Paulaga, the unknown foes who wanted him dead would go unharmed.

He recalled Paulaga's second, the man named Loussat. He had been at the quartermasters' office in the U.S. Barracks. Could Loussat be one of the members of the Ring? Lew thought it likely. The man may have hired Paulaga and then accompanied him to arrange the duel. Or was his presence merely a coincidence? Lew did not believe in coincidences.

Cécile met Lew in the courtyard, as usual. He wondered how long she sometimes waited and watched for him, for the time of his arrival varied by hours.

She did not come to him, but gazed across the space separating them, her eyes roaming their tender touch over him. As Lew came nearer, he knew that she had somehow become aware of the coming duel. The worry showed in the tiny crow's feet at the corner of her eyes.

"You know about tomorrow," Lew said.

"Yes. Such news about a placée's man travels swiftly in the Ramparts."

"We shall not talk about it. Tonight will be like all the past ones."

She shook her head in the negative. "I want to dance as we did that first night you came to this house."

"And will you play for me as you did then?"

"And make love to you like never before."

"Can I stand that much?" Lew said with a grin.

Much later, when the deep darkness arrived, the rain came again to the city. The wet wind whistled dismally late into the night as Lew lay and held Cécile close to him. He begrudged the swift, short passage of the night.

Lew heard the vehicle stop in the street below.

One short whistle sounded. Baudoin had arrived to transport him to the dueling place.

Lew had drawn the charges from his revolver and replaced them with fresh powder. Now he flipped off the caps and pressed five new ones over the nipples. He shoved the weapon into its holster and buckled it on.

He bent and touched Cécile's hair, shiny and black in the lamplight. She looked up, her eyes dark pools of worry.

She said nothing. It had all been said in the night.

Lew went swiftly from the cottage and into the darkness on the street. He was surprised to see a third man in the buggy.

"Good morning, Tim," Baudoin said.

" 'Morning, Yves."

"This is Doctor Chandler, Tim. He is the best surgeon in New Orleans."

"My pleasure to meet you," Chandler said.

"Thank you for coming," Lew said. "I hope you do not have to practice your skills this morning."

"So do I," said the doctor.

The buggy moved off in the damp night. Near the river, the fog thickened, smothering the sounds of the city. Lew felt his clothes absorbing the cool water vapor. The mist formed droplets on his eyebrows and his cheeks became wet. He flicked the moisture away like so much sweat.

They passed a gas streetlight, a dull-yellow stain

on the drizzly night. The light faded away behind them, and the foggy gloom enshrouded them again.

Baudoin finally halted the vehicle on the side of the street, and the men sat without speaking.

The uncertain light of the dawn came. Lew could make out the three ancient oaks, called the Three Sisters, that marked the favored dueling spot in the city park.

The gray damp twilight brightened. It gave way gradually to the day, as it had ever since time began its travel across the stars.

Somewhere in front of Lew and his comrades, and buried in the fog, the iron-rimmed wheels of a vehicle rattled in and came to a stop. Shortly another vehicle stopped behind Baudoin's buggy. A man in black clothing walked past and entered the park.

"The judge of duels has arrived," Baudoin said. "It's time to go."

"I'm ready," Lew said. He stepped down to the ground.

The surgeon climbed down beside Lew and the three men strode after the judge of duels.

The sun rose big and round over the swamps to the east. The fog immediately began to lift. It thinned rapidly in the warmth of the morning.

The rays of the sun struck the park. The night dew lying thickly on every blade of grass began to sparkle like a million diamonds covering the ground.

The men made their way across the park in the direction of the Big Sister, the largest oak in the grove. Their booted feet killed the glistening diamond points of light and left behind a black path leading to the dueling place.

21

LEW ignored the men near him in the park and watched the strengthening morning light. The last bit of the night fog was unraveling from under the Big Sister and rising upward to vanish among the branches of the tall oak tree. Overhead, the pigeons, hungry after the long black night of fasting, flapped by with a beat of wings in the direction of the waterfront. The sun, an orange ball, inexorably mounted the gray heavens.

"Sunrise has come, Wollfolk, let's begin," Paulaga called in a belligerent voice.

Lew heard Paulaga but did not reply. The confidence of the dueling instructor was in his voice.

"Mr. Baudoin, is your principal prepared to begin the duel?" the judge of duels asked.

"Tim, are you ready?" Baudoin said.

"Yes. Let's get it over with."

"Let me have your revolver," said Baudoin.

Lew lifted his Colt from its holster and handed it to Baudoin.

"Are you satisfied with the loads in it?" Baudoin asked.

"Yes. I've checked them."

Side by side the two men walked nearer the judge. Paulaga and Loussat approached.

Dr. Chandler joined Paulaga's surgeon at a position several steps behind the judge. They spoke short greetings. Then, holding their satchels containing probes, scalpels, and other medical paraphernalia, stood silently observing the ritual of killing.

"Colt revolvers are the agreed-on weapons," the judge of duels said to Loussat and Baudoin. "Are those the weapons you hold?"

"Yes," Loussat said.

"Yes," Baudoin said.

"Let me inspect them." The judge glanced quickly at the revolvers and returned them to the seconds. "Hand the firearms to the duelists," he directed.

Loussat and Baudoin offered the pistols to their principals. Each man accepted his pistol and lowered it to hang at his side. The seconds moved away to stand by the surgeons.

The judge spoke. "The number of shots is unlimited with the firing to continue until one man falls. The distance shall be thirty paces and I will count them off. Upon completing the pacing, stop, turn, and await my call to fire. Obey my instructions exactly.

"Take your places here in front of me. Stand back to back." The judge counted, and the men stepped off in opposite directions.

Lew took very long steps. He should have asked

for a greater number. He finished the last pace and turned.

The dueling judge nodded his approval and retreated out of the line of fire to a place just in front of the seconds and the two surgeons.

No one spoke. A deep hush fell upon the park. Not one leaf stirred on the three large oaks. The duelists were as motionless as the boles of the trees.

Paulaga stared at the young Wollfolk. The range was much longer than he liked. However, he had taken several practice shots at that distance the evening before, and his accuracy had been very good. He selected a spot over Wollfolk's heart. That would be his point of aim.

Lew saw Paulaga turn to the side to present the narrowest possible target to him. Lew turned sideways also. He wondered how much the man had been paid to force a duel with him. Would Paulaga earn the money in the next few seconds?

Lew jerked his thoughts to the imminent deadly action. Every strand of his attention focused on the judge, waiting his call. He clasped the pistol, positioning it just right in his hand.

"Fire," cried the judge, and his hands smacked together with sharp report.

Lew snapped his pistol up. The old, familiar revolver felt light as a feather. He pressed the trigger as the gun came level. The Colt crashed. The gray gunpowder smoke geysered out in front of him.

Lew heard his bullet hitting solidly against flesh

and bone. But Paulaga did not fall. Lew braced himself for the return strike of Paulaga's gun. Swiftly he thumbed back the hammer for a second shot.

Paulaga staggered at the punch of his opponent's bullet. God! How could a man be so fast.

He struggled vainly to sight along the iron barrel of his revolver. But he could not see the sights of the weapon. Nor Wollfolk. An ocean of blackness was rushing at him. He squeezed the trigger as a ghastly expression washed over his face. Paulaga crumpled, falling limply, his face plowing into the grass of the park.

For a few seconds, all the men remained standing stock-still. Then Paulaga's surgeon broke his trance and ran to kneel at the side of the fallen man. He jerked the shirt open on the still form.

After a short moment, the surgeon removed his hands from the body and looked up. He shook his head. "It is done. He is dead."

Baudoin and Loussat moved forward together to look at Paulaga's corpse. A bullet hole showed on the side of the man's ribs precisely in line with the heart within.

Baudoin shook his head. Paulaga had got off but one wild shot. This had not been a contest. It had been an execution.

"Loussat, I think you have made a very bad mistake," Baudoin said. "I would not want Wollfolk for an enemy."

Loussat did not respond to Baudoin. Angry at Paulaga's failure to kill Wollfolk, he pivoted away from the corpse. He saw Wollfolk bearing down upon him with long strides. The young man's expression was grim as death.

"Loussat, the day has begun with one killing. Do you want to make it two?" Lew's words were like darts flung through the air.

Loussat had killed men in duels. Yet he shivered now at the challenge thrown at him. Somehow he sensed that, should he fight this man, he would surely die.

"No." Loussat's voice choked in his throat.

Lew spoke harshly again. "I think you planned this duel, and for me to die. But I did not. Take Paulaga's gun. There are still four rounds in it. Stand over there and let's you and me try this game all over again."

Loussat spun away from the threatening man. He broke into a rapid walk toward the edge of the park.

"Take the gun and fight me, you cowardly bastard," Lew's whiplike voice chased after Loussat.

Loussat's pace increased. He reached the sidewalk and plunged away.

"The false Wollfolk would be a very bad man to face in a fair fight," Morissot said to Tim as they watched Loussat hasten from the park. Morissot's thoughts continued on silently within his mind. He would not fight the impostor fairly.

"Where did the man come from?" Tim said,

mostly to himself. "Where did he learn to shoot like that?"

"I agree, it is strange that a man so young is so skilled with guns. And he showed not one sign of fear."

Morissot and Tim stood together on the north side of the park. Tim had come, drawn by the duel, but mostly by the desire to watch the impostor. Morrisot had insisted upon accompanying him.

"Lezin, the impostor has told me he believes there is a group of men trying to destroy the Wollfolk Company. He thinks my uncle was murdered and that man Loussat could be one of the members of the gang that did it. He was present at the opening of the bids on the military contracts. Now the impostor has challenged him to a fight. Do you know anything about him?"

"No," Lezin replied. "But we can find out who he meets with after failing to kill the man he thinks is Timothy Wollfolk. I'll follow him."

"Wait. Let me tell you this first: two other men who may be involved are Stanton Shattuck and Farr Rawlins. Watch for them too."

Morissot felt the sudden tenseness at the mentioning of Rawlins. Over the past years, he had killed two men for Rawlins. Lezin did not know Shattuck, but if he was connected with Rawlins, then he too was suspect.

"I've heard of Farr Rawlins," Lezin said. "He has been around New Orleans for a long time. I thinks we should find Rawlins and follow him also. I'll have a friend help us."

"That is a good plan. Have your friend do it."

"Right." Lezin broke into a trot across the park. By cutting through the wooded section he should be able to overtake Loussat before he was lost.

As Morissot closed on the woods, a large man came out of a dense clump of trees and hurried off at right angles at him. The man looked back over his shoulder for an instant. Morrisot recognized the bearded face of Kelty. The presence of the Irishman here gave an added depth of danger to the game, whatever it was, that was being played out. The Wollfolk impostor could be correct about the conspiracy to destroy the Wollfolk Company. The best and surest way to do that would be killing the owner. Now that Paulaga had failed to kill the man he thought was Wollfolk, would Kelty strike to complete the job??

Morissot hurried on. Answers, he must have answers. Should Tim be identified as the true owner of the Wollfolk property, Kelty or someone else might strike at him. Tim would not be as able as the impostor to defend himself. In many situations, Morisot would not be able to protect him.

Lew and Tim left the park together. As they reached the street and walked toward the waterfront, Tim glanced sideways at the man who impersonated hm. There was still the steely tautness in his face. The gray eyes were half-closed as if he were in deep thought.

"Lezin Morissot watched the duel with me," Tim said. "He is following Loussat and will find out who he meets and talks with. I told him your suspicions about Farr Rawlins and Stanton Shattuck. He knew Rawlins, but not Shattuck."

"Can Morissot be trusted?" Lew asked without turning.

"Yes. He is an honorable man."

"There is something about him, a look in his eyes that makes me think he could be a very violent man."

"You seem to know a lot about guns and violence. Where did you learn that?"

"The use of guns seemed to come natural to me the very first time I tried one." Lew said no more, but lapsed into silence.

Tim also remained quiet. He had received the requested documents from the people in Cincinnati who would substantiate his true identity over the claim of the impostor. Further, the banker was coming to New Orleans on business within a few days. He could appear in person to testify to the truth.

Yet Tim was not ready to bring down the law on this man who had appeared out of nowhere to falsely claim the Wollfolk inheritance. There was a great unknown danger to anyone named Wollfolk. This strange man so quick with his gun and fists . . . let him run the risk and take the brunt. That would serve him right for his crookedness.

Lew and Tim strode on for several blocks with neither man voicing his private thoughts. They turned onto Gallatin Street, a street lined with gambling shacks, sailors, boardinghouses, and barrel houses where a man could get drunk for a dime.

They came opposite the open end of an alley. A ring of shouting men squatting or kneeling on the ground surrounded two multicolored fighting cocks battling with their quick beaks and deadly steel spurs, sharp as needles, fastened by the men over the less dangerous natural ones.

The smaller cock launched itself at its opponent. They fought for a full minute in a flurry of feathers and steel spurs. Then with a powerful flap of his wings, the smaller cock tore free.

A spray of blood jetted out from the neck of the second cock. Its right eye hung half an inch from the eye socket, held there by the torn optic nerve. In but a few seconds the cock's lifeblood covered the ground. It quivered and fell to the side. Its strong legs kicked, stirring the dirt. Then it became very still.

A portion of the men groaned. They began to hand money to the other men.

"Damn early for a cockfight," Tim said.

"They don't fight good when it's hot," Lew replied. He speeded his step. They had yet to find workers for a second shift.

Several early-morning pedestrians ahead began to talk excitedly and hurry off the sidewalk and into the street. Two sailors, bleary-eyed from drinking and with uniforms that appeared to have been slept in, looked about to see what was causing the sudden, scurrying exodus of people.

A soldier called out from the street. "Clear the

sidewalk, you dumb swabbies. Get off before you get your heads cracked."

A group of nine rough-looking men carrying wooden cudgels, some in their hands, most stuck in the backs of their belts, were swaggering along the sidewalk. Custus led, his shirt hanging in tatters and half-torn off him. He grinned wickedly as he bore down on the two sailors. His cohorts crowded close behind, an expression of pleased anticipation on their faces.

"Off the sidewalk," the redheaded Custus shouted at the sailors. But before the two men had the opportunity to move, the big man was upon them. He grabbed the nearest sailor and slung him to the rear. His followers immediately fell upon the man with vicious blows.

The redhead struck the second sailor a hard wallop to the head, knocking him up against the wall of the house abutting the sidewalk. He closed quickly on the half-unconscious sailor and began to slug him in the stomach.

The sailor slid down the wall. The redhead continued to hit him, his fists walking up the sailor's body as it slumped to the sidewalk.

The body of the first sailor was flung out of the mob and landed with a thud on the street. Custus caught hold of the second seaman and heaved him onto his mate.

"We'd better give them the sidewalk," Tim said to Lew. "That's part of the Live Oak Boys from the Swamp. Looks like they've been up all night drinking and carousing. They're a mean lot. Probably heading back to the Swamp."

"What's the Swamp."

"I only know what Morissot told me. He said it's a place of whorehouses, dance halls, and gin mills, and the home of the worst scoundrels in all New Orleans. No law officer has been there for twenty years. Sometimes the men come out to prey on the town. They often set something on fire, a house or business, and then loot it in the excitement."

"Nice fellows," Lew said. "Do you have your pistol?"

"Yes. Why do you ask?"

"You once said that you could shoot a man. Do you still think you can?"

Tim argued the question with himself.

"Better make up your mind," Lew said, his sight scouring the faces and weapons of the Live Oak Boys walking straight at them. "I'm not leaving the sidewalk for anybody."

"If there was a real need to, then I could shoot somebody." Tim said. "But all we have to do here is step out of the way and there'll be no trouble."

"Just answer yes or no." Lew's voice crackled. "Move into the street like a cur dog, or stand with me."

Tim bristled at the harsh rebuke. "Dammit," he said, and braced himself for trouble.

"Don't weaken, or it's going to be mightly unhealthy in half a minute."

Lew raised his hand to the front of his jacket. A faint icy smile creased his cheeks.

"Off the sidewalk," Custus called out.

"It's a public sidewalk," Lew replied. "My friend and I'll use this half." He gestured to the portion near the wall of the building. "You and your friends can use the other section."

"We need it all. Get out of the way," growled the redhead. "Or you're going to get a terrible headache." He pulled an oak club from the rear of his belt and began to smack it in the palm of his hand.

"I don't think I want a headache," Lew said. He reached inside his jacket and took hold of the butt of his Colt.

The redhead came on. He heard the tread of his gang behind him, their booted feet drumming on the wooded sidewalk. He measured the two well-dressed men in his path.

"Boys, these dandies are going to be more fun than we've had all night." He looked at Lew. "Mister, I've whipped three men your size with my fists this past night. You'd be nothing to me. But my fists are sore from busting all those hard heads, so I'm going to break your skull with this." He raised his club above his head.

Lew slid his pistol from its holster and brought it into view.

"Sam, I'll shoot the redhead," Lew said in a voice loud enough to be heard by the gang. "You shoot anyone else who tried to use a club or pulls a gun."

The gang abruptly halted at the sight of the gun and the cold words.

Lew cocked his weapon, and in the stillness it was like a thunderclap. "Go around me," he warned.

"We haven't got guns," said the redhead.

"That's lucky for you. If you did, they would just get you killed. Now, walk around me, and no one will get hurt."

"Custus, these uptown cowards won't shoot," said the man on the redhead's right.

"You're the second man that'll get a bullet," Lew told the man.

The man swallowed hard and became very quiet.

Custus evaluated the two men blocking part of the sidewalk. The blue-eyed one seemed nervous as he held his uncocked pistol. The gray-eyed man stared back with a sure and certain purpose.

"I think that fellow would use his gun." Custus made a motion at Lew.

"You've read me right," Lew said.

The gang leader hesitated a moment more. Then he reached behind and shoved his cudgel into his belt. He stepped out into the street.

"I'll not forget you. We'll meet again."

Lew shrugged. "Bring all your men. You'll need them."

"Let's go," the redhead told his followers. His men left the sidewalk and fell in around him. They were grumbling to each other as they went down the street.

Tim put his pistol back into his holster and he

watched the departing backs. "There wasn't any reason for that argument," he told Lew.

"Yes there was. Bully boys like those have to be faced down." And I wanted to see how you would react when threatened by the gang, thought Lew.

"But now you have made more enemies."

"I do agree that we have all the enemies we need. Are you afraid?" Lew intently studied Tim.

Tim stared back without blinking. "No," he said, and knew that he meant it.

"You'll do," Lew said. He clapped Tim on the shoulder.

22

THE morning grew cold as Lezin Morissot waited. From time to time, he peered in through the open door of the barroom at Russee Loussat sitting at a table in a shadowy corner. Loussat drank steadily by himself, staring at the top of the table. He had looked no man in the face since Wollfolk's duel earlier in the morning.

Morissot knew what the expression on Loussat's face meant. It was the look of a man who had discovered that he feared a man. He would forever hate the man who had made him see the sour blackness of that cowardice.

Near noon, Loussat fell unconscious across the saloon table. The bartender called his young assistant and gave him instructions. The assistant left the saloon and trotted off to the west in the direction of the Garden District.

Half an hour later a surrey, driven by a black man in red silk livery, rolled up to the barroom. The man halted the team of horses and entered the establishment.

A moment passed and he emerged with the bartender, Loussat supported between them, his feet dragging. The drunken man was placed on the rear seat of the vehicle and the thick curtains drawn closed to hide the unconscious form. The surrey driver climbed into the front seat, picked up the reins, and drove off.

Morissot fell in behind a block to the rear. The servant would take Loussat directly home. Morissot wanted to know exactly where that was.

For five days, Morissot spied upon Loussat's mansion. The man never once left the house. Several times visitors came, but they were always met at the door by a servant and turned away.

Farr Rawlins came. Old Ella trailed him, staying far back. Rawlins was not admitted and walked away, his cane pecking on the sidewalk.

Morissot had paid Ella and set her to following Rawlins. She could easily keep pace with the crippled man. Either Rawlins or Loussat would lead them to the fourth member of the Ring.

In the morning of the sixth day, Loussat left his home. Driven by the black man in red livery, he visited the offices of three dock-owners. He spent a few minutes in each and then went to his own place of business.

Morissot recognized the office of Rawlins. Stanton Shattuck's name was on the front door of his building. The third business was called the Mississippi Company. Morissot asked questions of the black porter of the small hotel across the street and learned the owner of the company was named Edward Tarboll. The last enemy, the fourth member of the Ring, had been identified.

Morissot hastened off to find Tim and the impostor. He thought it odd that he had begun to think of the impostor as an ally. But that was just a temporary situation. Soon now would come the time to slay the man.

Lew moved with long, purposeful strides along the street. He wanted to see a man's face. Lezin Morissot had found Sam and Lew on the docks. He reported Loussat's visits to Rawlins, Shattuck, and a third man named Edward Tarboll. Lew and Sam had agreed that Tarboll must be the fourth member of the Ring. Lew intended to find out for certain.

Since it was noon, there was less than half the number of people normally on the street. Their faces were strained with worry as they hurried along on some private errands. Two hearses passed, each carrying three coffins packed tightly together in the limited space of the vehicles. Every coffin was smeared with lampblack. No procession of

255

mourners followed to send off the deceased with the wailing of laments at their deaths.

Several wagons, buggies, and surreys went by loaded with men, women, and children, their bedding, and a few supplies to subsist on as they fled the city.

The heavy, sour smell of garbage, human waste, and smoke filled Lew's nose. To the northeast where the nearest cemetery lay, a pillar of gray smoke climbed to merge with the low-hanging clouds. Funeral pyres were burning the dead that had no grave.

The old blind fiddler man was slumped in a chair in his habitual place on the sidewalk. His fiddle had fallen and lay on the damp brick. The bow hung loosely in his hand.

"Hello, old man, wake up," Lew said, stooping to retrieve the man's instrument. "You've dropped your fiddle."

The man did not stir, and Lew bent to shake him by the shoulder. The man's head fell backward. His mouth gaped open. The glazed eyes in the bronze face of the dead man stared up at Lew.

"Goddamn," ejaculated Lew, hastily removing his hand from the man's body. Then in a kind voice, Lew said, "I'm sorry, old man."

He glanced around for someone to tell about the dead fiddler. A man and woman were watching him from the open door of a print shop, but they jerked their eyes away when Lew looked at them, and moved back into the shadowy interior of the shop.

A wagon with two corpses wrapped in bedsheets rolled by on the street. Lew shouted at the driver. "Can you take another body to the cemetery?"

The driver pulled his animals to a stop. He cast a look at the man in the chair. "How much money does he have?"

"How much does it take to get buried?" Lew asked.

"I'll take him for twenty dollars and five dollars for the gravediggers."

"Do it." Lew took out his wallet and gave the man some bills.

"Help me load him," said the driver as he clambered down over the wheel of the wagon onto the ground.

Lew assisted the driver in placing the body of the fiddler on the bed of the wagon. He lay the dead man's instrument near him.

"Bury that with him," Lew said.

"All right."

Lew stared after the vehicle as it continued down the street. The fiddler's death and the frightened expression of the people on the street saddened him. New Orleans was a bleak, dismal city filling with death and rapidly becoming deserted by the living.

Near the corner of Clay and Iberville streets, Lew entered the office of the Mississippi Company. The desk in the front office was vacant.

"Anybody here?" Lew called.

"Yes, what do you want?" A man spoke from somewhere in the back.

"I want to see Edward Tarboll," Lew said.

Shortly a man in shirtsleeves appeared from a side door. The skin of his face was rough and there were deep squint wrinkles at the corners of his eyes, as if he had spent much time in the sun and wind. He sported a reddish, heavily waxed mustache extending out in little spikes from both sides of his mouth. He halted and looked at Lew with sharp brown eyes.

"Are you Edward Tarboll?" Lew said.

"Yes."

"I'm Timothy Wollfolk."

The man blinked. Lew saw the man's recognition of the name and the wariness that came into him.

"So what does that mean to me?" Tarboll asked.

"Quite a lot. You're number four. I wanted to see what you looked like. If I ever need to come looking for you, I want to be sure to get the right man."

"I don't understand. Why would you want to find me?"

"If you or any of your three friends cause me any more trouble, if anyone tries to harm me or interfere with my business, I'm going to come and make you a sorry son of a bitch."

"Are you threatening me?"

"You're damn right I am. Get yourself a gun and I'll do more than threaten you."

Tarboll said nothing. The lids of his eyes lowered. The young Wollfolk had just made a grievous error. A man should never tell an enemy that

258

you know who he is and then threaten him. You should kill him as swiftly as possible. Tarboll almost laughed.

Lew caught the amused twist to Tarboll's mouth before the man hid the emotion. Laugh, you bastard. But don't send another paid killer at me.

"Is that all, Mr. Wollfolk?"

"For now."

"Then close the door as you leave. I expect no more customers. The business of the city is almost dead, as are many of its people." Tarboll turned and went back through the door he had entered by.

Lew stared at his retreating back. The man had shown no fear. And such a fearless man would now have to attack him. The attack would be strong, and it would come soon.

Honoré Savigne sat in Mayor Crossman's office with the other men called to the emergency assembly. He held his notepad on his knee, a stub of pencil ready as he listened to the discussion. However, he was having difficulty catching all the words, for an echoing drum inside his temples was growing louder, the percussive beats jarring and thunderous. His skull was straining to explode.

He heard Tigorson, the board-of-health chief speaking to the mayor.

"Charity Hospital has thirteen hundred patients. The Marine Hospital has nearly two thousand. Beds of the ill are crammed in every ward, hallway, and storage room. At the Marine Hospital hundreds of Army tents have been set up outside. They are overflowing."

"What is the death rate?" Crossman asked.

"About three hundred a day," replied Tigorson.

Dr. Carstensen spoke. "An equal number of people, and perhaps more are dying each day among the sick lying in thousands of homes throughout the city. We will never have an accurate accounting of the dead. I personally believe it is much worse than we imagine."

Crossman faced the head physician of the Louisiana Medical College. "Doctor Smythe, why can't you discover the cause of this dreaded disease? You have been given many thousands of dollars to search for it. Yet you have found nothing."

"It is sad that we don't know the cause," replied Dr. Smythe. "We have studied many things, to no avail. The disease may be picked up from some invisible pestilential effluvia from the swamps or riverbanks, because it seems to be associated with dampness. However, it may be some miasma riding on the dust specks in the air. Or something we have never even contemplated. It strikes in the most unexpected places. We don't know how it is passed from victim to victim, or if it actually is contagious."

"Damnation, Doctor, do we get that kind of answer after thirteen years of study by you and the full staff of the medical college?" the mayor said in dismay. He looked around the room at General Drake, commanding officer of Fort Jesup and the U.S. Barracks, and the three ward alderman.

"Gentlemen, what do you recommend we do to combat the disease?"

"Mayor Crossman, my soldiers are at risk, same as the civilian population," said General Drake. "The Army doctors know no more than do the doctors at the college. I stand ready to do whatever I can to help you.'

"Thank you, General Drake," Crossman said.

The mayor waited a minute for the aldermen to speak. When they remained silent, he stood up and walked to the window. He stared for a long time out from the second-floor room of the Cabildo and down at deserted Jackson Square.

The mayor faced back to the gathering of men. "We must do something, and do it now. This terrible disease must be driven from New Orleans."

"We must purify the air," Tigorson said.

"How do we do that?" asked the mayor.

"By loud noise and smoke," said the chief. "We have tried that before during epidemics, and it has been of some help."

The mayor looked at the head physician of the Medical College. "Do you think that would be effective?"

"Possibly. I agree with Tigorson that it has seemed to be somewhat effective in the past. If this thing is alive or is carried by something alive, then extremely loud noises and dense smoke might indeed drive it away."

"Doctor Carstensen, your opinion?"

"Let's do something. If it does nothing but lift

261

the spirits of the citizens, then it's worth the effort."

"General Drake, you have cannon at Fort Jesup that will not be going to General Scott in Mexico, isn't that so?" asked the mayor.

"I have over two hundred cannon and a hundred howitzers."

"Will you bring all of the guns to the city and fire them at short intervals? Make as much noise as possible."

"I will certainly do that. I can have them in the city and set up by nightfall."

"Begin firing them as soon as they are ready," said the mayor. "Place at least one near each hospital and one near the row of sailors' boarding-houses on the waterfront. Those places seem to be the centers of the worst infections of the fever." The mayor turned to Tigorson. "Assemble all the city employees that are still on the job. Order them to round up every tar barrel they can find. Go across the river to Algiers and confiscate the tar from the shipyards. Take a policeman with you to be sure no one prevents you from getting the tar. Burn a barrel at every major street intersection in the city."

"The people must be told why the cannon are firing, or they'll panic more than they already are," Savigne said from across the room.

"That is why I asked you to come, Honoré, to inform the people. Is the *Louisiana Courier* still staffed to print a newspaper?" asked the mayor.

"Yes."

"Then you tell the citizens what we are doing," said the mayor. "And tell them to pray."

Honoré Savigne clenched his teeth to keep from moaning with the horrible pain in his head. His skull felt swollen to the point of bursting. His mind seemed to flicker off as the pain soared to a crescendo. Then the pain relented step by step, and his thoughts became clear and solid again.

Honoré's sickness was getting worse. He must hurry. He picked up a pen from his desk and dipped it in the well of black ink. He wrote the lead sentence, "The scourge of death, yellow fever, disguised in its mask of bronze, is laying waste to New Orleans . . ."

Savigne lifted his pen and listened to the three printing presses clanking away sheet by sheet on the day's paper at the far end of the building. Another typesetter came in through the front door. A puff of wind followed him and fluttered the *baire* that hung from the ceiling and enclosed Savigne's desk. The movement of the *baire* set off an impotent buzzing of the cloud of mosquitoes that could not get inside to him.

He peered out through the window as a cart jolted noisily over the cobblestones in front of the building. A corpse wrapped in a red blanket and tied with twine was being bounced obscenely about in the bed of the vehicle as it hustled off to the cemetery. No longer were there the sedate and dignified funeral processions the dead deserved.

The gravediggers could not keep up with the

demand for their services. They were now on strike, demanding their wages be increased from twenty cents a grave to five dollars. The families of the dead were digging their relatives' graves. Often the excavations were but shallow trenches hardly deep enough to hide the corpses. On the side street near Saint Louis Cemetery Number Two, Savigne had seen families lighting funeral pyres to cremate their dead. In normal times it was common to see large mausoleums and tombs costing ten, twenty, even thirty thousand dollars. Now a man was fortunate to get a dozen shovels full of dirt thrown on him to hide his rotting body.

Savigne felt the pain stirring again inside his head. He clutched his skull, squeezing hard, trying to equalize the tremendous pressure that was building rapidly within. His ears filled with a roaring sound.

The pain subsided, leaving behind a throbbing drumbeat. Savigne grabbed up his pen, dipped it, and began to write swiftly. He had tried to mislead his own thoughts that the headache had nothing to do with the fever. But he truly knew better. This was the first symptom. At any moment the chills would come. Then he would not be able to hold a pen to write. He hastened even more, the script flowing out behind the scratching pen.

Savigne finally laid down the pen, the article completed. He picked up the pages of paper and stood. The chill came upon him like an ocean of ice water. His body shrank within itself. His teeth began to chatter so hard he thought they would shatter. He clamped his jaws together and still he could not hold them still.

He began to shake uncontrollably, his muscles involuntarily fighting one another in the body's instinctive method of warming itself. The very core of him became frozen as if his heart was pumping frigid blood.

Honoré sank back into his chair. He wrapped his arms about himself. He struggled to hold on, every fragment of his mind fighting the growing panic.

The chill gradually passed. But not the fear. Savigne knew his luck had run out. He had escaped many epidemics of the fever. He would not escape this one.

He took up the pen again. At the bottom of his story he wrote a word in heavy, bold strokes. Finis. Finished. This was the last article he would ever write.

He caught up the sheets of paper again, swiftly shoved aside the *baire,* and walked toward the printing room. The mosquitoes swarmed upon him in a black fog. He felt their stinging bites before he reached the end of the hallway.

Savigne handed the papers in under the *baire* protecting the printer. "Be sure this gets on the front page of today's paper," he told the printer.

"Right. I saw you working, so I held it." The printer looked at the article. "There's no headline. What do you want me to use?"

" 'Death Comes.' Just those words, 'Death Comes.' "

"Comes to who?" asked the printer.

"The list of names is incomplete and far too long to print. And mine will be among them." Savigne turned and hurried from the newspaper office. His teeth began to chatter uncontrollably again as he hit the street.

23

JULIUS RUFFIER shouted and the black stevedores broke from their work and hurried to form another line on the dock in front of Tim, the paymaster. They called out their names as they moved past Tim's table. He handed them their week's wages.

"Because of illness and death and men leaving the city to escape the yellow-fever epidemic, we have but a half a crew," Julius said to Lew, who stood nearby. "Tomorrow we'll be lucky to have a dozen men working."

"I can't blame the men for being scared and running," Lew said, "but it doesn't hurt us too badly, because some of the ships due to arrive are refusing to come to the docks. Every captain knows New Orleans has the yellow fever. However, the Irishmen are hanging tough. They'll be here for the night shift."

"They've only been here a week. Soon they'll be catching the fever."

"I think you are probably right." Lew had hired the Irishmen coming straight off the ship from Ireland. He had come upon the foreign men when he had boarded a steamship on the river and had negotiated with the captain for dock space. As the men came down the gangway, he offered each a job.

The Irishmen had assembled around their leader, Ira O'Doyle, and talked among themselves. Then O'Doyle came and talked to Lew. The men had made the long journey without their women and children. Many were penniless. Lew advanced money for food and rented all the rooms of a boardinghouse near the waterfront for their lodging.

The Irishmen had grown somewhat soft-muscled during the nearly fifty days at sea. But they were used to hard work and recovered quickly. Now each man was loading as many tons of cargo as were the black men of the day crew.

Tim finished paying the men. He folded his portable table, lifted it to his shoulder, and walked briskly up the side of the levee toward Lew and Julius in the warehouse.

"Sam seems to have completely healed from his gunshot wounds," Julius said, gesturing at the approaching man easily carrying the table.

"Don't you mean the injuries he got from a horse falling on him?" Lew said.

"No. Bullet wounds."

"How do you know that?" Lew felt a sudden apprehension.

"I saw them one day when his shirt was open. He has one on the side and a second on the shoulder. I've seen bullet wounds. I've got one myself. There's no mistaking them."

Lew felt a jolt as the pieces of a puzzle came together. For days he had been mystified by some of Sam's words and expressions. Now he knew their meaning. Sam Datson was Tim Wollfolk. The wounds had been received when the robbers had shot him. His experience as a bookkeeper had not been obtained in Saint Louis but in Cincinnati. Yet Lew had seen him fall into the river and disappear . . . What of that?

"Sam stays with Lezin Morissot," Lew said to Julius. "Isn't he a river fisherman?"

"Yes. And he has a very beautiful daughter. I've heard Sam and she are very friendly."

"What section of the river does Morissot fish?"

"Above the city. He says fish below the town are bad because they eat all the garbage thrown in the river."

Lew knew Morissot had somehow found Tim and saved him from the river. Being the true Wollfolk explained the quickness with which the man had accepted the job of accountant offered by Lew. And also why the angry look sometimes came to his eyes. Why had the man not had Lew arrested?

Lew walked away as Tim approached the top of the levee. He needed time to think. He angled down toward a broad-beamed steamship just dock-ing after a voyage from Vera Cruz with some of General Scott's ill and wounded soldiers.

The last ship's line was made fast to cleats on the dock and the gangway rattled down. The walking wounded came streaming ashore first.

Sailors and medical corpsmen began to carry litter patients off the ship. The army doctor came down to the dock. He called a corpsman to him and sent him off toward the town.

The doctor saw Lew watching the unloading. He nodded a greeting.

"My name is Wollfolk," Lew said. "This is my dock. Is there something I can do for you?"

"I have one hundred and seventy litter patients," said the doctor. "I need to transport them to the Marine Hospital. I've sent a messenger to the hospital to ask for their ambulance wagons. I hope they send them quickly."

"I doubt the hospital will send their wagons soon, for they are busy hauling away the dead."

"It's that bad, is it? And I've got more fever victims here. At least half of them."

"Your patients shouldn't stay long on the riverbank. It'll soon be dark and the mosquitoes will come like a fog. They're terrible uptown, but here they get so thick in the night a man could walk across the river on their backs."

"Can you tell me where I can find enough vehicles to haul the men to the hospital?"

Lew decided he would act one more time as Wollfolk. "I can help you. Line up your litters on the dock. I'll have my drays come and take all of you uptown."

"Great. The men will appreciate that." The doctor hustled off shouting orders.

"Julius, stop the drays from hauling cargo. Tell the drivers to go to that hospital ship and take the patients to the Marine Hospital."

"The navy captains won't like that," Julius said. "They've been telling me all morning to hurry the loading of their ships. They want to get away from the fever."

"They'll understand those sick men come first."

"I think so too."

Julius gave instructions to the drivers of the drays, and the vehicles rattled across the dock to the line of litters. Shortly the drays were loaded with the sick and wounded. They moved off in a long caravan.

Lew watched the procession disappear over the levee. For a few moments longer, he stood without moving, pondering the discovery of Sam's true identity. He knew there was only one solution to the situation: Tim had to be told why Lew had taken his name.

Lew turned to Tim, who had been silently observing the change in the work of the drays. "We must talk," Lew said.

"Sure. What about?" Tim said.

"Something that happened a few weeks back," said Lew. "Let's sit over there." He gestured at the desk in the end of the warehouse.

They sat directly across from each other. Tim said nothing. The impostor laid his arms on the desk and leaned forward.

"One morning about two months ago, I was coming south just above New Orleans. I saw three men rob and shoot a traveler on the riverbank. This traveler fell into the river. I thought he was dead. Until today. That man's name was Timothy Wollfolk."

Tim held his face impassive. This might be a ploy to trick him into some kind of comment that would give him away. "But you are Timothy Wollfolk," he said.

Lew spread his hands. "Wrong. You are Timothy Wollfolk. All these many days you've watched me play the fool."

"What makes you think I'm this Wollfolk?"

"Julius told me."

Tim cocked a disbelieving eye at Lew. "Julius told you what?"

"He said he was certain you had been shot. That your wounds were not from a horse falling on you. Then the rest came to me. The timing of your wounds. Morissot the river fisherman being with you. Your skill as an accountant. It all added up to the fact that you are actually Wollfolk."

Lew hesitated a few seconds, waiting for the man to speak. When he did not reply, Lew continued. "I know that I'm not Wollfolk."

Tim's face hardened. "Yes, I'm Timothy Wollfolk."

"Why have you not said so before?"

"Why should I tell a thief that I know he is an impostor until I can prove it?"

"You've had plenty of time to prove it. There has to be another reason."

"If there is, then surely I would not tell you."

Tim saw the look of shame in the eyes of the impostor. He felt his resolve to severely punish the man begin to weaken. Without doubt, the man had saved Tim's life. And the Wollfolk Company still existed because of the man's drive for business.

"What happened to the men who shot me?"

"I killed them. No. I executed them, for I saw them shoot you and I thought it was murder. I know they intended to murder you. I dumped them in the river like the filth they were."

"Then you looked at my papers and decided to become Timothy Wollfolk?"

"That's right. At the time, I thought all the Wollfolks were dead. So there was nobody to be cheated, to be robbed." Lew rose. "But there is a Wollfolk alive. What belongs to him must be given to him. Come, let's go to the lawyer, Rosiere and have him prepare the papers necessary to give you back your inheritance."

"Very well," Tim said. He climbed to his feet. "What name shall I call you?"

"Lew Fannin."

"Mr. Lew Fannin, what was your occupation before you became a thief?"

Lew knew the name thief was totally correct.

He could take no affront at the truth. "A Texas Ranger," he said.

"The office is closed," said the dark Creole law clerk of Gilbert Rosiere. He was alone in the outer office, filling a leather satchel with papers. "We are packing to leave the city."

"This will not take long," replied Fannin. "Tell Mr. Rosiere this is important and must be done today."

"I doubt that he will want to delay his departure to talk with a client now." The Creole's face held a skeptical expression.

"Try him," said Fannin. "Let him make up his own mind. Tell him Timothy Wollfolk is here."

"I know who you are," said the Creole, his voice hardening. He walked toward the rear, where Rosiere's office was.

Rosiere came in with hurried steps. "Good day, gentlemen," he said.

"Mr. Rosiere, we need a paper drawn up," Fannin said.

"Can't it wait? The epidemic is getting worse and I want to take my family away from the city."

"This should take but a moment of your time. Can we talk in your office?"

"Very well," Rosiere said in a reluctant tone. "Follow me."

He sat at his desk and dipped his pen in ink. "What do you wish written?"

"A document that clearly states the identity of Timothy Wollfolk," Fannin said.

"What do you mean?"

"My name is Lew Fannin. That man is the true Timothy Wollfolk." Lew nodded at Tim.

Rosiere looked from Lew to Tim, and then back. "I should think that strange statement needs considerable explanation."

"I'll explain," Tim said. "I hired Mr. Fannin to take my place."

Lew held his surprise in check. Why was Wollfolk saying he had hired him? To have him arrested was more in order.

"Why would you do that?" asked Rosiere.

"My uncle died under suspicious circumstances. I thought there might be danger to me. Mr. Fannin is an ex–Texas Ranger. He is quite capable of protecting himself. He agreed to help me. As it turned out, my uncle had several enemies."

"I've heard of your trouble," Rosiere said. "But why could you not confide in me?"

"We did not know who to trust in New Orleans, a city neither one of us had ever been in," Tim said. "But we now know that you are an honest man. That is why we are here. These are dangerous times with the epidemic raging. We wish to have the record accurate."

"I understand. Give me a moment and I shall draft a statement for your and Mr. Fannin's signatures."

Rosiere wrote swiftly. Finishing, he handed the paper to Tim. "Examine this closely. If it is satisfactory, then I will draft a duplicate. Thus in the event one becomes lost or destroyed, there will still be a record."

Tim read the document. He handed it to Lew. "It explains the situation adequately," Tim said.

Lew scanned the paper. "I agree."

"Good." Rosiere swiftly drafted the copy. He laid both papers before the men and offered his pen. "Both of you sign."

"All right," Tim said. He returned the papers signed by both Lew and him to Rosiere.

"I'll put my name on as a witness to your signatures." Rosiere took the pen and wrote.

"Here is your copy, Mr. Wollfolk. I shall keep the other one in my safe." Rosiere looked at Tim in a reproachful way. "I still wish you had taken me into your confidence. I vouched for the correct identity of Mr. Fannin as the true Wollfolk heir."

Fannin looked at the lawyer. "Perhaps you should tell those who ask that you were knowingly part of the deception. We certainly shall never say otherwise. Isn't that so, Tim?"

"I think that is a good plan," Tim said.

"Thank you, gentlemen. That is very kind."

"Mr. Fannin will continue to impersonate me for a few days longer, Mr. Rosiere. So please keep this paper confidential. Tell absolutely no one until I contact you."

Lew glanced at Tim. What game was Wollfolk playing?

"Our enemies are still running free," Tim said, returning Lew's look.

"I will do as you ask," said the lawyer. "Now,

gentlemen, if that is all, I bid you good day." He stood up.

"Thank you for your time," Tim said. "I wish you and your family stay safe from the epidemic."

"Good fortune to both of you," Rosiere replied.

Lew led the way from the lawyer's office. The law clerk was still packing his satchel in the outer office. Lew barely glanced at the man and continued on to the outside. Once on the sidewalk and away from the door of the law office, Lew wheeled around on Tim.

"What's this about me continuing to pretend to be you? Now that I'm not going to be arrested, I plan to join the army and ship out to Mexico."

Tim looked steadily at Lew. "I believe you meant me no harm. Further, I think you did execute the three men that shot and robbed me. I can even understand your logic to impersonate me. Perhaps I would have done the same thing had I been in your position."

"Maybe you would have. So what now?"

"I want to hire you to help me destroy the Wollfolk enemies, my enemies."

"Do you mean kill them?"

"If it comes to that, yes. I'm sure they meant for you to die in the duel. I'll pay you well for your help, whatever you want."

Fannin studied Tim with a measuring stare. "I want Cécile Pereaux."

"Agreed. What else?"

"Nothing."

"But there is something else you want. You

276

may have a half-interest in the *Honest Traveler.* I've seen how you look at her."

Lew was astounded at the offer. "But why? I do not ask for anything more than what I've already said."

"I called you a thief. I do not believe that. I think you are an honest man. And also a good businessman. The clipper ship will soon be ready for sea. Find her a good captain. Take Cécile and go with the ship. Make us both a lot of money. Between voyages, help me here in New Orleans. Live in the house on Rampart Street." Tim waited a moment, watching Lew. "I want you to be my partner."

"You're crazy," Lew said. "I want nothing else. I can't be your partner."

"If you do not help me, I won't be alive in a week."

"Probably not. But even if I help you, neither one of us might be alive in a week. We could be killed by either the yellow fever or the Ring."

"That may be true, but I think I have more of a chance to survive if you help me. Therefore, I'm not being too generous. My life is damned valuable to me. Shall we be partners?"

"We may end up being dead partners, but partners we shall be." Lew held out his hand.

24

OLD ELLA watched Farr Rawlins enter the office of Russee Loussat and the door close behind him. Then, exaggerating the slump of her shoulders, she shuffled across the street and moved past the front of the building.

She slowed as she passed the window at the end of the structure. The drone of a man's voice reached her through the open window covered with a mosquito netting.

Ella continued along the street for half a block and then turned and began to retrace her steps. The few pedestrians paid her no attention. There were no street vendors about to become suspicious of her movements.

Near the window of the office, Ella halted and sat on the sidewalk. She stretched her thin legs out on the brick and pulled the faded dress primly down to her shoe tops. She closed her eyes and her chin sank to rest on her bony breast. Just an old black woman asleep, or perhaps sick, on the street.

For five days, Ella had spied upon Rawlins. He was a punctual man, with a routine that varied hardly at all. She slept when he entered his house and the lights went out. When he sought out a restaurant for his meal, she ate from the food sold on the street by the vendors. Never once did she lose track of Rawlins.

A messenger had come to Rawlins' office in the late afternoon. Immediately Rawlins had left and, leaning on his cane, walked the short three blocks to Loussat's place of business.

Ella shifted her head slightly, placing her ear at the very edge of the window. The voice of a man came to her through the *baire* swaying to the slow, damp wind.

"We should not meet so openly, and in one of our offices," Stanton Shattuck said. "This had better be damned awful important."

"Nobody is thinking about rigged bidding for military contracts," replied Loussat. "The city's half-deserted and the remaining people are hiding in their homes or preparing to leave."

"We're still here," Shattuck said.

"But only for a very short time," Tarboll said. "I'm about ready to leave too."

"The same here," Rawlins said. "Loussat, why did you send for us?"

"My nephew, the one who works as law clerk for Rosiere, came with important news just a few minutes ago. What he told me will change how we handle Wollfolk." Loussat looked at one face after the other.

"Out with it, Loussat," Shattuck growled.

"Wollfolk is not who we think he is. That accountant Datson is really Wollfolk."

279

"Then who in the hell is the man that has been passing himself off as Wollfolk?" Rawlins asked.

"A Texas Ranger named Lew Fannin."

"A lawman from Texas has no jurisdiction in Louisiana," Rawlins said.

"He used to be a Ranger. Now he's hired by Wollfolk to take his place."

"How did your nephew come to find this out?" Tarboll asked.

"Wollfolk and Fannin came to Rosiere to draw up a paper to set the record straight. They must be afraid the yellow fever might strike one of them. My nephew heard it all."

"That's good news indeed," Shattuck said. "This new Wollfolk will be much easier to kill."

"The timing is excellent," Rawlins said. "The city is in turmoil with the law busy either picking up dead bodies or trying to stop looting of vacant homes and businesses. Wollfolk can be disposed of without danger to us."

"We will use Kelty this time," Shattuck said. "He'll not fail."

"But is he still in the city?" questioned Loussat.

"Kelty's afraid of nothing, not even Bronze John," Shattuck said. "I know where to leave a message for him. Perhaps I can still get hold of him today."

Tarboll spoke. "Since the Wollfolk Company has put on the night shift, Datson is usually working on the dock or at the warehouse until dark. I've seen him there. Kelty can catch him on his way home."

"I want to get this thing done today," said Shattuck.

"If Wollfolk's not on the dock, Kelty can find him at that mulatto Morissot's home."

Ella clambered to her feet and scampered off along the avenue. Lezin must be told at once of Kelty. He would stop the assassin from killing Timothy.

Or could he? When Ella was in the presence of Kelty that one time, she had felt the power and evil in the man. Maybe no one could stop Kelty.

Ella had visited Lezin's home and had seen the tender looks Marie gave the young white man. The girl had a great love for Timothy. Once, oh, so many years ago, Ella had possessed such a love for a man. She felt the glow of the pleasant memories of that time. But her man was long dead. Marie's man must not die.

Ella lengthened her stride almost to a run. Her old heart with its paper-thin walls beat and thrashed against her ribs as she sped block after block.

"What's that noise?" Shattuck said. He had heard the scuff of feet at the open window. He hurried across the room, flung aside the *baire*, and looked out.

"Just an old nigger woman passing," he said. "That's all." He reseated himself.

Tarboll spoke to the group of men. "Have you thought of what the Texas Ranger will do if we kill Wollfolk? The Ranger was at my office earlier today. He said he wanted to see what I looked like, that I was number four. That means he knows the three of you. He is aware of the Ring. He threatened to come and kill me if anyone tried to hurt him or damage his business."

Tarboll studied the three men. Shattuck was grinning as if a joke had been told. Tarboll thought the man was anticipating a fight with the Ranger. Loussat and Rawlins were not grinning. Both had felt the deadly threat of the Ranger. Rawlins had been slapped half-senseless and knocked to the floor of the Saint Charles. Loussat had been challenged and had tucked his tail between his legs and ran.

"So we must kill the Ranger Fannin too," said Shattuck, looking at Tarboll. "And more than that, this is the time to destroy the Wollfolk docks."

"You are right," Tarboll said. "I have no doubt that Fannin will come after us when we strike at Wollfolk. I mean to hit him before he hits me. I know many men in the Swamp. I'll gather a bunch of them and we'll burn the Wollfolk docks and warehouse. We'll do it late tonight. If Fannin is there, we'll shoot him while he is busy fighting the fire. If not there, then we'll go to his placée's house on the ramparts and finish him."

"I'm coming with you," Loussat said. He had to conquer his fear of Fannin. The Ranger's deadly accuracy with the pistol had unnerved Loussat. But that was passing. To redeem himself in his own eyes and those of his comrades, he had to slay the man with his own hands. "You must let me kill Fannin," Loussat told Tarboll.

"All right, Loussat," Tarboll said. "You get the first shot at Fannin."

Morissot took a two-pound channel catfish from the hook on the trotline and tossed the flapping creature into the bottom of the pirogue. Bait was fastened to the hook and the trotline released to sink back into the water of the Mississippi. The boat floated free, picking up speed and drifting with the current.

Lezin inserted the oars into the oarlocks and stroked for the bank. The day had been profitable. Some fifty pounds of fish had been taken from his seven trotlines. At three cents per pound, he had earned one dollar and fifty cents, an average day's wage for a laborer.

Morissot had enjoyed the simple honest pleasure of the fishing. He wished he truly was only a riverman who traded his hard-earned catch of fish for the necessary things of life. But he had long ago passed beyond that simple existence. Now, nearly two score of dead men lay behind him. He was thankful that he had no son and that the line of assassins would end with him.

The pirogue reached the riverbank and Lezin stepped out. He dragged the craft out of the water and secured it with a chain and lock to a big sycamore. The fish were packed into a burlap sack. Lezin lifted the sack to his shoulder and climbed up to his wagon on top of the levee. The mellow feeling of an enjoyable day on the river still held him, lingering as a pleasant glow as he drove the horse and wagon in the direction of his home.

Old Ella and Marie were in the carriageway when Lezin came into sight on the wooded lane to the house. The women hastened toward him. Lezin's pleasant mood vanished at the sight of Ella's face so full of dread and fear.

"Lezin, I'm so glad you have come," Ella said as the wagon came to a stop. "Kelty is coming to kill Timothy."

"How do you know that?" Lezin asked.

"I heard Rawlins and some other men agreeing to hire the man to do it."

"Where is Tim?" Lezin asked Marie.

"He hasn't come home yet," Marie answered. Father, you must warn him."

"Ella, tell me all that you know," Lezin said.

The old woman swiftly described how she had followed Rawlins to the office of a man named Loussat, and the conversation she had heard.

"How many men were there?"

"I heard four different voices. I did not see any of the men except Rawlins. They know Timothy stays with you."

"Marie, take Ella and go to Jonathan's home. Kelty may come here and he would harm you and Ella. Stay with Jonathan until I come for you, and don't go outside, for Kelty may see you. Tell Jonathan no one must learn that you are there."

"What of Tim?" Marie asked. There was a tremble in her voice. "Ella told me Kelty is a wicked man and has killed many people."

"Ella exaggerates."

"I don't either," Ella snapped.

"Father, keep Tim safe for me," Marie said, catching him by the hand.

"I will. Now go to Jonathan's like I say."

"I'll pack some things at the house."

"No. Leave this very second."

Lezin watched the two women scurry off through the woods on the worn path to Jonathan's. Then he drove on to the house and tied the horse. He climbed the steps to the upper floor.

From the closet in his bedroom, Lezin dragged out an iron-bound chest and unlocked it. He dug into the chest and laid out his cache of killing weapons, an assortment of knives, handguns, and two garrotes.

Rarely did Morissot use a gun to carry out the contracts he made to execute men. However, this time he was not going against ordinary men, but against Kelty. He loaded one of the Colt pistols with measures of powder, rammed home the five lead balls, and pressed a cap over each nipple. He put the gun in his belt. A long-bladed, two-edged knife was strapped to his waist. The remaining weapons were once again placed into the trunk and locked away hidden in the rear of the closet.

Morissot walked slowly down the stairway of the house. On the ground, he gazed back, letting his eyes roam over the old house where he had lived all of his life. Where Marie had been born and grew to beautiful womanhood. He recalled old joyous memories, savoring them as they flitted through his mind. He should be hurrying, but there was a growing premonition that he might never see his home again.

Morissot whirled around and leapt into the wagon. The whip cracked an inch above the horse's ears and the animal broke into a trot easterly toward New Orleans.

Behind Morissot, the sun watched with half a red and bloody eye showing above the flat horizon. Ahead cannon began to boom, jarring the city as if it was under military attack. Smoke was streaming upward in many locations.

He knew what the cannon fire and smoke meant. Once again the officials were beginning their defense against the yellow fever. The number of dead must be very large.

Gustave Besançon stopped pounding on the door of the barroom and looked through the darkness at Leandre and Maurice standing near him. "Locked tight, and nobody answers," he said.

"I want a drink of rum," Leandre said. "Step aside. I'll give it a few kicks that'll wake even the dead." He assaulted the door, and it rattled loudly on its hinges and against the lock. He ceased kicking and listened through the boom of the cannon. There was only silence from within. "We must have tried nearly a dozen barrooms and every one is closed," he said.

"The Flatboat Saloon won't be closed in the Swamp," Gustave said. "Those hellions down there have never given in to any epidemic, either yellow fever or cholera. They just draw lots to see who will dig the graves for the dead, and the rest go right on drinking and whoring."

"The Swamp is a damned good idea," Leandre said. "And we're not going to let old Bronze John spoil our good time either. Let's go visit those rascals in the Flatboat."

The three Creoles waded off through the night lying dense with ropy smoke from burning tar.

Gustave stopped just inside the entrance of the Flatboat and stared around. "We've made a long trip for nothing. The place is nearly deserted." He gestured down the saloon.

A pair of men stood at the bar and sipped at beers. One of the card tables had three players. The craps table was covered with a dirty Indian blanket.

"We might as well have a drink while we are here," said Leandre, leading toward the bar.

"Maybe Custus is around and knows where something is happening that will entertain us," Gustave said.

"Back again," said the bartender, recognizing the young Creoles. "Don't shoot anyone this time. I don't have enough customers to spare even one."

"Business does look lean," Gustave said. "Is Custus around?"

"He's in the back with a couple of gents from

uptown," said the bartender. He chucked a thumb in the general direction of the rear of the saloon. "Go on back. They're probably someone you know."

"Order me a drink too," Gustave said to his friends as he turned and headed off.

He parted a pair of ratty curtains and entered a short, dark hallway. A sliver of weak yellow lamplight shone from under a closed door at the end of the passageway. He heard men's voices.

As Gustave approached the light, the voices became clear. Custus was speaking.

"All right, I'll help you burn the warehouse and as much of the docks as will burn. My charge is two hundred dollars."

"That price is acceptable," a second unknown voice said. "How many men can you get?"

"As many as you want," Custus announced.

"The Irishmen might help Wollfolk fight us off," the first man said. "We'll get only one chance, and that'll be a surprise. Fifty men or so will be needed. That would be enough to keep the Irishmen busy and still leave us with some men to set the fires."

"That number won't be any problem," Custus said. "How much pay do the men get to help me?"

"We want men who can swing a hard club," said the first man. "The pay is a double sawbuck for an hour's work."

"I can find men who'll work for that. What about the military cargo? After we soak the warehouse and the docks with coal oil and light them, we're not going to be able to control the fire."

"We don't give a damn about the military supplies. So don't you worry about them. Now, here's the plan."

"I don't need your help to do this," Custus said.

"You're going to get it whether you want it or not." The first man spoke quickly and angrily. "And you'll follow it or I'll get somebody else to do the job."

"All right," Custus agreed in a mollifying tone. "Take it easy."

"Good. Now, the first thing is that your men must not know who hired you."

"They won't find out."

"Be sure of that. Here is how we'll organize your men. First there'll be a frontal attack on the warehouse and docks by the bulk of the men. Second come ten men with coal oil and lucifers. Have four men with axes go around the border of the fight and cut the lines of the ships tied up at the docks. Those ships must drift out into the river so the sailors can't help Wollfolk. The ships' crews will be sleeping, so that should be easy. Is all this understood?"

"Yes. Give me the money now. And there's one thing you got to know: even if we fail to burn Wollfolk's property, we keep all the money. For, sure as hell, the men I pick to do this job won't give it back."

"That's agreeable," the first man said. "When can you be ready?"

"In an hour, just as soon as I can round up the men."

"Make the attack just as I told you," the first man warned. "I'll be watching."

Gustave backed away from the door and hastened along the hallway. He slowed at the doorway and sauntered to the front of the saloon.

"Did you find them?" the bartender asked.

"They had the door closed and I did not want to disturb them," Gustave said. He sat and picked up his glass of rum. "We got to get out of here," he said under his breath. "Drink up."

"What's the problem?" Leandre said.

"There's a hell of a fight coming and I think we can get in on it. I know which side we should be on. I'll tell you the rest outside." Gustave drained his glass of rum and headed for the door.

25

THE crashing boom of cannon fire rumbled across New Orleans and hammered the city and its frightened inhabitants like a great thunderstorm. At a hundred street intersections, tar barrels burned and sent up their putrid smoke.

The cannon positioned by the row of sailor's boardinghouses exploded, jarring the buildings and rattling the windows near Kelty. He heard the clattering fall of stones as ancient bricks softened by age and shattered by the concussions of the gun rained down from the buildings to the sidewalk.

Kelty stole on, slipping through the army of night shadows crowding the waterfront streets near the Wollfolk warehouse and docks. The man Shattuck had said was named Fannin walked sentinel duty on the river's edge. The mulatto Morissot guarded the inland side, stalking Jackson Square and the dark streets that lay adjacent to the waterfront. That action of the two fighters told Kelty that his prey was there on the docks. However, he would have to get close to identify a man he had seen but twice, and that at a distance.

First Morissot must die. That would leave the direction toward the city open for escape after Kelty killed Wollfolk. Kelty also knew he wanted to slay Morissot for another reason. He had sensed the presence of a man in the woods near his home one night. He believed only Morissot would have done that and then could have escaped so easily before Kelty could catch him in the dark.

The assassin moved into the gloom-filled recess beneath the long portico of the Cabildo and settled to wait. Morissot had made a mistake. As the hours had passed, his vigil had taken on a predictable path. Now Kelty lay in ambush along that path.

Morissot tried to ignore the cannon fire as he strained to spot movement or a form that could be Kelty. The street was a murky black canyon, for the streetlights hung unlit: the lamplighter either had abandoned his duty or was dead. The only light was the now-and-then flicker of flame from a burning tar barrel.

Lezin sought the deepest shadows and hugged the walls as he prowled warily along. Smoke boiled up from the tar barrels to mingle with the night. The dark mixture seemed to have a palpable density that Morissot had to push aside as he moved down the street. His nostrils were clogged with the heavy sooty smoke, and his eyes burned with acrid fumes.

Morissot knew it was dangerous, even foolhardy, to be stalking Kelty, for the man could be hiding in ambush in any one of a thousand places. But Morissot had no choice if he was to locate the assassin before the man found and killed Tim.

He had first gone to Kelty's home, hoping to catch the man there. But the house had been empty. There was only the clothes and other personal things of a single man living alone.

Morissot stared hard all the way around. He had been prowling the waterfront for many hours watching for Kelty. It was far past midnight now, and the time stretched long and weary. Fannin, guarding the approach from the river, must also be growing tired.

Tim worked with the Irishmen carrying cargo aboard the two military chartered ships tied up at the docks. The captains had argued strongly that their vessels must be loaded and ready to sail by daylight—before their crewmen caught the hated fever. Tim had decided to help O'Doyle and his men to meet that deadline. Morissot had thought the plan not a bad idea, for Tim would then become one of the dockworkers. Should Kelty slip past Fannin or Morissot, he would find it very difficult to pick Tim out from the thirty other white men laboring in the frail lantern light on the docks. However, when the day arrived, a better method must be devised to keep Tim safe.

Morissot crossed Jackson Square and turned to pass in front of the Cabildo, with its giant portico supported by the four thick stone arches. This most popular place in all the city was totally forsaken, the night-walking whores gone and even the saloons closed. He veered from the sidewalk and into the street to put space between himself and the black caves beneath the arches.

As Morissot stepped into the street, the black shadowy form of a large man tore free of the other shadows beneath the nearest Cabildo arch. The man made one long bound and hurled himself upon Morissot.

Morissot had time to only spin toward the attacker and partially thrust out his arm to fend him off before they crashed together with a bone-jarring force. He felt the jolt of a blow on the chest, a knife blade hitting a rib. The stout bone deflected the stabbing blade, sending it slicing with ice-cold heat along his side from front to back. A searing pain sprang to life.

Kelty's hard body slammed Morissot backward, rolling him on the ground. Kelty held his own footing. He gathered himself and sprang again to the attack.

Lezin stopped his wild tumble and surged to his feet. Kelty was leaping toward him, his knife thrusting out.

Morissot dodged to the side. His move was late. Kelty's knife caught him, passing through his left arm, up high.

Before Kelty could strike again, Morissot grabbed for the pistol in his belt. The weapon was gone, lost in his roll on the ground. He snatched the knife from its sheath. Held it ready to defend himself and kill when the opportunity came.

The large figure of Kelty, knife poised to deal the death stroke, circled Morissot, closing upon him. "Tonight you die," Kelty said.

Morissot laughed out through the gloomy night. Perhaps he could make the man angry and therefore reckless. "Kelty, you bastard, you had both the first and second blows with your blade. Yet you failed to kill me or even to hurt me badly. For all these years people have overrated you, feared a man who can kill only weak men, and those poor fellows from ambush."

Kelty ceased his circling movement. He growled and advanced. Morissot moved warily to the left. A man can cut most quickly and strongly while moving left rather than to the right. Kelty pivoted to keep facing his foe.

Morissot felt the blood pouring from his wounds. He was losing the precious life fluid at a fearsome rate. Already his pant leg was wet with blood from the waist to the bottom. Soon he would fall unconscious.

The fight must be short. He lunged at his adversary.

Kelty jumped clear. His knife swung in a quick, hard counterstroke, barely missing the mulatto. Then, with amazing swiftness, he sprang in on Morissot's side.

Fighting Kelty was like fighting a phantom, thought Morissot as he spun to meet the new attack. But this phantom must be killed to keep Marie's man safe.

Kelty made a roundhouse sweep with his knife and rushed upon his opponent. Morissot grabbed for the man's knife arm, caught a firm hold on it. Instantly he stabbed out powerfully with his own knife. But his hand was caught, halted in midstroke.

The momentum of Kelty's charge rode the two men down to the cobblestone street. Each held his grip on his adversary's knife arm. They rolled and cursed and fought on the hard pavement.

Morissot struggled mightily, his heart beating with great pulses of blood. He dredged up the ultimate ounce of his strength to break free so he could cut with his knife.

But Kelty matched the increased pressure, and then even more. Morissot's arm began to tremble. The knife wounds were sapping his strength.

Kelty lowered his head and rammed it forward with terrible power. Morissot felt his nose and teeth break against the man's skull. He was half-stunned. Pinwheels of light whirled and exploded, flinging burning stars off to every corner of his brain.

Again, viciously, Kelty slammed his head into Morissot's face. For an instant Morissot's grip on Kelty loosened. Kelty ripped his arm free. He drove his knife into Morissot's stomach—and again instantly, higher up in the chest, the blade plunging in between two ribs.

Kelty rolled away from Morissot. The knife, wedged solidly, was left behind protruding from Morissot's chest.

Kelty sat upright. He peered across the short distance separating him from Morissot. "That should send you to hell," he said. He began to laugh, a harsh, brittle sound.

Morissot caught hold of the knife and tried to pull it from his body. But the weapon was anchored firmly and his feeble strength could not budge it. He released the blade and lay trying to collect enough strength to sit up. He smelled the cloying odor of the hot blood draining from his body.

He struggled to a sitting position. He was not going to lie there and die like a stuck hog. He reached out with his hands to brace himself on the pavement.

Something was beneath his hand, something metal. He trembled. Unbelieving of the sudden turn of fortune. His fingers closed upon the butt of the pistol he had lost. He swung the weapon, cocking back the hammer. He fired at the center of Kelty.

The shadow that was Kelty was flung to the pavement. Morissot shot again into the body.

He collected his strength and crawled painfully to Kelty's crumpled form. He reached out and caught the man by the throat. The big vein in his neck was pulsing feebly, barely detectable and erratic. Morissot said, "Kelty, can you hear me?"

The figure quivered. A thin ghost whisper came. "Yes."

Morissot must verify the information he had about the Ring. All the enemies must be known. He had to accomplish that quickly, for he held the dying man's thought by only a little spider's thread. "Who hired you to kill Wollfolk?"

Kelty did not reply. A spasm shook him like a deep chill.

"Tell me, Kelty. It doesn't mean anything to you now."

"Shattuck," gasped the man.

"How many members in the Ring?"

"Four . . ." Kelty's voice trailed off.

"I'll speed your trip to hell now," said Morissot. He fired the pistol into Kelty's head.

Morissot staggered to his feet. He had to reach Jonathan with his healing hands. He stumbled to the corner of the Cabildo, turned along the street that paralleled the side of the building, and entered the park at the rear. He untied his horse and laboriously climbed up into the wagon. He reined the horse in the direction of his home. Black unconsciousness caught him like a thunderclap. He fell heavily into the bed of the vehicle.

A tremendous pain ripped through Morissot. He opened his eyes to the light of a lantern and Jonathan pulling strongly on the knife embedded in his chest. The knife came free.

The cold unconsciousness reached for Morissot again. He fought it back and lay still on the bed of the wagon.

Morissot tried twice before he could speak, and then his voice was but a broken whisper. "So that old horse found its way home," he said to the healer.

"I've been waiting and watching for you to return. I heard your wagon come," Jonathan said.

"And Marie?"

"She is safe."

"Good, tell Tim that Kelty is dead. Shattuck hired him to murder his uncle. The members of the Ring are four, as we thought. Fannin and Tim must find and kill them."

"I'll tell him that."

"Do it soon."

"Yes."

"And what of me, Jonathan?" Morissot asked.

"Old friend, your wounds are many and deep. I can't help you to live. You'll be dead before the morning comes."

"I know that you speak the truth." Morissot fell quiet. He felt death rising like a black tide at the borders of his consciousness. He looked at the knife stained with his blood. "Jonathan, put the knife in my hand."

"Why do you want it?"

"I see all my old enemies, all the men I've killed there in the shadows. I believe they mean to harm me. I must show them the steel of my blade to keep them off."

Jonathan pressed the knife into Morissot's hand. The fingers closed upon the handle.

"Jonathan I've slain so many men that I have lost count. Now I go into their world. From now to eternity, I must fight them."

Morissot's hand that held the knife rose as if to ward off a blow from some invisible foe. His hand fell. Morissot died.

26

FANNIN walked the wooden planking near the river's edge. He passed Cadwaller the night watchman. Shortly he moved through the lines of Irishmen carrying cargo to the two ships tied up at the wharves. The men labored silently as they trod heavy-footed and bent under large loads along the lane of light cast by burning lanterns.

A slow wind came off the Mississippi, keeping the smoke of the burning tar over the city. Millions upon millions of mosquitoes had fled the smoke zone and congregated along the river. Invisible in the darkness, the black-winged pests droned around Fannin. The grease he had smeared on his face gave him but scant protection from the stinging bites.

He reached the downriver edge of the Wollfolk dock and turned to head along the border in the direction of the levee. He thought of Cécile. She had read the *Courier*'s description of the many deaths from yellow fever and had urged him to take her from New Orleans until the epidemic ended. He knew she had good reason to be afraid. But he had refused to leave and tried to get her to go alone. She would not go without him. Now both remained in the pestilential city. God! How he hoped the deadly disease did not strike her.

He looked ahead in the direction of the city. For hours the cannon, hidden in the smoky night, had rumbled without stop. The flames of distant funeral pyres showed as dirty red splotches on the darkness. A dismal sight.

The two pistol shots came close together, just beyond the levee and near Jackson Square. Fannin barely heard them between the crashing booms of the cannon. He halted and stared hard through the formless vapors of the night. Had Morissot found Kelty? Were they fighting in the darkness? A third shot rang out.

Lew watched for Morissot to appear in the light on the docks or at the warehouse. Morissot did not appear. That was a bad sign. Fannin hastened forward.

He stopped on top of the levee in the edge of the cloud of tar smoke. He would go no farther, for he must be near if an attack was made on Tim.

Squatting on his haunches, Lew watched in the direction of the city for a long time.

The weary minutes passed. Sleep began to pull at his eyelids. He climbed erect and shook himself awake. He looked upward at the pinprick holes the stars made in the black dome of the heavens. The day could not be far away. He moved off along the top of the levee toward the lighted warehouse.

Iron wheels rattled on the stone pavement of Front Street. A few seconds later, a wagon pulled by a trotting horse bounded out of the night and whirled up to the warehouse. The Negro driver shouted and O'Doyle hurried to him.

O'Doyle called down over the docks. Tim separated from the stevedores and hastened up the slope to the wagon driver. They spoke together.

Tim saw Lew approaching. "Lezin is dead. Kelty killed him."

"I'm sorry about Morissot," Lew said. "What of Kelty?"

"He's dead too. They fought and wounded each other. Before Lezin died, he told Jonathan that there were four members in the Ring and that we should hunt them down and kill them."

"I don't have to be told to hunt them," Lew roughly replied. "I've had enough of giving them the first blow."

"Lezin is dead and Marie is all alone," Tim said sadly. "I must go and be with her."

"Wait," Lew said. "Some men are coming. They may mean trouble."

Three men walking swiftly along the levee top came into the full light of the lanterns. "Hello, Wollfolk," one of the men called.

"Gustave Besançon, what brings you here?" Lew asked.

"My friends and I have come to pay you back for the favor you did us. And to get in on the fight," replied Gustave.

"What fight?" Lew said.

"The fight when Custus and his Live Oak Boys from the Swamp come to burn your warehouse and docks."

"Tell me more," Lew said.

"About fifty of them will be here in an hour or so. They'll have coal oil and lucifers. Some uptown men have hired them to burn you out."

"We can guess who they are," Lew said.

"Who would that be?" Gustave said.

"There are four of them, men named Shattuck, Rawlins, Loussat, and Tarboll."

"We know them. You pick strong enemies. But we're not worried. I'd like to introduce you to Leandre and Maurice. All three of us would like to join you. A little fight would get our blood flowing."

"Join if you like. But there must be no killing if we can help it." Lew's mind raced as he surveyed the warehouse and the dimly lit dock. He spoke to Tim. "Send the old black man home," Lew said. "He's done his part."

"Jonathan, please go and take care of Marie," Tim said.

Jonathan nodded and reined the horse away from the warehouse. Man and wagon vanished into the night.

"O'Doyle, call your men together," Lew said. "They have a right to know we will soon be attacked."

"All right," O'Doyle said. He faced about and whistled shrilly through his teeth.

The Irishmen gathered at the end of the warehouse. They looked curiously from O'Doyle to Lew.

"That's all of them," O'Doyle said.

Lew nodded. He began to speak to the assemblage of men. "In an hour or so, a gang of head-knockers called the Live Oak Boys from the Swamp will come here to burn the warehouse and docks. They have been hired by our competitors to destroy the Wollfolk Company. I'm telling you this so that you may leave before the attack comes."

The men were silent, shifting their feet, looking from Fannin to O'Doyle.

The Irish leader stepped closer to Lew and faced his countrymen. "If the warehouse and docks are burned, then our jobs are gone," he said.

An angry growl rose from the men. "I wouldn't like that," a man shouted. There was an answering chorus of agreement.

"The men who are coming are tough," Lew said. "But those of you who stand with me will get a week's pay. Anyone who gets hurt and unable to work will receive full pay until he is well again."

"Irishmen are tough too," O'Doyle said. There was a roar of approval at the statement. As the noise subsided, O'Doyle said, "I for one am standing with Wollfolk. He helped us to get started in a foreign land. But those of you who think this fight is not yours can leave with no blame thought toward you. But leave now, for we got to know our strength."

O'Doyle waited, looking from face to face. Not a man moved. "Damn good fellows," he said with a broad grin. "Wollfolk, tell us what you want done."

Lew made a quick count. Thirty-five men against fifty or so. Damn poor odds, and there was so much area to protect. Yet they had no choice but to fight. It would be impossible to prevent determined men from starting fires and doing damage. A hard smile stretched Lew's lips. There might yet be a joker who he could deal the Live Oak Boys.

Tim watched Fannin's flinty face and slitted eyes as they sat at the battered desk in the warehouse. Fannin the strategist had devised the defense. Tim could not find fault with the plan. Every door in the warehouse was opened to its full extent to allow a clear view in almost every direction. About two-thirds of the men were positioned in the warehouse. They appeared to be working; however, they were merely shuffling the mounds of military supplies from one location to another within the building. Barrels had been emptied of their contents and now were spaced about, full of riverwater and soaking burlap sacks to be used to swat out fires.

The last third of the men were near the river. Hundreds of buckets of water had been splashed upon the beams and planks of the dock. They would not burn easily.

Every man had found a hard cudgel of some sort and carried it in his belt. There would soon be many broken heads. Men could die.

Lew turned his gimlet eyes on Tim. "You once said that you could kill a man if the situation was right. Well, I think tonight is the right time. The Irishmen have no guns. Some of the Live Oak Boys will surely be carrying them. Those armed men must be shot, and you and I have to do the shooting."

Tim breathed in and out. The sound was like a sigh, yet held an undertone of anger.

Lew's voice came sharply, questioning, "Can you help me shoot every Swamp man that has a pistol? If we can't, they will surely kill these men who are helping us."

Tim could feel the wolf rising in his heart. The Texan was correct. There was a time to meet violence with violence, to kill your enemy if you could. "Yes, I can shoot them. I think my uncle would approve."

"I'm certain of that," Lew said.

Tim pulled his pistol from his belt and checked the set of the lead balls on the powder and the condition of the firing caps. He slid the weapon back into its place.

The two fell silent. The wind washed over them in hot, damp waves as they waited for the impending battle to begin.

Lew stiffened. He knew the enemy had come, was hidden just out there beyond the reach of the lantern light.

"They're here, Tim," Lew said quietly. "Take your club and walk down to the other end of the warehouse like we planned. Remember, don't let our men get shot. Kill any Oak Boys that pull a gun. If they don't use guns, then it's only a fight with clubs. Maybe there'll only be broken heads and nobody will die tonight."

Tim walked among the piles of cargo. "Get ready. Get ready." He repeated the words in a low voice again and again to the men until he came to the far wall of the warehouse.

Edward Tarboll felt his pulse pounding with the excitement of the imminent attack. Nine years had passed since he had last led his band of pirates. The Boston-bound merchantman had been overtaken just off the east coast of Cuba after a three-day chase. He and his band had stormed aboard the ship with pistols banging and cutlasses swinging. Once they had boarded the ship, the fight to clear the decks of resistance and rout the last holdout defenders from below had taken less than ten minutes.

Capturing Wollfolk's docks and setting all afire

would be little different from capturing the merchantman. Probably even less difficult because Wollfolk and his Irishmen were not expecting to be boarded.

"I see that Texas Ranger, Fannin, there at the desk," Loussat whispered.

"So do I. We'll both go for him. Once he's dead, the other men will run."

"Remember I get the first shot at him."

"Then don't fall behind me. Soon as Custus attacks and Fannin is fighting them, we'll catch him from behind."

Tarboll crouched with Loussat in the dark at the foot of the levee. They were beyond sight of Custus and his gang of Live Oak Boys, and he could hear nothing from them. But unless he was mistaken, he could smell coal oil. He liked that. Soon Wollfolk and his property would be no more.

"What's Custus waiting for?" Loussat said in an aggravated voice.

"Have patience," replied Tarboll. Old pirates had learned much patience.

The shrill, savage battle cries pierced the night like daggers. An instant later, a long line of running men armed with clubs broke from the darkness and charged up the sloping face of the levee. A group of the men veered off at an angle and tore past the end of the warehouse toward the docks. The major portion charged directly at the long side of the building.

Lew grabbed up his club from the desk and

sprang to meet the assault. A tall man yelling in a wild voice rushed upon him.

Lew blocked a hard swing of the man's club. Then, before the fellow could recover, he struck him on the side with a rib-cracking blow. Another whack of Lew's weapon laid the man out cold on the dirt floor of the warehouse. Lew whirled, looking for another foe.

No one was close and he threw a look along the length of the warehouse. Men fought with clubs. And swords flashed, for the young Creoles were using their sharp blades to cut arms, legs, to cripple men and put them out of the fight. Clubs were no match for the swords. Lew was glad the Creoles were with him.

Shouts and the clash of weapons rose to fill the building with a great clamor. Men began to fall as their opponents overcame them. Moans rose to mix with the shouts of victory.

At the foot of the levee, a second line of men, widely spaced and carrying metal cans, came out of the murky night. Part of the line peeled away, as had happened with the first wave, and ran toward the docks. The largest number of men climbed straight up the levee to the warehouse.

Lew barely had time to see the new threat before a man with an ax handle was flailing at him. They circled, darting in at each other, parrying and hammering, striving to find an opening, a weakness.

Tarboll slipped out of the darkness beside Loussat. Though his eyes were focused on Fannin, he saw the strong resistance of Wollfolk's armed Irishmen. How could they have been so well-prepared for the battle? Somehow they must have been warned. Still he could win, for fires were beginning to burn at half a dozen places on the side of the warehouse and one end wall.

Loussat raised his pistol to aim at Fannin fighting a man swinging a club. The gun crashed. A jet flame lanced out at Fannin's back.

The man bore in, swinging his club mightily at Lew's head. Lew dodged to the side. He bent forward and, reaching out to the limit, rammed his club into the man's gut.

As Lew started to straighten, a bullet nicked him on the side of the head. He flinched and ducked. The second bullet whizzed over his head.

Lew pivoted to the rear and dropped to a knee. Two men with pistols were moving upon him. One held his gun leveled and was sighting down the barrel.

Lew dropped his club. His hand caught the butt of his pistol, lifted it, fired.

Loussat's eyes opened wide in terrible surprise. He stumbled, his legs giving way. He fell with a thump.

Tarboll saw Loussat's shot stagger Fannin. But then, unbelievably fast, the Texan drew his revolver and killed Loussat. Tarboll jerked up his gun, aimed quickly.

Lew hurled himself from in front of Tarboll's pistol. Even as he fell, he swung the barrel of his pistol, brought it into alignment with the man's body. The gun roared and bucked in his hand.

Tarboll's face twisted with the shock of the bullet ripping through him. He collapsed, slack and lifeless.

Lew leapt erect, his eyes searching for another man with a gun. He saw only men in hand-to-hand combat.

A pistol shot boomed in the far end of the warehouse. A second shot, from a different gun answered. Then a third shot rang out.

Lew broke into a streaking run, dodging swinging clubs and leaping over fallen, bloody men. A Live Oak Boy yelled a harsh cry and tried to hit Lew as he passed. Fannin's speed carried him safely beyond the reach of the club.

Lew slid to a stop at the opposite end of the building. Tim leaned against the wall. A redheaded man lay on the ground. Blood leaked steadily from a hole in his chest. He breathed once, then no more.

"Are you hurt?" Lew asked.

"No, I'm okay. That's Custus, the man we had trouble with on the street. He tried to shoot me."

"He's done for. Go help the Irishmen. I'll help the men on the docks."

"The fire's getting a good start." Tim pointed at the oil-fed flames climbing the stanchions and sides of the warehouse and licking at the rafters.

"The fire can wait a few minutes longer. Help

the men." Lew snatched up a club from the floor and dashed down onto the docks.

"Now! Now," Lew shouted as loud as he could above the screams and curses of the fighting men.

As if in answer to his call, the deckhouse hatchways of the two ships tied at the dock were flung open. A mob of seamen swarmed out onto the decks and down the gangway. Their voices rang out savage as a pack of hunting dogs. Swinging belaying pins, the seamen sprang into the fray.

A Live Oak Boy, the first to be overrun by the sailors, screamed out in a harrowing voice as he was struck several times. A second Swamp man chased by two seamen raced full-speed into the darkness. Another man, badly hurt, tried to crawl away on hands and knees, but an Irishman spotted him and knocked him unconscious with a bone-breaking lick from his club.

More Live Oak Boys fell or fled. The front of the battle zone retreated toward the warehouse.

A sailor shouted out, "They're running. Yahoo! Look at them run."

Like a wave, the knowledge of which side was winning swept across the docks. Struggling groups of men broke apart. One side ran.

A great cheer swept across the docks. Men began to laugh. The Irishmen called out happily to the sailors who had come to their aid and helped defeat the bully boys from the Swamp.

The captain of one of the ships saw Lew and raised his hand in salute as he approached.

Lew, smiling broadly, called out, "Damn glad

to see your seamen come tearing off the ship, captain."

"I couldn't let them destroy my cargo or endanger my ships," said the captain. "It was a good plan to draw them all into the open and then beat the hell out of them."

"It worked just like we hoped," Lew replied. "Now, if you'll have your medico look at the wounded, I'll take the rest of the men and put out the fires those fellow started."

"Can't be much damage done by the fire in such a short time. Some charred timber, but not enough structural damage to put you out of business. I want you to start loading cargo again just as quickly as you can. When daylight comes, I want to see the last of New Orleans and be on my way with military supplies for General Scott."

"You'll be loaded by then." Lew began to shout orders at the men around him.

27

Tim stretched his aching muscles and watched the orb of the sun crest the curve of the earth and a bright, clear morning rise from the swamp on the flat eastern horizon. The lingering purple shadows of the night began to burn quickly away.

He felt his impatience. The battle had been won, the fires quenched, and the ships loaded. Now he wanted only to hurry to Marie, hold her in his arms, and comfort her for her father's death.

He looked at Lew standing near the river. The last ship was pulling away from the dock with a throb of its steam engine. Lew turned and walked toward Tim.

"Is your pistol loaded?" Lew asked.

"Yes. Why?" Tim was afraid he knew the answer to the question as he looked into Lew's taut face and eyes cold as a panther's.

"Tarboll and Loussat are dead. That leaves us with two enemies, Shattuck and Rawlins. Those men are most likely the toughest of the Ring. Surely the smartest, for they are still alive and their friends dead. The failure to burn the warehouse and docks and to kill us last night won't stop them from trying again." Lew pointed up at the yellow disk of the morning sun. "Daylight is here. Now it's time we killed some men."

Tim saw the pitiless anger in Fannin. Nothing would prevent him from hunting the men. He made an excellent friend, but an implacable and terrible foe.

Lew's hand touched the butt of his pistol. The fingers seemed to caress the wood and iron. To Tim that understated threat lent an eerie emphasis to what Lew was thinking. Tim felt his own sharp edge of hate. Never until now had he thought of searching for a man with one single purpose in mind: to deliberately slay him.

"They may have left town."

"Maybe, but I believe they are still in New Orleans. They've started a war and now can't leave until we are dead. My guess is that they'll be at one of their warehouses waiting for us."

With the warming of the morning, the heavy tar smoke that had lain in the streets all night began to rise in writhing black plumes. Some of the wooden barrels had given way under the charring fingers of the fire, and the bubbling tar had spread in a flaming blanket, nearly blocking some of the streets.

Lew led, avoiding as much of the lung-searing smoke as possible and setting a fast pace along Front Street. Now that the search for Shattuck and Rawlins had begun, he wanted the final battle to end quickly.

The avenues seemed foreign without the cries of the street vendors, the cake sellers, knife sharpeners, and fish peddlers. The merchant shops were closed. Lew had seen a few scurrying figures dart along the street and vanish into the houses. New Orleans was a desolate, frightened city. It was a fitting time for killing an enemy.

Lew and Tim came upon a large fire burning in the middle of the avenue. Pieces of wood, tables, chairs, a door ripped loose from somewhere, and other burnable odds and ends were used as fuel. In the center of the flaming, crackling mass, a human corpse was being consumed.

They had traversed but a short distance beyond the funeral pyre when a piercing, tortured screech came from behind them. They whirled.

A yellow buggy with the top laid back came hurtling along the street toward them. The driver, a woman with her hair blowing out behind in a wild, whipping tangle, stood spraddle-legged in the vehicle and viciously lashed the running horse with a whip. The wheels of the speeding vehicle struck the edge of the funeral pyre and sent sparks and burning embers flying. The buggy bounced and swayed violently, on the verge of overturning. But the woman maintained her footing with an inhuman agility, and the conveyance settled back into its original wild ride.

Clots of sweat foam flew from the laboring flanks of the straining horse. Its head was outthrust, the nostrils flairing as they sucked at the air. The beast's back was cut in scores of places, and blood welled out to mix and thicken with the sweat. Still the woman struck with the whip again and again, driving the horse at the top of its speed.

The woman threw back her head and shrieked, an animal sound that peaked at an intensity of madness that made Lew's spine tingle.

Annette Grivot saw Lew and reined the carriage directly at him. She brought the horse to a halt, the bridle bit cruelly cutting its mouth. The whites of her eyes showed and the pupils narrowed as she locked her sight with an insane light on Lew.

"You bastard," the woman screamed, foam and spittle spraying from her mouth. Her whip snaked out amazingly fast. A piece of skin was jerked from the side of Lew's face, torn loose by the metal tip of the whip.

Annette struck again. Lew dodged and threw

up a hand to protect his eyes. The whip tip peeled away a piece of the back of his hand.

"You killed my husband for me. Then you rejected me for a nigger when I came to you with my love. I'll cut out your eyes for that." The long whip snaked out again.

Lew was backing swiftly out of reach. The metal tip, traveling at tremendous speed, missed his face and cracked like a small-caliber pistol just in front of his eyes. Even as Lew retreated from the hurtful whip, he knew sorrow for the woman. Her half-madness before had now been driven to complete lunacy by the death of her husband and the horror of the epidemic, the booming cannon, and the pall of smoke.

The woman cast a feral glance at Tim, then suddenly she was looking past both men. "It's Enos! See him there on the street!" She stared, bending forward as if peering through a fog. "My husband is not dead. It's all a lie. I'll catch him. He'll always love me."

Lew looked in the same direction. He saw only an eddy of tar smoke trapped between the buildings and drifting along the street. The deranged mind of the woman saw something that could not exist.

The woman slashed the horse. It bolted down the abandoned avenue.

Lew heard the sobbing cry of the tormented woman. "Enos, wait for me! Oh, please wait for me!"

"Who in God's good name was that?" Tim asked in shocked surprise.

"Just a madwoman," Lew replied, staring sadly along the street.

The yellow buggy, and the woman standing upright with inhuman agility, raced on and on.

"It's Shattuck," Fannin said, gesturing at the tall man standing in the open doorway of the big warehouse on top of the levee. "I thought he'd be the kind of man who would fight and not run."

"Rawlins is there too, farther back inside," Tim said.

"I see him. They're ready for us, Tim. How do you feel?"

"You name the game. I'll play it out to the end with you.

Lew looked at Tim, so ready to follow him into battle. He did not want to lead him to his death. But one man could protect another just so far. Then each man must fight his own fight, and die if his luck was bad.

"Fannin, we've been waiting for you," Shattuck shouted. "You took your damn good time getting here."

"You'll be dead soon enough without rushing it," Lew shouted back.

Shattuck laughed. "You got your story ass-backward. But I'm glad you got Wollfolk with you. Rawlins and I want to get this over with."

"How many other men do you have with you?" Lew called, walking slowly forward.

"Just Rawlins and me, and no more. Hell, that's all we need."

"Come outside where we can see both of you," Lew said.

"No. I've got a better idea. You come into the warehouse. Then we'll shut all the doors. You and I'll fight in one end and Rawlins and Wollfolk in the other end. Only the men who are left alive will see the daylight again."

"What do you say, Tim? Rawlins will be hard to kill."

"Those two had my uncle murdered. They've tried to kill you and me. We have no choice but to fight them. Their way is as good as any."

Lew watched the warehouse as he mulled what Shattuck had suggested. He smelled the air heavy with the odor of burning tar. The cannon were still banging away in a desultory manner, the gunners weary after so many hours of loading the noisy weapons. The awful smoke and the loud booms might drive away whatever caused the fever and thus stave off more deaths from that cause. But there was nothing that would prevent death from finding Tim and Lew in the darkness of the warehouse.

Lew spoke to Tim. "Once we are inside, quickly find a spot and don't move until your eyes get adjusted to the little light in there. Make Rawlins come to you. Out wait him. The man who moves can be seen easiest." He raised his voice and called to Shattuck, "We agree. Wollfolk and Rawlins will close the doors while you and I watch to see that there's no tricks played."

"Right. Rawlins will close them on the river side and Wollfolk the opposite side."

Lew walked inside, his eyes scouring the half-empty warehouse. He saw nothing suspicious. He focused his attention on Shattuck and Rawlins.

Tim and Rawlins began to move from one big door to the next, sliding them tightly shut. Shattuck, his sight hard on Fannin, backed toward one far end. Lew trailed, angling off to the side. The last door banged shut.

Lew sprinted straight ahead through the half-darkness. A dozen long strides took him in between piles of freight. He turned abruptly left down an aisle, then angled to the right into another aisle. He halted, pressed tightly against some wooden crates, and stood stone-still.

He felt the sweat beads as he remained motionless, waiting for the foe to come stalking. He recalled other battles he had fought as a Texas Ranger, his pistol against another man's. He had learned much from those times. He wished he had given Tim more guidance on how the fight should be waged. Let him not become impatient and walk into the sights of Rawlins' gun.

He counted, marking off the minutes with his fingers. Five, and then five more. The outlines of the mounds of cargo were visible now in the light coming from the open door and the cracks up high near the eaves. The black depths of the warehouse were merely murky shadows.

At fifteen minutes, Lew knew something was wrong. He was playing a game that Shattuck had devised. That was bad, No attack had been made on Lew. That left only Tim. He was in deadly danger. Rawlins could draw Tim's attention while Shattuck crept upon him from behind. Once Tim was dead, both men would come for Lew.

Crouched low, Fannin ran on cat's feet. He passed the middle of the warehouse.

A shot rang out among the freight some distance away on Lew's right. Then silence for a few heartbeats. Abruptly two shots boomed, the concussions coming so close together that they blended into one prolonged explosion. The loud sound bounced off the walls, became distorted among the piles of freight, and died in eerie echoes in the gloom in the far distant corners of the building.

Tim shouted out in a high, excited voice. "Lew, I killed Rawlins."

Lew screamed out in fear for his friend. "Tim, run! Hide! Shattuck is there. He's close."

A crate fell with a loud thump. Lew heard men struggling. A sharp cry of pain came.

"Fannin, I got Wollfolk," Shattuck called in a gloating voice. "I got his head bent back to the limit. One tiny pull and his spine will break."

"What do you want from me?" Lew asked.

"Rawlins is dead, Fannin. That leaves just me. I think you are a vengeful man and would hunt me until we fought. You may be better with a pistol than I am. I'll let your friend go if you fight me with fists."

"You are a professional boxer, so I've been told," Lew said.

"Well, you're a Texas Ranger, and a professional with pistols. So we're both professionals. But I've got Wollfolk. Do we fight without guns, or do I break this fellow's neck?"

"We fight."

"Good."

Fannin came warily into the gloom-filled aisle between two long rows of piled cargo. Shattuck held Tim's half-unconscious body in front of him. Tim's head was pried back to such a degree that Fannin thought the neck must surely be broken.

"Let him loose," Fannin said. "I want to see if he is all right." He moved three steps closer as he spoke.

Shattuck released his hold on Tim's hair. Tim straightened his neck and shook his head, flinging out a spray of red droplets from his broken nose and mouth.

"He's not hurt much," Shattuck said. "I just hit him a few times to soften him. Now, throw your gun away and let's finish this with fists."

Fannin knew Shattuck would never let Tim live. Once Lew was unarmed, both he and Tim would die. He took another step closer, peering intently through the murk of the warehouse.

Shattuck remained hidden behind Tim. Only the side of his face and one wicked, staring eye was visible.

"Do as I say," Shattuck warned. "I can snap Wollfolk's neck before you can reach me." He again took hold of Tim's hair and jerked his head back.

Fannin lifted his pistol and fired. Shattuck and Tim tumbled backward in a tangle of arms and legs.

Fannin breathed deeply in and out. Was Tim still alive? Fannin knew with the certainty that only truly competent men have that his bullet had gone exactly to his point of aim. But had Shattuck, in being slammed by the bullet, broken Tim's neck?

A moan came from the pile of bodies. Tim rolled to his knees. He halted in that position and stared down at Shattuck.

"My God, Lew. You shot out his eye."

"Having just one eye might be a blessing in hell. For sure that's where he's going."

Tim chuckled happily. "Damnation, I'm glad I never had to fight you." He climbed erect and stood swaying in his feet.

Lew hastened to Tim and caught him by the shoulders. "How are you, partner?"

"I'll live."

"That's good to hear. You are one bloody mess."

"That doesn't mean a thing now. We're both alive." He pointed a finger at Shattuck's still form. "Our last enemy is dead. Maybe now we can have some peace."

"I'll give both of them a fiery journey to their destination," Lew said. He began to gather boards, broken crates, and other burnable items from the warehouse and pile them on the levee. After he had accumulated a large mound, he carried the corpses of Shattuck and Rawlins outside and placed them on top of the wood. He found a can of coal oil and liberally doused everything with the flammable liquid.

Lew lit the fire with a lucifer and backed hurriedly away. The flames ignited with a loud swoosh. In a handful of seconds, the crackling fire was a raging flaming mass.

"Let's go," Lew said.

"Tim, do you know what will make you feel better?" Lew said as he walked down the side of the levee.

"What?"

"Some loving care from a beautiful woman."

"You are exactly right," Tim said. "I'll head home and find one who'll give me some. I suggest you go find one too."

Dr. Carstensen left the hospital ward jammed with the beds of yellow-fever victims and went out onto the balcony. The space there was equally crowded with the ill. He threaded a path among the beds to the railing.

The gunners at the cannon positioned a block to the east of the Marine Hospital were taking a rest. Thank God for a respite from the thundering, ear-bursting noise. The smoke from the burning tar rose directly upward and no longer suffocated the patients.

Below Dr. Carstensen, on the sidewalk, a young man hurried past, a big smile on his smashed and bloody face. What did he have to smile about? Damn strange.

Carstensen started to return to his work, then halted. Something was different. Then he recognized what that difference was. The damp, sultry air was gone. A hot, dry wind was blowing strongly in from the West. Overhead, there was not one cloud, the yellow sun hanging in a clear blue sky. And there were no mosquitoes.

He had seen this type of weather come to New Orleans before, just as an epidemic of yellow fever reached its peak. Thereafter, as the hot, dry wind continued to blow, the number of fever deaths declined rapidly.

Carstensen realized that in some manner the change of weather halted the spread of the disease. He did not know why or how, only that it did.

THE soldiers at Fort Jesup, located just outside New Orleans, had a saying: "Mud and water reach to the boot tops, mosquitoes cover everything above." The fact that yellow fever was transmitted by the bite of a mosquito was unknown in 1847 and remained so for another fifty years.

Epidemics raged off and on in New Orleans for more than one hundred and fifty years. Yellow fever was joined by cholera in an epidemic in 1832–33. Ten thousand people were known to have died, one in every eight inhabitants. Five hundred died in one day at the peak of the dual epidemics.

The peak of dying during the 1847 epidemic was reached in August, when twenty-two hundred people died. By the first of October, the number of deaths had decreased to a rate of eighty per month. In total some eight thousand people died.

The year of 1853 saw a resurgence of the yellow fever, and seven thousand two hundred citizens died.

Even with all the dying, the population of New Orleans swelled rapidly. At times it grew by more than a thousand a week as shipload after shipload of new immigrants arrived from a score of foreign lands.

The publishers hope that this
Large Print Book has brought
you pleasurable reading.
Each title is designed to make
the text as easy to see as possible.
G.K. Hall Large Print Books
are available from your library and
your local bookstore. Or, you can
receive information by mail on
upcoming and current Large Print Books
and order directly from the publishers.
Just send your name and address to:

G.K. Hall & Co.
70 Lincoln Street
Boston, Mass. 02111

or call, toll-free:

1-800-343-2806

A note on the text
Large print edition designed by
Pauline L. Chin.
Composed in 16 pt Plantin
on a Xyvision 300/Linotron 202N
by Marilyn Ann Richards
of G.K. Hall & Co.

AOB-XM
12-8-97
4-2-02